KILLER DOLLS

PART 2

Buy

♥

for Melodrama

KILLER DOLLS

PART 2

NISA SANTIAGO

This is a work of fiction. All of the characters, organizations, and events portrayed in this novel are either products of the author's imagination or are used fictitiously.

www.melodramapublishing.com

Library of Congress Control Number: 2015912544
ISBN-13: 978-1620780893

First Edition: May 2016
Mass Market Edition: November 2017

Model Photo: Frank Antonio
Cover Model: Nefertiti

Printed in Canada

BOOKS BY NISA SANTIAGO

CHAPTER 1

Aoki locked eyes with the perpetrator and frowned heavily. How could he? She'd trusted him. She'd believed in him, but now it came down to this.

"Dis how ya come fi me?" she said.

"I'm sorry," he said.

There was a strong moment of silence and eye contact between them. Three gunshots suddenly rang out, and Aoki knew she was a dead woman.

Surprisingly, it was AZ who collapsed face down on the concrete before her eyes, leaving her in shock.

Emilio emerged from the shadows, the smoking gun in his hand. He gazed at Aoki with concern. "Are you okay?"

"Me fine."

He looked down at AZ's body and then averted his eyes back to Aoki. They both then heard signs of life still coming from AZ. He was still barely alive. Blood pooled beneath him as he struggled to breathe.

Emilio pointed the gun at the back of AZ's head about to fire, but Aoki shouted, "No! Don't!"

Emilio looked at her quizzically. "Why not? He wanted to kill you!"

"Just don't," she said.

Emilio frowned and angled the gun away from AZ's head. He looked too cool after shooting AZ and showed no contrition.

"Emilio, run! Leave! Please, for your safety," Aoki said.

"You need to come with me," he said.

"I can't."

"You have to. You're not safe here."

"Just go! Me can take care of myself."

Emilio's jaw tightened as he looked at her one final time. He was hesitant to leave her side, but he took her advice and ran from the scene.

It was late and quiet, except for the gunshots that had pierced the air. Aoki knew the cops were probably on their way. She hadn't shot AZ, so she wasn't overly concerned. She could easily come up with some bullshit excuse. She could still hear AZ struggling to breathe, fighting to stay alive.

AZ had been shot twice, though Aoki had heard three gunshots.

AZ was trying to remain calm. He looked up at her.

She crouched near him and looked at him deadpan. "Was ya really gon' do it? Was ya gon' shoot me?" she asked him.

AZ could only stare up at her, his eyes pleading for help. He didn't want to die.

Aoki was torn over whether to call the paramedics or to allow him to bleed out and die right in front of her eyes. She

10

looked into his eyes and then at the gun by his side, and she felt some type of way. Was he going to kill her? What did she do? As a man who couldn't kill anyone, could he have started with her?

As Aoki was wrestling with her conscience, a black SUV came barreling down the street haphazardly and came to a grinding stop right by her. Two armed men stormed from the vehicle, pistols outstretched and aimed at her, as she looked on wide-eyed and helpless. Everything was happening too fast.

When she saw B Scientific emerge from the vehicle after the armed assailants, Aoki was terrified. Was it her time to die right along with AZ?

She glanced AZ's gun and was tempted to reach for it, but her chances of surviving were slim. They had the drop on her.

"Yo, look at this shit here," B Scientific exclaimed. "Two birds already down and out for me to fuckin' pluck!"

Aoki had to smarten up and think quickly. It was obvious B Scientific hadn't come by for a social visit or a booty call. He was there to kill and create havoc. She had to do something fast.

Aoki burst into tears and shouted, "Please help me! He needs a hospital!"

B Scientific looked at AZ shot up and bleeding on the concrete. No police around yet. He pointed his gun at AZ, ready to finish what he thought he had started. B Scientific thought it was his bullets tearing AZ apart from the inside and that Aoki didn't know about his attempt on AZ's life.

Aoki jumped into the line of fire, covering AZ with her petite frame. "Nuh, please don't!"

"Get the fuck out the way, Aoki!" B Scientific screamed.

"Ya kill him, then ya kill me too!" Her eyes red from crying, she was serious. She didn't know why she was protecting him, when just minutes earlier, he'd had a gun in her face.

"I've been thinking about it, and you're tempting me," he said.

Aoki continued to cry out. B Scientific had never seen her like this before. It was painful to hear.

Aoki locked eyes with him, tears flowing down her face like a river, but her look toward him was still fierce.

For some reason, her cries touched B Scientific's heart. Though he wanted to murder her and AZ, there was something about her that rendered him hesitant and somewhat forgiving. He wanted to scoop her up into his strong arms and love her. He couldn't bring himself to kill her, and he didn't want to create any more pain for her.

"Him not gon' make it!" she screamed, holding AZ in her arms.

Thinking Aoki didn't know he had shot at AZ, B Scientific asked, "What happened to him?"

"Someone shot him. I came home and someone tried to ambush me. He saved my life," she lied.

Aoki wanted to protect the two men she cared for. She wanted to protect Emilio from any heat coming his way, and AZ from B Scientific. Ri-Ri told her that B Scientific was trying to murder AZ. If she told B Scientific someone else had shot AZ, perhaps he would chill. The fact that AZ's eyes were closed and he was unresponsive actually helped.

One of B Scientific's men suggested, "Yo, *B*, we need to go soon. Either dead this nigga or don't."

B Scientific hesitated for a moment before looking at Aoki and jumping into action. "Yo, put that nigga in the truck," he ordered his goons.

His men looked at him, bewildered by his choice.

"What?" one of his men exclaimed.

"Muthafucka, you heard me! Put him in the truck. We takin' him to the hospital," B Scientific shouted.

Reluctantly, his goons followed orders. They quickly picked up AZ from the ground, his blood dripping everywhere, and placed him in the backseat of the truck.

Aoki was grateful, but she didn't show it.

B Scientific had his reasons for his mercy. Besides Aoki's horrific wailing pulling on his heartstrings, B Scientific's story could be that AZ was shot at Aoki's place and he'd helped him, not tried to kill him if AZ snitched about the earlier shooting.

B Scientific picked up AZ's gun from the ground and tucked it into his waistband. He jumped behind the steering wheel, and with AZ dying in the backseat, he peeled out and raced toward the nearest hospital.

It was crowded in the backseat. AZ was silent and unresponsive. Aoki was worried and didn't want him to die because she needed answers.

B Scientific hurriedly drove down Linden Boulevard, toward Brookdale Hospital. Aoki still clutched AZ in her arms as he was sprawled across the backseat, her hands and clothing covered in his blood. It was a nightmare. It could have been her laying there bleeding and dying. Shit was becoming hazy for her.

She looked at B Scientific. "What make ya come at me like dat, *B*? Why ya drive up 'pon de block all crazy and shit wid a gun?"

B Scientific continued toward the hospital, ignoring her questions. He came to a stop in front of the emergency room at Brookdale, and the doors swung open. Everyone exited the truck, carrying AZ from the backseat.

"We need a fuckin' doctor here! He's been shot!" B Scientific shouted.

A handful of emergency room employees came flying out of the hospital, one pushing a gurney, and quickly tended to AZ. They strapped his bullet-riddled body to the gurney and hurried him inside as B Scientific and Aoki looked on.

AZ was immediately rushed into surgery. They were losing him. His vitals were very low. He was touch and go.

One nurse stayed behind and started to question Aoki and B Scientific about the incident.

B Scientific frowned and said roughly, "Yo, you need to get the fuck out my face with these questions and go save that man's life!"

"But, sir, we need his information," the nurse returned.

"I don't know shit!"

The nurse looked appalled and dumbfounded, but the look on B's face sent her running back into the hospital.

B Scientific turned and glared at Aoki. Suddenly, the nice-guy routine was gone. He snatched her up by her shirt and dragged her away from the hospital entrance and to his truck.

Aoki protested the manhandling.

"Get the fuck in the truck, Aoki!" he growled.

She cursed at him, and he cursed right back. He forced her into the truck, and he and his men jumped inside.

"Ya don' lost ya fuckin' mind."

"Shut the fuck up, Aoki!" he shouted.

B Scientific sat shotgun and placed his gun on his lap. Now it was time for him to get his own answers. Aoki was in the backseat with her face scrunched up. B Scientific spun around and aimed the pistol in her face, his finger on the trigger.

Aoki didn't budge. "So now ya gon' shoot me? After all dis?"

"Where the fuck is my chain?" he asked. "The one I gave to you."

At first, Aoki didn't say a word to him. She smirked. *His chain.* She had totally forgotten about it. She was turned off that this rich nigga was pointing a gun at her over a stupid chain, no matter the sentimental value.

Before she could respond, B Scientific leaned closer and slapped the taste out of her mouth for smirking and being silent.

"You think I'm playin' wit' you, bitch?" he shouted. "I've been nice and cool because I like you, but don't play me for a fuckin' fool, Aoki!"

Aoki shed a few tears while gazing at him. She looked him dead in the eyes and replied, "I lost it!"

"You lost it?"

"Yes!" she cried.

B Scientific wasn't buying it. He was determined to make her admit what she'd done. He had lost so much respect for her. She'd caused crazy drama in his life, from making Brandi lose his baby to pawning his brother's rosary chain, and playing his ego.

"Aoki, I swear on everything that I love, I'll beat you the fuck down until there's nothing left to beat if you don't tell me where my motherfucking chain is!"

She wondered why he didn't believe her. "Me swear to ya, me lose it. And dat's de God's honest truth."

"Yo, your parents smoke crack?" B Scientific asked out of the blue.

She was stunned silent. Why was he asking about her parents? None of it made any sense.

She looked at him and answered honestly, "Yes, dem both had ah serious drug problem. But dem didn't steal ya chain, no matter what ya heard."

"Don't worry; we gonna get to the bottom of everything," B Scientific assured her.

"Me can pay for ya chain, if ya want."

"I fuckin' told you, that piece of jewelry was sentimental to me. You think you can just pay for it and everything's gonna be fuckin' cool?"

Aoki felt like she was fucked.

The truck pulled over on a dark, secluded block in

Brooklyn. The silence was eerie, witnesses nonexistent.

B Scientific rushed out of the truck and opened the back door. Then he dragged Aoki out by her hair and pushed her to the ground. His two goons surrounded her, both of them glaring at her and waiting for their cue.

B Scientific placed the tip of his gun to her head. "You got three seconds to come clean about every fuckin' thing, or I swear on my unborn child, I'm gonna leave your fuckin' brains all over the sidewalk. You pawned my shit then you beat down my bitch and made her have a miscarriage. Right?"

Pawned? Beat down his bitch? She didn't know what he was talking about. She was shocked by the accusations against her.

"One!"

Aoki felt the cold steel of the gun pressed against her temple. B Scientific was boiling, like a volcano ready to explode. She suspected someone was setting her up. Someone probably found the chain in the dumpster and pawned it, and now she was taking the fall. But the beating of his baby mama was an absolute fabrication. Aoki was convinced she was being set up.

"Two!"

"Me being set up!" she shouted.

"What?"

"B Scientific, dem set me up. Lemme prove it! Dem lie 'pon me!" she said. "Give me some time to prove me innocence."

B Scientific looked pensive. He didn't want to admit it to himself, but he had really fallen in love with Aoki. As much as he felt he should kill her, like he felt she'd killed his baby, he just couldn't.

Aoki had convinced him to allow her to live so she could prove to him that she was being set up. He lowered the gun from her head and sighed.

His goons looked at him like he was crazy, their eyes saying, *"You ain't gonna murder this bitch?"*

CHAPTER 2

B Scientific and Aoki rode alone in silence back to her place. It had been a long night. Aoki had been reprieved from death for now, but she wasn't out of hot water just yet. Someone was out there spreading lies about her, trying to get her killed. In order to stay alive, she was going to have to smoke out the muthafuckas who lied on her.

B Scientific stopped in front of her home and killed the ignition. Aoki's eyes scanned the house and stopped on AZ's bloodstain on the concrete. Apparently no police had come around, and everything looked back to normal, but it was far from normal.

She didn't know if AZ had survived surgery or not. She then wondered if Emilio was safe.

"Let me escort you inside and spend the night. You know I miss you," B Scientific said to her, like everything was copacetic.

Aoki couldn't believe he had the audacity to want some pussy after all that had happened. He looked at her lovingly, like he was ready to kiss her passionately and fuck her.

"Me tired, B Scientific. It's been ah long night."

He looked at her with a combination of hope and desperation. "You love me?"

She was convinced he was bipolar. He'd wanted to murder her hours ago, and now he wanted to love her and act like tonight never happened.

"Me just exhausted and need to go inside and be alone for a moment. Come by tomorrow an' we'll talk."

"I wanna fuck you," he blurted out.

She couldn't understand why his dick was hard after a night like this. Maybe B Scientific had some kind of twisted fantasy of sex after violence.

"Come by tomorrow and me give ya what ya need. Now I just need to sleep."

Aoki started to get out, but B Scientific quickly jerked her by her arm, pulling her back into the truck.

"Aoki, you better be around tomorrow afternoon, or else. I want my chain back, and I want you!"

"Me will be here, B Scientific, ya nuh need to worry. I just need time alone to meself."

B Scientific nodded as he released his tight grip from Aoki's arm.

Aoki stepped out of the truck and walked toward her front door. She didn't look back, but she could feel his eyes on her, watching her every move.

She went inside, closed the door, and started to peel away her bloodstained clothing. She went to the bathroom, drew a bath, and immersed herself in the hot, soothing water. She closed her eyes and exhaled. She had a lot to think about.

Now she understood why B Scientific showed up at her place with a gun, yet she didn't understand why his bitch had her name in her mouth. Nor did she understand why AZ showed up to murder her. Then there was Emilio, also with a gun. What was going on? It was all too perplexing.

Aoki knew today's drama was just the beginning of things to come. B Scientific was coming by tomorrow afternoon, and he expected some pussy and his chain. It was going to be hard to fuck him after he'd put a gun to her head. She had to keep her cool, though, stay focused, and figure out what was happening.

After her hour-long bath, she toweled off, donned a robe, and collapsed on her bed. She fell asleep right away.

Aoki was able to get a couple hours of sleep, until the morning sunlight percolating through her open bedroom windows stirred her awake. She looked at the clock and the time read 9:45. She looked at her phone and saw a slew of missed calls from Ri-Ri, but she didn't have any time to fritter away. She needed to make moves. She quickly showered, got dressed, and rushed out of the door. She climbed into her truck and sped toward the city, NYU to be exact.

She parked near Washington Square Park and walked toward Emilio's dorm room. It was a breezy fall day, and students were just settling into school and their dorm rooms. The area was flooded with undergraduates and locals, many students sporting clothing with the university's logo.

Aoki walked briskly toward Goddard Hall, the six-story dormitory on the city street near Washington Square East. She piggybacked her way into the building, walking closely behind a group of girls. She looked as if she belonged with them, wearing her knapsack and basic clothing. She made her way toward Emilio's room on the sixth floor. She knocked twice and waited.

He opened the door and looked surprised to see her.

"Can I come in?" she asked him.

He nodded. He stepped aside and allowed her into the room.

He was packing up his things. School had just started up, so why was he leaving? "Ya goin' somewhere?"

"I am. I'm quitting school and going back to L.A."

"Why?"

"We gonna stand here and play this game, Aoki?"

"What game?"

"You don't have to thank me for saving your life, but you've ruined mine. You told on me, didn't you?"

"Tell what?"

"I got your voice message the other day about you threatening to tell on me for drug-dealing in the school. I tried to call you back a couple of times, but you refused to answer. I rather leave school than do time in New York. I can't risk getting locked up."

Aoki looked wounded by his words. She stepped closer to him, saying, "Me would never tell on ya, ya hear? Me was just upset. Only said dem words out of anger. Ya done so much fo' me. I apologize. Me love ya."

It slipped out, but she meant every word of it.

Emilio looked touched by her words. "I love you too."

She smiled. Suddenly she had an afterthought about something. She looked at Emilio with some concern and asked him, "Why were ya at me house with a gun?"

Emilio didn't miss a beat answering her.

"It was only a precaution. I'm always carrying a gun when I go into Brooklyn; I'm no fool. I came to apologize to you."

"Ya didn't come to hurt me?"

Emilio touched the side of her face. "I could never hurt you. I came to see you and say that I was sorry. I didn't mean to threaten you about the bodies I found in your yard. I'm no snitch. I wasn't raised like that. It was just unexpected, that's all. I should have been a man and come to you for an explanation, instead of leaving like some bitch."

"Ya could have been killed." The thought frightened Aoki. "Ya could have walked right into an ambush."

"I hold my own. But what was that about last night? Why was AZ there to murder you? Y'all got beef over us?"

Aoki shook her head. "Me don't know yet. AZ's no killer. 'im a good dude."

"I saw the look in his eyes, Aoki. He was going to pull that trigger had I not been there. Is he dead? Did I put that nigga to sleep?"

"I hope him not dead. We, um, I got him to the hospital."

Emilio didn't know if he should be relieved or not. He felt indifferent. "I regret that shit had to happen." He didn't come to New York to pick up from where he'd left off in Los Angeles, murdering his enemies.

"We all have our regrets."

"I definitely do. I need to tell you something." Emilio took Aoki by her hand and pulled her deeper into the room.

With the door shut, they sat on his bed. He looked at her. "I'm no angel myself," he started, "and I don't have any right to judge you. Back in L.A., I used to gangbang, and I've done and seen a lot of things—crazy shit—back home. I believe I'm a changed man now, but those bodies I found in your yard almost made me revert back to my past."

Aoki listened to him intently. She knew he wasn't a choirboy; she always felt that Emilio had an edge to him. She held his gaze and said, "Me don't want to lose ya. Me want to tell ya the truth."

Emilio nodded.

Aoki started telling him the truth. Partly. She told him that her father was strung-out on drugs and killed her mother. When he finally came down off his high and realized what he'd done, he then took a hot shot of heroin and overdosed. Being a minor and not wanting to be turned over to ACS, she hid the bodies in the barrels in her backyard. It was a dumb mistake, but she was scared and felt she had to do what she needed to do.

Emilio believed every word. He wrapped his arms around her like a thick blanket. Aoki had never felt so strongly about a man. Yes, he was definitely the one. She cared for AZ, or used to, but she was in love with Emilio.

He gazed at her. "You're absolutely beautiful, Aoki."

She smiled. Her heart started to beat fast, and she didn't want to leave his comforting embrace. She looked into his eyes, and they showed real compassion.

Emilio leaned forward and kissed her passionately. His lips against hers always felt so blissful.

Just as they were about to get into it, her phone chimed. *Perfect timing*, she thought. She looked at the caller ID and saw it was Ri-Ri. She knew she needed to pick up, but she couldn't yet. She needed to wrap things up with Emilio.

"Is everything okay?" He sighed, regretting his question after seeing the look on Aoki's face. "I'm sorry. It was a stupid question. I know you're going through a lot right now. But I'm here for you, Aoki, and I don't plan on going anywhere. I got your back, and your secrets are safe with me."

"Thank you." Aoki felt secure and assured with him.

Emilio leaned into her again, and they locked lips. Their kiss was magnetic. He slowly peeled off her clothes and touched her body lovingly.

"Is de door locked?" she asked.

"We're good. My roommate won't be home for another hour or so."

Emilio continued to remove her clothes and his too. They continued to kiss passionately.

Emilio climbed between Aoki's thighs as she lay on her back. He rolled a condom on his erect dick and thrust inside her, moaning as the pleasure of feeling her overtook him.

Aoki moaned and wrapped her legs around him. She closed her eyes and exhaled. He thrust, their bodies intertwined on the small twin bed.

"I want you," he said into her ear. "I want you forever!"

Fucking in the missionary position, Aoki dragged her nails down his back and moaned beneath him. Her cell phone sounded again. She knew it was Ri-Ri calling again and how important that call was, but her interests were elsewhere right now.

Emilio placed his lips against hers and sucked on her tongue. He loved the taste of her cherry lip gloss. He loved how the walls of her vagina contracted when he rammed himself deep inside her, and he loved the faces she made.

He felt himself about to explode inside of her. He pressed his body against hers closely, moving his hips between her thighs, clutching the sheets as he maneuvered his erection in a circular motion inside her pussy, going from left to right then up and down.

Aoki squirmed beneath him. She closed her eyes and felt her own orgasm about to abrupt.

"I need you," he whispered in her ear. "I want you."

"Me want ya too," she said.

His chest rubbed against her nipples. He gripped the back of her thighs and continued pounding and penetrating his way into her bliss.

"I'm coming!" he announced.

"Me too!"

Their bodies shuddered against each other from the strong orgasm. Emilio released a breath of liberation and collapsed against her. Aoki was satisfied with the experience. He knew how to make her come. The two lay together in silence for a moment.

"I needed that," he said, trying to regain his normal breathing.

She nodded in agreement.

Aoki said to him, "Don't quit school. Stay for me."

He took a deep breath. "I won't."

Aoki's phone started to ring again. She looked at the caller ID. It was Ri-Ri yet again. She looked at Emilio. "I need to take dis. She gon' continue to call if I don't answer."

"Handle your business. I need to take a piss anyway." He got up, put on a pair of jeans and T-shirt, and left the room to use the bathroom in the hallway.

Once he was out of sight, Aoki answered the phone.

"Where the fuck have you been, bitch?"

"Ri-Ri, me so sorry. It's been a long night. So much has happened that me can't explain. Did ya find out why B Scientific shoot at AZ and Heavy Pop?"

"Not really, but the hood is talking and people are saying that AZ owed B Scientific some money for fucking up ten kilos. They think the beef is over some coke."

"Wait. What?"

"Yeah, that's what I heard. But Tisa heard that AZ and Heavy Pop had robbed one of B Scientific's stash houses."

Aoki knew both stories were just hood gossip. "Me don't think these things are true."

"Aoki, I really don't care about that right now. I called because I have some bad news."

"Me know about AZ getting shot last night after you called me. Let's not talk 'pon the phone. What I need ya to do is find out if they okay. They still alive?"

"For now. I heard neither one of them is going to survive another night."

Aoki's heart dropped. She couldn't lose AZ before having a chance to speak with him. "Just sit tight and me come ya way later. Understood?"

"Okay. Just hurry."

Aoki hung up and started to get dressed. As she was buttoning her shirt, Emilio walked into the room.

"You leaving so soon?"

"Me have to go and handle some business."

Aoki had her rendezvous with B Scientific this afternoon. It was almost noon already. She didn't want to be on his bad side and she needed answers.

She kissed Emilio goodbye and hurried out the door and almost ran toward her truck. She started the ignition and raced back to Brooklyn like Tony Stewart. By the time she crossed over the Brooklyn Bridge, B Scientific was calling her phone, letting her know he would be at her place in an hour.

CHAPTER 3

Aoki quickly showered and changed clothes. She didn't want to smell like sex when she met with B Scientific, and she wanted to look nice for him. She needed to get back on his good side and regain his trust. Someone had lied on her, and she didn't have a clue who.

The only thing that put a smile on her face was thinking about her fun with Emilio this morning. Now it was back to business and survival. She was waiting coolly for B to show up.

B Scientific knocked on her front door ten minutes after one p.m. Aoki answered with a smile. He came alone, looking clean in a brand-new outfit, fresh haircut, and a shiny whip.

Aoki was dolled up in a sexy button-down denim minidress and high heels. The outfit made B smile as he looked her up and down, nodding his head in approval.

He said, "Let's go!"

She climbed into the passenger seat of his Escalade, and they drove to the pawnshop to retrieve his chain. Aoki was a little nervous. She was clueless about who had pawned the jewelry.

They arrived at the Brooklyn pawnshop, and Aoki apprehensively walked behind B Scientific into the building. He went straight to the counter, where the owner of the pawnshop was taking care of a customer.

B Scientific stepped toward the counter with a frown. "I'm here to collect my shit!" He tapped on the glass counter, where numerous jewels were encased.

"Do you have your ticket?" the man asked him.

B Scientific looked at Aoki. She stepped toward the man and said, "It's in me name."

"You have ID?"

Aoki removed her driver's license and presented it to the man, who entered it into his computer system. He looked at her picture and then looked at her. The name and address matched the ticket. But there was one problem—she wasn't the one who'd pawned it.

"I still need your pawn ticket."

B Scientific yelled, "Yo, she just showed you her fuckin' ID! It shouldn't be a problem! I just want my shit back!"

The owner was coveting the expensive piece of jewelry. He looked at them both and said, "There's a problem."

"What the fuck is the problem?" B Scientific shouted. "I just want my shit back! Ain't no need for it to be an incident in this fuckin' place!"

"She wasn't the one who pawned the chain," the man said.

"What?" B Scientific was baffled.

Aoki exhaled, hearing the owner say those magic words out loud. Her wrongdoing was cleared. She kept her composure and held off celebrating too soon.

"What the fuck you talkin' about, nigga? She ain't the one who pawned my shit?" B Scientific pointed at Aoki. "Then who, muthafucka?"

The owner nodded. "No. It wasn't her."

"Who the fuck was it then?"

"She was older with long black hair," the owner said.

Aoki and B Scientific both knew he was describing Gena. Aoki was fuming, but B was fuming harder.

"Look, I don't know who the fuck you talking 'bout, but it ain't her! Just take out my chain, and I'll pay whatever for it. It's obvious, nigga, that you been lied to, and you got something that you shouldn't have in the first place."

The owner was reluctant to release the chain. It was a beautiful piece of jewelry, one that he could sell for a lot more.

Aoki remained quiet, while B Scientific and the owner argued intensely. She knew Gena was in hot water. It was clear to her that Gena had always hated on her, but how did she get the chain? Aoki figured that Gena must have stolen it from her daughters. Aoki didn't want to get her friends' mom in trouble, so she didn't call Gena out. She knew B Scientific would kill her.

"Yo, nigga, you gonna give my muthafuckin' chain back!" B Scientific shouted angrily.

"I don't want any trouble," the owner said.

"Fuck that! My shit is leaving with me today, nigga!"

B Scientific was furious, realizing he had been played. He knew Gena had two daughters, who were both friends with Aoki. Gena must have gotten wind that he was fucking Aoki, got jealous, stole the chain from her somehow, and set Aoki up to get murdered. He planned on dealing with the devious bitch later.

Aoki could see B Scientific bubbling with rage. She knew he wouldn't hesitate to take his chain back by force. The owner wasn't backing down either. He had his registered gun on his hip. Things were growing ugly in the store.

While they were arguing, Aoki discreetly dialed 911 and reported the incident. She then tried to calm B Scientific down, but his anger was already unleashed. That piece of metal meant so much to him.

Shortly thereafter, the NYPD came walking into the pawnshop seeing the two men in a heated argument. B Scientific saw them and figured one of the pawnshop employees had called the police. The officers quickly intervened, and when both sides had told their stories, the cops were on B Scientific's side.

"Her name is on the ticket, and she has her ID to prove it's her. That is what your store policy states, right?" one of the cops said to the owner.

He scowled. "But she don't have her ticket!"

"It doesn't matter. You release that property over to her, or we'll arrest you right now for grand larceny, sir," the cop threatened.

The pawnshop owner continued to frown. He was pissed.

B Scientific smirked. It was the only time he was grateful to see a cop around. He paid the ransom for the chain and was a happy man. His brother could rest in peace again.

The cops left without having to report an incident, and B Scientific and Aoki were walking right out the door behind them. B Scientific had his precious rosary dangling around his neck.

As the two got into the Escalade, B Scientific realized that if Aoki didn't pawn his chain, then perhaps she also didn't jump Brandi and make her lose "their" baby.

He started the ignition, looking at Aoki. "You hungry?"

"Yes." She nodded.

B Scientific took Aoki to a quaint Jamaican restaurant in Crown Heights. The place was known for having some of the best oxtails, curry goat, and beef patties in the city. They got a corner table and ordered their meals.

Aoki took a sip of pineapple soda and said, "Me would never betray ya, B. That hurt me."

He didn't respond to her comment, feeling somewhat like an ass for doubting her in the first place.

They talked while dining on jerk chicken, oxtails, plantains, rice and beans, and coco bread. The meal was delicious.

"Me don't know who could do dis to us! Did de description sound familiar to ya?" Aoki wanted to know if he suspected Gena.

"Nah, not at all." B Scientific wiped the corners of his mouth with a napkin then looked at Aoki. "Can you continue to keep it one hundred with me?"

"Me have no reason to lie to ya."

He tried to gauge her expression. "Did you have anything to do with my girl Brandi being jumped?"

"B Scientific, ya already know de answer to that. Why would I do that? I don' told ya I'm in love wid AZ, and I the one dat told ya to stay wid ya girl."

B Scientific cringed when he heard Aoki say she was in love with AZ. But she was right; it didn't add up. "You right," he said.

"Me need to ask ya someting."

"What you need to ask me?"

"Did ya shoot Heavy Pop and shoot at AZ?"

B Scientific didn't want to get into details. He looked Aoki squarely in her eyes and said, "They don't need to worry about me anymore."

"What ya mean by dat?"

"Should your friends pull through, I'm good. So they need to make sure they're good too—no retaliation. If it's a problem with them, this time, I won't miss," he said in a calm voice.

"Why ya beef wid dem so? What dem do?"

B Scientific chuckled. He realized she was absolutely clueless. "It was all a misunderstanding over some bad intel. I'm gonna leave it at that."

Aoki knew she wasn't going to get anything else out of him. He shut down tighter than security at the White House.

They finished an early dinner and climbed back into B Scientific's truck. B Scientific's phone rang during the ride home, and he was on his cell phone the rest of the way to Aoki's place.

Aoki didn't mind him being distracted. She was just hoping he didn't want to fuck next. Her pussy was still sore from being with Emilio earlier.

When he came to a stop in front of her home, he paused his cell phone conversation and said to Aoki, "Yo, I'm gonna take a rain check on fuckin' you today. Something came up, and I gotta handle it."

It was music to her ears. "Ah, everyting okay?"

"Yeah, just business."

"Just gimme a call."

"I'll do that, maybe later on tonight."

They tongue-kissed momentarily, and she climbed out of his truck and walked toward her front entrance. B Scientific sped off.

The minute he was gone, she jumped in her vehicle and drove to meet with Ri-Ri.

CHAPTER 4

Aoki pulled up to the Pink Houses and sat with the truck idling. She called Ri-Ri on her cell phone to inform her that she was parked outside her building.

"I'll be right down," Ri-Ri said.

Aoki took a deep breath and exhaled. She felt like she was in a horrible B movie. The hood was quiet. She didn't see a single soul anywhere—no corner boys or hustlers lingering in the parking lot or on the block, no hood rats walking around. Usually, around this time of the day, the projects were flooded with activity and people, but it looked like a ghost town.

Abruptly, Aoki's passenger door swung open, startling her. She was about to reach for her pistol.

It was Ri-Ri hopping into the truck.

"Ya scared me half to death," Aoki shouted.

"I'm sorry. You knew I was coming down."

Aoki felt a bit on edge. She wanted to curse Ri-Ri out, but she had other issues to deal with. She pulled away from the curb and started to drive toward the hospital.

Aoki asked her, "Any word on AZ?"

"They sayin' he's out of surgery and stable."

"That's good. Him strong. He gonna make it. I know he is."

"What happened? First, Heavy Pop and then AZ. Yo, the entire hood is losing they mind, going crazy and shit! Niggas at war or somethin'?" Ri-Ri rambled on.

"Me don't know."

"You ain't heard about anything? It might be retaliation for somethin', Aoki."

"Me don't know, Ri-Ri."

"Aoki, you gotta know somethin'! AZ and Pop are shot up and you don't know shit? You don't know how AZ got away only to get shot up later? Did B Scientific get at him?"

"Me don't know," Aoki remarked dryly.

"You know who did it, don't you? Was it B? Are you planning to get revenge for AZ?" Ri-Ri was asking a hundred and one questions.

"Ri-Ri, let me just get there. Me don't have ah fuckin' clue who did it. Me in de dark just like you."

Ri-Ri pouted.

Aoki drove on Linden Boulevard, trying to fight the evening traffic. It felt like every car around her was purposely moving slow and going against her.

"Move out de fuckin' way, bitch!" she yelled at a car slowing down in front of her while there was a green light ahead. "Dem drivin' like pussies!"

As they got closer to the hospital, Aoki looked at her friend and decided to shed some light on what had happened. Ri-Ri was the only person she felt she could trust.

"AZ came to me house last night wid a gun. Me think him was gon' kill me," Aoki said.

Ri-Ri's mouth dropped open. "What! You can't be serious!"

"I am!"

"Why would he come at you? Y'all been best friends forever and y'all dating! That's your boo!" Ri-Ri was bewildered. Then it dawned on her. She looked at Aoki and was almost afraid to ask, but she did. "Did you shoot him?"

"Nuh, it wasn't me."

"Then who, Aoki?"

Aoki remained silent. There was no way she was going to bring up Emilio.

It didn't make any sense to Ri-Ri or Aoki. There had to be some kind of reasonable explanation. If AZ was a murderer, then what did he need them for?

"This shit is crazy, Aoki, so fuckin' unreal."

"Me know."

"We both know that AZ wasn't gon' kill you. If he could kill, then why pay us?" Ri-Ri took a deep breath. "The only reason he was at your place is because *B* had just tried to murder them and had shot up Pop. Maybe he was just being cautious, Aoki. Shit has been crazy in the hood lately. I heard B Scientific was beefing with him, but I ain't believe it. But word is, and I didn't want to come at you like this, but people are seeing you hanging out with B Scientific, like on some more-than-just-friends shit, and that ain't cool. Keep it real wit' me—You still fuckin' B Scientific? Is all this about you and this affair?"

"B Scientific didn't shoot AZ."

"How you know that? You said you don't know who shot him."

"Ah get ah good look at 'im face, and it was someone different, not someone from our hood."

"So you never saw this nigga before?"

"No!"

"You think one of Peanut's men came back at AZ?"

"Ah not sure," Aoki replied.

Ri-Ri was reveling in the gossip and going into her investigation mode while Aoki hurried toward the hospital.

"Aoki, I've known you most of my life, and I can't shake this feeling that you're not keepin' it one hundred. Whatever it is, you gotta know you could trust me."

Aoki couldn't keep lying to her best friend. And with so many things going on with all the men in her life, she needed her girlfriend by her side. Before they got to the hospital, she said, "Ah don't know why B shoot at AZ and Heavy Pop. And it's true dat B did put Pop in the hospital. But on me life, B didn't shoot AZ. There's a puzzle that I gotta piece together, and ya moms plays a part."

"Gena?"

"Gena pawned B Scientific's chain in meh name, the chain dat Tisa said she lost after the hit. Dat stolen chain almost cost me my life."

Ri-Ri's entire body turned around to face Aoki. "What?"

"She did. I was wid him earlier at the pawnshop."

"You think all this is over a chain? And now the beef is squashed?"

Aoki shrugged. "Ah don't know, I keep tellin' ya."

Ri-Ri sighed. She knew Aoki was telling the truth; her mother was just that devious. She also knew that Gena couldn't have done it on her own. Her grimy mother and sister were both down together.

"Aoki, I'm sorry for what that bitch tried to do to you. I had no idea. If I had known, it wouldn't have even went down like that. I'm so sorry."

"Ah know ya didn't know," Aoki said.

"I should fuck Tisa up!" Ri-Ri said, heated. "That shit was so petty."

"We don't know dat Tisa had anything to do wid it, only Gena."

"That jealous-hearted bitch was down. She was the last one wit' your shit, talking 'bout she dumped it in the trash." Ri-Ri sucked her teeth. "You can't keep defending Tisa."

"Ah don't."

"You do—She left us for dead on the Peanut hit and you let her keep money she didn't earn."

"It ain't easy takin' a life, Ri-Ri."

Ri-Ri felt more connected to Aoki than her own sister. "We gotta teach this bitch a lesson, Aoki. We just cut Tisa off. Fuck her! She can't be trusted. Trust gotta be earned!"

Aoki agreed.

"Did you tell B Scientific about Gena?"

"Ah didn't." Aoki just didn't want to see Ri-Ri and Tisa become orphans like herself. "He would see Gena dead for that rosary. His dead brother owned it."

"Tisa is so fuckin' stupid!"

"Ya keep talking 'bout Tisa when me focusing on Gena! Me wanna bash her fuckin' face in."

Ri-Ri was horrified. "Aoki, no! You can't . . . you just can't disrespect my moms. She's my mother, Aoki, and you can't violate."

Aoki was quiet. "Me wait."

Ri-Ri knew that if Aoki jumped on her mother then she would be forced to jump in to help Gena, and Tisa would do the same. Aoki wasn't the type to take getting jumped lightly and would most likely come back to retaliate which could mean three more bodies added to her backyard.

"No, Aoki, please . . . promise me you won't go after Gena. I'm begging you as a friend. As your one and only true friend. As your sister," Ri-Ri pleaded.

Aoki was touched. "Me promise."

They arrived at the hospital, and it was crowded with people, from the entrance to the lobby. There were so many recognizable faces from their hood, it looked like a block party, like the entire projects had come to the hospital to support AZ and Heavy Pop.

Aoki was suddenly swamped with people offering their support. It was no secret that she was his girl and he loved her. Emotions were running high in the lobby. AZ's goons were ready for war, and they were looking to Aoki for some answers, desperately wanting to know his condition.

Tim said, "Yo, we ridin' for our nigga, Aoki! We got ya back!"

"Niggas gon' pay for this shit!" a young, pugnacious goon named Leon shouted, clapping his hands together as he talked. "I came as soon as I got the word, Aoki! I'm ready to body some niggas, yo! Them my niggas up in this fuckin' hospital!"

Aoki was showered with love and encouragement from everywhere. A few females were comforting, and assured her that whatever she needed, they would be there for her.

Security and other visitors in the lobby looked nervous amid the circus. Supporters of both AZ and Heavy Pop could be intimidating.

In the shadows though, lurking in the corner of the lobby, she spotted Connor. He was quiet as a mouse, but pretending to be hard, trying to look like he belonged with the rough, boisterous group of men. He and Aoki quickly locked eyes. Though he talked shit about her, and to her face, she somewhat felt sorry for him. He had to pretend to be something he wasn't to see the man he loved. But him being there was a liability to AZ.

She walked toward Connor, looking at him seriously. People were looking, watching, and wondering who Connor was, questioning his presence.

"Ya can't be here," she said to him in a low tone.

"I need to see him!" he said back in a strong whisper.

"Not now."

"When? I'm going crazy, Aoki. I need to know something."

"Ah will keep ya informed."

Aoki knew if word got out about Connor, he wouldn't make it out of the hospital alive, and AZ's reputation would be destroyed.

The wolves walked toward them, Aoki knew they were coming her way with concern and questions.

"Aoki, who this nigga?" one goon asked.

"He AZ cousin."

"Cousin?"

"We ain't know the nigga had a cousin."

"He from outta town—New Jersey. Ah call 'im," Aoki told them.

Some still looked on with suspicion, but they mostly backed off.

For a split second, Connor's eyes showed gratitude. If it wasn't for Aoki, they would have torn him apart.

"I just want to see him, Aoki, only for a minute," he said.

Aoki sighed. She nodded. She walked toward the Intensive Care Unit, Connor right behind her. She was determined to see AZ, and no security guard or doctor was going to prevent that.

AZ and Heavy Pop were going to pull through, but neither was conscious for more than a few minutes each hour because of the heavy sedation they were under. They were both extremely lucky to be alive, especially AZ. One bullet had penetrated his right lung three inches, and it partly collapsed. They removed fragments of the bullet as he underwent three hours of surgery. Now, his vital signs were stable.

The minute Aoki and Connor walked into the room to see AZ, they both burst into tears and grief. He was unconscious and looking like he could play a part in *The*

Matrix movie with the wires and tubes running in and out of him.

Connor's macho act came tumbling down immediately. He walked over to AZ's slumber state and took his hand into his. He took a deep breath, and his tears continued to fall. "You're so stupid, AZ! You hear me? I love you! But you had to go and get yourself shot! You could have been killed."

Of course he didn't get a response. Connor stared at AZ dejectedly and continued to wipe the tears from his face.

Aoki stood her short distance from him. Though she was in tears, she still felt betrayed by AZ. She wanted him to wake up and explain what he was doing at her house with a gun in her face.

Their moment with AZ was short-lived.

The moment two detectives showed up at the hospital, the crowd of thugs in the lobby began to scatter. When they came to AZ's room, Aoki frowned at them. They quickly started to question her.

"I'm Detective Blake, and this is my partner, Detective Sloan. Who are you to the victim?" he asked. Blake was a tall and lean middle-aged white man with short hair. Both men were dressed in suit and tie.

"Me his girlfriend and him best friend," she replied snappishly.

"And you?" Blake asked Connor.

"I'm his cousin."

The second detective was white also, an inch or two shorter than his partner, and older in the face, with a grayish goatee and dark hair with dark, experienced eyes.

"Where were you last night?" Detective Sloan asked.

"Wid a friend," Aoki told them.

"And you?"

"I was home," Connor said.

They asked a few more questions, and Aoki and Connor answered them efficiently. They were simply doing their job. Aoki just hoped and prayed that they didn't link her back to the shooting, and that she wasn't captured on camera when B Scientific dropped him off at the hospital.

Blake handed Aoki his card, and he and his partner headed out.

Cops made Aoki nervous, but she handled herself calmly and kept her cool.

"Ya need ah ride somewhere?" Aoki asked Connor when they got outside.

"I'm okay. I have my own transportation, thank you," Connor replied, pressing the alarm button to his silver Benz. He walked across the street to his car and climbed inside.

Aoki watched him with a blank stare. It was still hard for her to swallow. *AZ a batty bwai and fucking him.*

Aoki climbed into her own vehicle and headed home. Then it dawned on her that she had no idea where Ri-Ri had gone. She shrugged it off, assuming that when the cops came, Ri-Ri left with one of the guys in the lobby.

CHAPTER 5

Scientific felt like a fool. He had been bamboozled. Doing seventy on the freeway with his gun on his lap, he was ready to make the culprits pay for their sins against him. He took a few puffs from his cigarette and then flicked it out of the window. Brandi was a liar, and lying about having a miscarriage was the ultimate betrayal and violation to him.

He parked in front of his home, tucked his pistol in his waistband, and walked inside with a different look.

Brandi was lying on the couch in her underwear, watching a movie in the dark, still playing the role of a woman losing her baby from a beating.

"Hey, baby, I missed you," she said, smiling.

He decided to play her game for the moment. "I missed you too. You okay?"

"I'm doin' fine, baby. Still recovering, but sad though. It still hurts."

"I know it does. We can always try again."

"You really mean that? I really want to have your baby," she said. "I hate that fuckin' bitch for what she took from us. You need to take care of her, baby."

"I will," he said coolly. "Believe me, baby, it's gonna all be handled."

B Scientific cringed inside, knowing it was all a lie. He smiled and sat next to her on the couch, pulled her into his arms, and kissed her lovingly.

Nestled in his arms, she said, "Baby, I'm thirsty. Can you bring me a bottle of water and some fruit from the fridge?"

"I got you." He stood up and went into the kitchen.

Brandi appeared to have difficulty getting up from the couch to use the bathroom, clutching her stomach like she was still in great pain. B Scientific wanted to applaud her for putting on such an award-winning performance. Every fiber in his body told him that it was all an act.

But he continued to be kind and amiable to her as they snuggled on the couch watching a movie.

Brandi continued talking about the ordeal. "I wanted to give you a son, baby. I knew I was going to have a boy," she said tearfully, "and he was gonna be so beautiful."

B Scientific remained silent.

"You cheated on me wit' that bitch! You know it's hard for me to forgive you for cheating on me wit' that dirty bitch! And she the reason why I lost your baby."

"Baby, I already told you I'm sorry," he said, holding his tongue.

"Sometimes sorry isn't enough! That bitch put me through a lot!"

"I told you I'm gonna take care of that bitch—she's a dead woman."

"You take care of that bitch, baby . . . for our unborn son. Make that fuckin' bitch pay."

"Oh, I will. Believe that."

B Scientific had his own plan, which he was going to put into action the following day. There was a lie in Brandi's tale; something wasn't right. He believed she'd had an abortion. But one thing for sure, tonight was going to be the last night he would be played for a fool.

As they watched the movie, B Scientific tried to get frisky with Brandi on the couch, but she wasn't in the mood because of the alleged miscarriage. And they ended up falling asleep on the couch, with the television watching them.

The next morning, B Scientific woke up early, feeling bright. He stared at Brandi still sleeping like she was a baby, curled up on the couch in her underwear.

He nudged her. "Get up, baby. I got something special planned for you today."

Hearing that, she woke up with a smile on her face, looking up at her man. "Oh, you do?"

"Yeah, it's gonna make you feel a whole lot better. So let's get dressed."

Brandi leaped up from the couch and threw herself into B Scientific's arms. They hugged each other, her petite frame pressed against him firmly. B Scientific started growing hard.

She started to kiss the side of his neck and nibble at his earlobe. "Baby, you know I'm impatient when it comes to surprises." She slid her hand into his pants and stroked his penis from the tip to the base.

B Scientific turned into putty, moaning lightly.

Though he was enjoying her sexual advances, he found it odd that just the night before she clearly wasn't in the mood to have sex. One mention of a surprise, and Brandi was all over him like a cheap suit.

"I love you, baby," she said as she continued to jerk him off.

"I love you too."

"So tell me what my surprise is."

"I'm taking you to the Diamond District to buy you that Audemars watch you always wanted."

Brandi burst into joy. "Ohmygod! Are you serious?"

He nodded. "I owe it to you, baby. After what you been through, you deserve the best."

She leaped into his arms. The kisses came like raindrops. They were all over him. Brandi was almost foaming at the mouth. She ran into the bedroom to get dressed.

B Scientific smirked. Her lie continued to unravel little by little. When Brandi ran into the bedroom to get dressed, she didn't look like she was in pain at all. All that slow-walking and moaning and groaning was gone.

Brandi emerged from the bedroom dressed in a tight skirt, nice top, high heels, and a smile so wide, it got her ears wet. They climbed into B Scientific's truck, and he drove off. Brandi couldn't stop telling him how wonderful, considerate, and handsome he was, but B Scientific drove without saying much.

Fifteen minutes in the truck, instead of getting onto the highway that took them to the Brooklyn Bridge and into the city, B Scientific continued straight and drove deeper into Brooklyn.

Brandi realized they weren't heading toward the Diamond District. "Baby, you missed the ramp onto the highway. Where are you going?"

He ignored her.

Brandi continued to question him, but he had nothing to say to her. She soon found herself in front of a doctor's office in downtown Brooklyn.

"Why are we here?" she asked him, perplexed.

B Scientific turned and looked at her. He killed the engine and said, "Since the miscarriage, I've been worried about you, so I made an appointment for you to see a doctor. I want you to get a full physical done. I want to make sure that you can still have babies. After this, we'll go and get the watch."

Brandi looked shaken.

"And you don't need to worry. I put my man on Aoki, and he's laying on her house right now to take care of that bitch," he lied.

"Baby, I'm fine. I-I don't need to see a doctor."

"Baby, you been through a lot. We need to make sure everything's okay with you."

"But I feel great. I mean, I know my body. I don't need a doctor."

"I would feel a whole lot better if you see this doctor and get a full physical. Then we can go shopping when you're done," B Scientific said firmly. He looked at her vigorously, and his stare was intense. It was hard for her to look him in the eyes.

Brandi started to fidget in her seat.

"Baby, forget the watch and let's just go home and fuck our brains out. Make love to me and put another baby in me, and that will prove to you that I'm fine."

"We here already," he said.

"I rather go to my own doctor. I can make an appointment next week."

B Scientific grabbed her by the collar and nearly broke her in half with his strength when he slammed her against the passenger door. He was all over her like acne on a teenager. He glared at her. "Did you fuckin' kill my baby? Or did you really have a miscarriage? And you better not fuckin' lie to me, bitch!"

She cried out, "No!"

He slapped her so hard, her face turned red. She was in tears.

"What happened to my baby? Did Aoki have anything to do with it?" he shouted. "Yes or no?"

Brandi was crying hysterically. Then suddenly she decided to sucker-punch him in the face and attempt to flee from the vehicle, but B Scientific snatched her back in. He punched her in the face repeatedly, blackening and swelling her eye and lip, leaving her screaming for her life.

He grabbed her by her hair and slammed her face into the glass, nearly shattering it from the might. He then grabbed her neck, tightening his grip, choking her.

"You better tell me what the fuck happened to my baby! And you better not lie to me, bitch!" he shouted.

Brandi's face was in a full-blown panic, never having seen this side of him before. B Scientific was waiting for an answer as he continued to clutch her neck, barely allowing any breath into her body.

Through tears and hysteria, she shouted, "There was never no baby!"

"What the fuck you talkin' about?" he growled.

"I was never pregnant! I lied to you!"

He released his hold from around her neck, breathing heavily and looking lost.

"You drove me to lie! I loved you so much, I couldn't stand to see you leaving me for some next bitch! I did everything for you, and you ain't shit—nothing but a cheating bastard!"

B Scientific thought he had heard everything. It placed an innocent woman in his path to get murdered and would've allowed him to go through with it. The fact that she was happy to be rewarded with a watch that cost nearly a hundred thousand dollars, after playing him for a fool, had him ready to break her neck. There was no coming back from this one—no forgiving her and her lies.

She wasn't the only one on his shit list; Gena was at the top too. They both thought they were smarter than him, treating him like nothing more than an ATM and a fool. They both needed to be punished.

B Scientific pulled out his gun and aimed it at Brandi. She was wide-eyed and frozen with fear. "You stupid bitch!"

"Ba—"

"Shut the fuck up!"

He started the engine and drove off, holding her at gunpoint while he drove.

A half hour later, they were parked on a secluded block in an industrial part of Brooklyn, with not many people or cars around.

He turned and glared at her. And then the attack happened fast. His fists rained down on her repeatedly, striking her head, face, and stomach.

He screamed, "You lie and play me, bitch! You fuck wit' me! You fuckin' dirty, deceitful cunt! I should fuckin' kill you!" He repeatedly pounded his fist into her eye and right temple.

"I'm sorry! Please! Help me! Please God! Please!" she screamed out for help, but to no benefit. She was alone with nowhere to run.

B Scientific tore into Brandi like a lion killing its prey. He picked up his gun and slammed it into her face.

She closed her eyes and whimpered.

"Look at me, you cunt bitch!" he ordered through clenched teeth.

Her eyes opened slightly, almost beaten shut and leaking tears.

"If you go to the fuckin' cops or tell anyone I did this to you, I'll kill you. You understand?"

For a moment, Brandi was confused and disoriented.

"Bitch, do you fuckin' understand me?"

She nodded her head.

"I will kill you and your whole family!"

She knew he would do it too. He had people that could go after her and everything she loved.

"You and me, we're through! I don't want to ever see you again. From now on, you don't exist to me, and I don't want to ever see you around. Don't come home and don't call!"

Brandi nodded.

"In fact, all that shit you got on, take it off!" he said. "The only thing you're leaving with is your life."

Brandi didn't hesitate. Her diamond earrings, ring, chain and bracelet all came off. The red bottoms came off, along with the clothes she wore, except her underwear.

He told her, "Leave the Chanel bag in the truck."

Brandi sat in the truck beaten and bloody in her underwear.

B Scientific continued glaring at her and shouted, "Get the fuck out my truck!"

After she stepped out of the ride barefoot, battered, and bleeding, he peeled off and never looked back.

The only reason he didn't kill her was because he'd loved her once. However, Gena was going to be a different story.

CHAPTER 6

Scientific walked into his apartment and plopped down on the couch. He sat brooding in the dark for a while. He had no remorse for what he'd done to Brandi. She was out of his life for good. Though, he was saddened that there was no baby. He'd always wanted a child.

He sat there in the dark for a long while, and then he stood up and marched into the main bedroom. He removed all of Brandi's clothes from the closet and tossed them onto the floor. Then he removed all her belongings from the drawers and the bathroom. He planned on getting rid of everything. He didn't want anything in the apartment that reminded him of her. Including pictures of them. As far as he was concerned, she had never existed.

He tossed it all into a trash bag and then took it out into the street and dumped it into the dumpster. "Good riddance, bitch," he said.

He went back upstairs and sat back on the couch. He sat silently in the dark, and then burst into tears. He was a cold-blooded killer and a dangerous thug, but the one thing he felt he would never be, was a father.

He leaned over with his elbows pressed against his knees and his face in his hands. He cried for a moment, becoming emotional. He felt like a fool for being so stupid and naïve. It was hard to hold it in. No one ever saw him cry, and he planned on keeping it like that.

No more! he thought to himself. *It ends today!*

B Scientific dried his tears and exhaled. It was time for him to take care of his business. He'd had his moment, but he was determined to never allow it to happen again.

He stood up, walked toward the window, and gazed outside. He lit a cigarette, transfixed in thoughts of Aoki. Now with Brandi gone, he could give her all of his attention. Carefully. He wasn't about to make the same mistake twice. He did want Aoki all to himself, but he knew he had to earn her love, not buy it.

CHAPTER 7

It was mid-afternoon on a sunny day when Aoki walked in the hospital with several bottles of Snapple and a large bucket of Popeye's chicken for the nurses on the fourth floor. She had just come from the place up the street and spent fifty dollars on food and drinks. In the mornings, she would bring bagels and coffee. The nurses gave her special privileges, like staying long past visiting hours. The expense was nothing to her; she had enough cash to splurge, though she hadn't fulfilled a contract in a while.

She strutted through the hallway in her high heels and hair down, looking like a runway model. She walked toward the nurses' station with a broad smile. "Hello, ladies."

Seeing Aoki, the nurses smiled. For two long weeks she had become a regular at the hospital. They all fell in love with her accent, and they believed she really cared for her boyfriend. She was the pretty girl checking up on her boo.

"Hello, Aoki," the nurses greeted affably.

"Me brought ya some lunch." Aoki handed them the large bucket of chicken and drinks, and they thanked her.

She had been running back and forth to the hospital each day, waiting for AZ to wake up. A part of Aoki truly cared about AZ's well-being, but then there was that part of her that was about her own business and well-being. She needed to talk to AZ and find out what went wrong between them.

As the nurses started to dig into the chicken, Aoki pivoted toward AZ's room.

One of the nurses said, "Aoki, we have some good news for you."

Aoki turned and looked at the nurse. She hadn't heard any good news in a while. "What good news?" she said.

"Your other friend, the heavy one, he's awake," she said.

"Fa true?"

The nurse nodded. "He's been up since early morning. I thought you would like to know."

Aoki smiled. "Tanks," she said to the nurse. Now maybe she could find out what went wrong.

Aoki decided to go see Heavy Pop first. She walked down the hallway with a sense of urgency. She hoped he was alone so they could talk in private. She got to his door and saw a nurse inside the room. She was checking Heavy Pop's vitals and jotting down some information on a clipboard. She stood in the doorway and observed. Not only was he awake, he was trying to flirt with the nurse, and it looked like she was flirting right back. Heavy Pop was bandaged up a little and connected to an IV, but still looking in good spirits after almost losing his life. So far, he hadn't noticed Aoki.

Aoki walked into the room, and Heavy Pop looked at her and smiled.

"Aoki, what's up?" he greeted her.

"Ya gave me ah scare, Heavy Pop," she said.

"I'm sorry. Shit just got crazy."

She smiled and stepped closer to his bed. She glanced at the nurse. "How him?"

The nurse smiled lightly. "He's fine. Just lucky to be alive." The nurse quickly continued her duties and said to them, "I'll give y'all some privacy." She walked out the room.

Aoki shut the door behind her.

Heavy Pop looked at her and asked, "What's up?"

"Ya didn't hear?"

"About what?"

"AZ's been shot too. Him down the hall."

Heavy Pop looked overcome with shock and serious concern. "What the fuck you talkin' about?"

Aoki told him the story, explaining that a stranger had shot AZ. "Him came out de dark," she said.

Heavy Pop shook his head in disbelief. "I need to go see him."

"Ya need to rest first."

Heavy Pop sulked for a moment, looking away from her.

"Tell me 'bout de shootin'," she said, sounding like a detective.

"It was crazy; it happened too fast. One minute we chillin' and shit, and the next, B rolling up on us, shouting somethin', and he opened fire. It sounded like he said your name, though. I ain't know we had a problem wit' that nigga until then."

Aoki sat there near his bed feeling so guilty. She'd listened to his every word. She felt consumed by blame. What if Heavy Pop had been killed? He had always been down-to-earth and about his business. And though he was a drug dealer, he always tried to avoid violence, whenever possible.

"Yo, you fuckin' that nigga, Aoki?" Heavy Pop said out of the blue.

"What? No!" she lied.

"It don't make any sense, though. Why he comin' at us like this? What beef we got wit' that nigga?"

"Me don't know."

"We ain't stepping on the nigga's territory; me and AZ made sure of that. We always been careful and respectful." Heavy Pop tried to read her. She was just too quiet for him. He looked her in the eyes as she sat there quietly. "Aoki, tell me the truth. We've been friends for a long time—You sure you ain't got nothin' goin' on wit' B Scientific? The only time a nigga really acts up like this is over some pussy, if it ain't over drugs and cash."

Aoki looked down at her hands. "Me got nothin' goin' on wit' him."

"AZ really loves you. He's loved you since we were kids."

"Me know."

"And it would break his fuckin' heart if he ever found out that you were fuckin' around on him. If you did, I'm not judging you, but just don't let him find out, because it would kill him."

"Me know. And everything has been handled."

The thing was, though, Heavy Pop was clueless to everything that had gone on between her and AZ. AZ was gay, and at first their relationship was only an act. Aoki knew he'd developed some feelings for her and wanted her for real this time. But the damage had already been done. B Scientific came into the picture, and her world flipped topsy-turvy.

"What you mean, 'handled?'"

"Me met wit' B Scientific, and him assured me that there is no beef between y'all."

Heavy Pop couldn't wrap his head around it. "Why'd he shoot at us, though? We never had any problems wit' him, not to my recollection."

"It was all ah misunderstanding."

"Misunderstanding? Several gunshots later, and it's all a misunderstanding? That's it?"

Aoki shrugged. "That's all him said."

"But who shot AZ?"

"Me told ya, it was dark and me never seen him before."

Heavy Pop shook his head. "It probably was them Staten Island niggas."

"Probably," she replied.

Though Heavy Pop looked fine, his body still ached in certain places, and he was still weak. He wanted to get up from the bed and visit AZ, but Aoki was against it. If AZ woke up, then she needed to speak to him first.

Aoki stood up. "Get some rest. We'll talk later," she said. She kissed Heavy Pop on the forehead, wished him well, and made her exit from the room.

She strutted down the hallway, turned the corner, and went into AZ's room, only to find that Connor was there, asleep in the chair next to AZ's bed. He'd probably been there since early morning or maybe the night before.

She was irritated. If AZ was awake, he would be furious. It looked bad, and luckily she was there to correct the scene before anyone else saw it. What man would sleep by another's man bedside? She shut the room door, walked over, and kicked Connor's chair, startling him awake.

Connor opened his eyes to see her glaring down at him. "Why ya here?"

"I'm worried about him," Connor replied.

"Ya need to leave."

"I can't. I love him. I deserve to be here."

"Him wouldn't want ya here," she said firmly. "Ya know him on de down low. Him don't need de trouble from ya."

Connor was furious. He stood up, frowning. "I'm not leaving!" He folded his arms across his chest and stood his ground. "I deserve to be here and watching over him."

"Ya can't out him like this! Ya gon' make more problems fo' him."

He shot back, "Who made you lord over his life? Huh?"

Aoki stepped closer to Connor, her eyes tapering into a harsh stare. She wanted to punch him in the face and drag him out of the room, but she didn't want to make a scene. Too much drama had happened already. They both argued, but in a strong whisper, out of respect and love for AZ.

Aoki was up in his face, her fists clenched. "Ya know what will happen if they find out 'im a batty bwai? Huh?

They will kill 'im and you!"

Connor continued frowning. Aoki was serious, telling him the truth.

"If ya really love him, then leave."

Connor stood silently for a short moment, looking at Aoki's. Without saying a word, he pivoted, collected his things from the chair, and left the room.

Aoki sighed with relief. She took a seat in the same chair Connor was in, looked at a comatose AZ and said, "What make ya have so much trouble?"

She planned on staying for a while. She had nothing to do today. She turned on the television and then got on her cell phone. The first person she contacted was Ri-Ri, to tell her to meet her at the hospital.

Aoki conversed with AZ, but it was a one-way conversation. She wanted to know if he would have pulled the trigger and taken her life. Why was he so angry with her?

CHAPTER 8

Ri-Ri walked into the hospital room and greeted Aoki with a hug and a kiss on the cheek.

When she turned and saw AZ lying there looking lifeless, she started to cry. "I hate to see him like this," she said.

"Him be fine; him strong," Aoki said.

Ri-Ri took a deep breath and said a silent prayer. It was hard to see AZ out of commission, and it was still hard for her to believe he was going to kill Aoki. There had to be a reasonable explanation for his action.

"Any word on the streets?" she asked Aoki.

"No news so far."

"I haven't heard anything either. They say Heavy Pop is awake."

"Him is."

"I need to go see him."

"Him doin' fine," Aoki said.

"I'm just glad they're both alive."

The two girls hung out in the family zone of the room and conversed and gossiped while flipping through the cable channels. Periodically, a nurse would come in to check on AZ's vitals and jot down some notes. The ladies made small talk with the nurse. When she left, they went to talking about the streets and business.

"I'm gonna keep my eyes and ears open, and if I hear anything, I'm on it, Aoki," Ri-Ri said.

"We just need to be cautious."

"I know."

Aoki's cell phone chimed, indicating that she had a text message. She opened the text and it was Emilio.

HEY BEAUTIFUL, SITTIN HERE THINKIN' BOUT U? WHAT U DOIN?

She smiled at his text. She texted back: AT THE HOSPITAL. WHERE ARE U?

I'M LYING IN MY DORM RM BUTT NAKED, WAITING 4 U 2 JUMP ON THIS DICK AGAIN. U WANNA SEE HOW HARD I AM?

She texted back: STOP BEING NAUGHTY.

I CAN'T HELP IT. I'M ALWAYS THINKING ABOUT IT AND U ALWAYS GET ME EXCITED.

He sent her a dick picture.

Aoki smiled at it. She knew she was wrong for sexting Emilio while AZ was lying in a coma right next to her. But she was in love. While her fingers moved incessantly, Ri-Ri was busy looking at the television.

As Aoki continued communicating with Emilio, B Scientific all of a sudden sent her a text too: I WANNA SEE

U TONIGHT. YOU KNOW WHAT I WANT.

She wasn't in the mood to see him.

I'M KINDA BUSY. AT THE HOSPITAL.

He came back with: SO, UNBUSY YOURSELF N LINK UP WIT ME.

I'LL TRY.

A minute later, B Scientific texted: U NEED TO TRY HARDER TO SEE ME. BEEN THINKIN' ABOUT U A LOT. I KICKED BRANDI TO THE CURB, NEARLY KILLED THAT BITCH FOR LYING ON YOU.

U KNOW HOW TO PICK EM.

WELL NOW I'M PICKING YOU. CALL ME WHEN YOU GET THE CHANCE.

Aoki wanted to see Emilio, but B Scientific wasn't taking no for an answer.

"You a popular girl, Aoki," Ri-Ri said, referring to her cell phone activity. "Who got your phone buzzing like that?"

"Just nonsense."

"Mm-hmm."

Aoki didn't want to share her business with Ri-Ri. She knew it was wise to keep her two affairs a secret. People talk, even friends, and the last thing she needed was her sex life to be exposed.

The evening progressed with them eating Chinese takeout and watching a movie on cable. Aoki didn't want to go home. She felt safe at the hospital, where she was able to get some rest and think.

After eating and talking, Aoki and Ri-Ri left the room. AZ's condition was the same. The only things they could do there were sit by his bedside and pray. The girls walked toward the elevators.

"I'll meet ya in de lobby," Aoki said to Ri-Ri. She needed to make a quick stop at the nurses' station.

"All right."

Aoki approached the nurses. She needed to take care of something important before she left the hospital. "Me need ah favor from y'all," she said.

The ladies were listening.

She asked them to limit the amount of time Connor was with AZ.

The nurses obliged her request. They were already chattering about the relationship. With Connor's frequent visits, tears, emotional outbursts, and over-the-top gayness, the nurses felt that AZ's beautiful girlfriend was being played.

Aoki and Ri-Ri strutted out of the hospital underneath the fading evening sun. AZ was just one of many victims being treated inside. Brookdale was a busy hospital in an ever-growing Brooklyn war zone, where gunshot victims came in constantly. AZ was being well taken care of. The doctors and nurses were doing their best to treat and comfort him, and Aoki was there to make sure of that.

Though everything seemed taken care of, and B Scientific said that he had squashed their beef, Aoki couldn't help but feel that something evil was brewing. Her name and reputation had been cleared, but something didn't feel right.

The girls crossed the street toward her truck, but before Aoki climbed inside, she noticed detectives parked nearby. She could see their silhouettes in the front seat of a Buick.

Who are they watching? Are they staking me out? Aoki wondered.

The NYPD were desperately searching for the Killer Dolls, who were on everyone's radar. They had New York's attention with the brazen murders they'd committed.

Always careful to cover her tracks, Aoki was certain that she'd given them no reason to suspect her of any wrongdoing. She looked their way for a minute.

Ri-Ri broke her trance. "Is everything okay?"

Aoki came back down to earth. "Everything fine." She climbed into the truck and started the engine. She pulled out of her parking spot and headed toward the Pink Houses.

Aoki drove down Linden Boulevard amid light traffic. She constantly glanced through her rearview mirror to see if they were following her. Unfortunately, she picked up their trail three cars behind. "Ri-Ri, we bein' followed."

"What? By who?"

"Dem two detectives."

Ri-Ri spun around to look through the back window. The only thing she saw was traffic behind her. "Which car?" she asked.

"De silver Buick."

Ri-Ri saw the Buick moving behind them inconspicuously.

Aoki continued doing the speed limit, constantly glancing in her rearview mirror, trying to predict the detectives' next move.

"What the fuck they want from us? We ain't do shit!" Ri-Ri exclaimed.

"We just need to keep cool."

"We ridin' dirty?" Ri-Ri asked.

Aoki nodded. "Yes."

"Fuck!"

Aoki drove several more blocks. "Me have a plan," she told Ri-Ri.

"What plan?"

Out of the blue, Aoki pulled over to the side of the road like she was being pulled over by police and put on her hazard lights. She put the truck in park and left it idling.

"Aoki, what the fuck you doin'?"

"We have nothin' to hide."

"We ridin' dirty! Did you forget that?"

"Dem don't know that."

Ri-Ri sighed heavily.

Aoki stepped out of the truck and walked toward the back.

Ri-Ri looked confused by her actions, thinking that her friend done lost her mind. "Aoki, you gonna get us locked up!" she hollered.

"Me ain't gon' run from no police." Aoki looked for the Buick and spotted the detectives coming her way. She smirked as their car slowed toward them.

The detectives parked and stepped out of the car simultaneously and looked casually at Aoki.

"Is dere ah problem, officers?" she asked.

"That's *detectives* to you," Detective Blake corrected her.

"Me sorry, detectives," Aoki replied indifferently. "Is there ah reason why ya followin' me?"

"Do we need a reason?" Detective Sloan asked.

"NYPD, such pillars in de community," she said.

Both men towered over Aoki and moved with prudence as they inspected her SUV from the outside and locked their eyes on both females with grave apprehension. They had nothing on the girls, but Detective Blake had his suspicions about Aoki. In fact, every fiber in his body told him that she was hiding something. When they'd met at the hospital a couple weeks back, something in her eyes gave him the chills. He'd decided to run her name and found out she had a violent rap sheet for such a young female.

Ri-Ri sat quietly in the passenger seat. She refused to entertain the detectives with any questions or eye contact. She frowned, wishing they would go away.

"Where are y'all two headed?" Detective Sloan asked.

"Home," Aoki answered bluntly.

Detective Blake tried to read Aoki. He could see the coldness in her eyes. She tried to look like the standard girlfriend or vulnerable female, but he'd been a cop for too long and had seen every kind of criminal. His intuition told him there was more to these two girls than met the eye.

Blake asked Aoki, "Are you hiding something?"

"Me have nothin' to hide," she returned calmly.

"That's what they all say," he countered. "But there's something about you that disturbs me, Aoki. You know, there have been some brazen killings lately by a group of young women. The newspapers are calling them the 'Killer Dolls.' Funny thing, I've done my homework, and some of the people murdered by these women are connected to your boyfriend lying in the hospital, like Peanut, Greasy Dee, and Polo. It seems like they all had some kind of trouble with your boyfriend."

"Shit happens, detectives."

"I know, shit happens. But I continued looking into you, and you know what else I find odd? That your parents have been missing for a while now. They just vanished like that"—He snapped his fingers. "No trace of them anywhere in the neighborhood."

"Me don't know what ya mean."

"Of course, you don't. What do you do for a living again, Aoki?" Detective Blake asked.

"Me, I'm a grievin' female."

"She's a funny one," Detective Sloan said.

"Yes, she is. And you know the funny thing, Sloan? They always think they can get away with murder, that they're so much smarter than the police."

"Look, dis is harassment, ya hear!" she spat.

"We're just having a friendly chat."

Aoki glared at the two detectives. "Me have things to do, detectives. Ya have ah warrant or probable cause? 'Cause me done talkin'."

Detectives Blake and Sloan smiled.

Blake said, "Just our suspicion."

"Can we go?"

"Yeah, but I'll catch you later, Aoki," Blake said. "Believe that."

Aoki turned and limbed back into her truck, upset that they were up her ass so deep. She sped off, not looking back.

"What the fuck was that about?" Ri-Ri said.

"Dem have nothin' on us, Ri-Ri. Dem fishin', that's all."

"We gotta be extra careful."

Aoki nodded. "Me agree."

Nosy detectives weren't going to deter Aoki from handling her business. They had nothing on her. Aoki planned on being extra careful and smarter, though. She couldn't afford to take uncalculated risks. She'd come too far in the game to be scared away by two snooping detectives.

The girls hurried back to the Pink Houses.

Things had become a lot more difficult, but interesting. Despite the heat from the detectives, the Killer Dolls were still going to be active. Aoki was a hard-core bitch down to the bone, and she was about her money. And her revenge.

Aoki came to a stop in front of the project buildings. Being a balmy night, everyone was outside, including a few of AZ's and Heavy Pop's goons. They were hanging on the corner, drinking liquor, smoking weed, and rolling dice.

Aoki killed the engine to her truck and exhaled like a deflating balloon. It had been a long day. She had a lot of spring cleaning to do—implementing her own investigation on why AZ had a gun to her face and also trying to clean up his mess with Connor.

"What you about to do?" Ri-Ri asked her.

"Me gon' go home to sleep and tink."

Ri-Ri nodded. "You do that. Call me later." She opened the door and stepped out of the truck.

Aoki watched her strut to her building. As Ri-Ri was walking away in one direction, Aoki noticed Tisa running toward her truck from a different direction, like it was an emergency. They hadn't seen or spoken to each other in weeks. Both Ri-Ri and Aoki had decided to not confront Gena or Tisa until AZ had woken up. Aoki wanted to deal with one situation at a time. In the meantime, Ri-Ri was to keep her ears and eyes open to see if Gena or Tisa slipped up and mentioned the stolen rosary.

Aoki wasn't in the mood to see Tisa. Poised like a cobra, she quickly gripped the handle of her pistol, ready to strike if Tisa even flinched wrong her way.

Though Tisa was a part of the Killer Dolls, she still hadn't proven her worth. She talked a good game, but when it came down to doing the deed, only Aoki and Ri-Ri got their hands dirty.

"Aoki, what's good?" Tisa asked.

"Ya tell me, Tisa," Aoki replied dryly. She was already giving the girl shade, looking at her apprehensively.

"Been tryin' to call you. I heard about AZ. How is he?"

"Him fine."

"What happened?"

"Me still don't know."

"Please, when he comes through, give him my love. Let him know that we're thinkin' about him and hoping he pulls through. That shit is fucked up what happened to him. Whatever you need, Aoki, I got you."

Aoki sat behind the steering wheel of her truck staring at Tisa stoically. "If me know somethin', ya know somethin'."

Tisa, dressed in a pair of tight jeans and Yeezy sneakers, looked disheartened by Aoki's nonchalant reaction.

Aoki kept her gun close. She didn't trust Tisa and started to dislike her actions. Tisa had been whoring herself around the neighborhood and spending money like it was going out of style. Aoki felt the bitch was creating too much attention on herself unnecessarily, becoming just like her mother, Gena.

The two girls had a sparse conversation before Aoki said, "Tisa, me need to go."

"Okay, Aoki, talk to you later."

Aoki drove away, leaving Tisa standing on the sidewalk. Tisa watched Aoki's truck drive toward the corner, where some goons were lingering, and Aoki stopped to converse with one of the men.

AZ's crony, named Nine, flagged Aoki down in her truck as she was about to turn the corner. He was a fierce soldier who lived like he had nothing to lose. He approached the passenger window, looking troubled. The two of them locked eyes, a mutual respect between them.

"Yo, Aoki, I ain't been down to the hospital to see my nigga because I can't see him like that, all fucked up and shit!" Nine said.

"Him cool, Nine."

"But, yo, whatever you need from me, call me. I'm ready to fuck a nigga's shit up, you feel me?" Nine lifted his shirt to reveal two pistols tucked snugly in his waistband. "I'm always ready. You know me, Aoki—I don't give a fuck! I'll kill anything moving!"

Aoki nodded with a smirk. She didn't feel threatened by him but was definitely impressed. She'd heard stories about how ruthless and deadly he was. He was also homophobic. Aoki had heard stories about him nearly beating a man to death because he thought the man was coming on to him at a party. He was known to shout out hateful and nasty slurs to homosexuals, and he wasn't shy about how he felt about them.

Nine let his shirt fall over the guns. "AZ's my nigga. I got mad love for him and Pop."

Aoki couldn't help wondering if that same love would still exist if he found out AZ was gay. If the truth ever came out about AZ, would he still have love for his friend, or would he put a bullet in AZ himself? The fire in Nine's eyes was something terrifying. Even Aoki was cautious around him, knowing he was temperamental and dangerous.

"Me tell him ya said wha' gwan when him come through," she said.

He nodded. "A'ight, you do that."

Nine stepped away from the passenger window looking serious. Aoki drove away and she felt that same feeling from earlier—something evil was brewing, and it gave even her a deep chill.

Tisa walked into the apartment and shut the door. She couldn't shake how she felt about the situation that'd developed between her, Ri-Ri, and Aoki. It was unusual. Her sister and best friend were keeping her out of the loop and acting like she had crucified them on the cross. She didn't know what was with the sudden change in them both. Tisa was frowning as she marched into the bedroom, where Ri-Ri was getting undressed.

Ri-Ri, in her matching bra and underwear, looked at Tisa frowning her way.

Tisa exclaimed to Ri-Ri, "Yo, what's with the shade?"

"What?"

"You heard me. I'm outside talking to Aoki, and she acting brand-new on me, like she didn't want to tell me shit."

"Bitch, stop trippin'." Ri-Ri shook her head.

"I ain't trippin, Ri-Ri! What's goin' on? What the fuck did I do?"

"You tell me."

"What? Tell you what?"

"I don't know. You sounding all guilty an' shit. Did you do somethin' to feel all paranoid and guilty about?"

"I ain't do shit." Visions of Aoki's rosary flashed before Tisa's eyes. She was sure both Ri-Ri and Aoki knew she had stolen it. But fuck it! They couldn't prove it.

"Then ain't shit goin' on. AZ was just shot, and Heavy Pop too, and you think it's all about you. Bitch, please. Aoki's got a lot more serious shit to deal with than to be worrying about your fuckin' feelings."

"So talk to me—I'm part of the crew too, right?"

Ri-Ri sighed and continued to get dressed in her yoga pants and tank. She knew now wasn't the time to go off on Tisa. She had to keep quiet and bide her time.

"Stop actin' thirsty!"

Tisa was relentless. She marched closer to her sister and spat, "What's goin' on? What the fuck did I do, huh?"

Ri-Ri rolled her eyes. "You ain't do shit!"

"Y'all ain't actin' like that! Y'all bitches actin' fake toward me!"

Ri-Ri sucked her teeth. "Tisa, you're fuckin' delusional, you know that? You're crazy."

"No, I'm not! I'm not stupid, Ri-Ri!" Tisa shouted.

"You could have fooled me, because right now I'm thinkin' you're a dumb-ass, grimy, stupid bitch!"

"Fuck you! What, y'all think because I didn't get my hands dirty like y'all bitches, that I'm not official? Huh? Is that it? I was there too when shit went down. I risked my life just like y'all did."

"Ain't nobody judging you."

Tisa screamed, "Yes, y'all are! Stop tryin' to fuckin' play me!"

"See, you're too emotional."

"I know y'all tryin' to cut me the fuck out. That's what y'all tryin' to do. I'm not stupid, Ri-Ri."

"Yo, ain't nobody calling you stupid. You need to calm down."

"Don't fuckin' tell me to calm down!" Tisa jumped into her sister's face, her fists tightened.

"Tisa, you better back the fuck down! I ain't the fuckin' one, bitch!" Ri-Ri warned through gritted teeth.

"Fuck you and Aoki! What, you think because you helped kill some people that you bad now?"

"Tisa, you need to shut your fuckin' mouth."

"Or what?" Tisa shouted. "Keep fuckin' wit' me, bitch, and I'll have you and that mixed breed doin' life!"

Rihanna couldn't believe what her sister let slip from her lips. Would she ever be angered enough to snitch? The thought gave her pause. "You won't get that far, bitch!"

They were like two alley cats, snarling and hissing at each other, claws out, the hair on their skin rising.

"What y'all bitches in here yellin' about?" Gena shouted, bursting into the girls' room. "The whole fuckin' neighborhood can hear y'all fightin'."

"She started it, Ma," Ri-Ri said.

"No, I didn't. She and Aoki are tryin' to play me."

"I don't care who started what. Y'all bitches take that shit outside of my fuckin' house. I ain't in the mood to hear y'all fuckin' bickering."

Tisa made a face like she'd sucked on an onion as she backed away from her sister. She scowled at her mother and exclaimed, "Fuck it, I'm leaving! I fuckin' hate it here anyway!"

Gena said, "Then pack your shit and leave out my apartment, bitch!"

Tisa pivoted, marched out of the bedroom, and stormed out of the apartment, slamming the door behind her so hard, it rattled a few pictures on the walls.

"Fuck her!" Ri-Ri said. "She a hatin'-ass bitch!"

"Yeah, but y'all still sisters."

Ri-Ri sucked her teeth. "Fuck that thievin'-ass bitch!"

"What the fuck you say?"

"Nothing."

CHAPTER 9

Under a dark sky sprinkled with shining stars, B Scientific pulled back the throttle of his red-and-black Ducati motorcycle and opened up the engine beneath him, accelerating to eighty. The bike came to life on the highway like a bat out of hell, its thick tires burning up the asphalt. Crouched forward with his eyes fixed ahead, he had complete control of his bike. He leaned into a curve, feeling like the motorcycle was an extension of his body. He downshifted when he came into traffic or a sharp corner, and then zigzagged between cars like a street racer before hitting just the right amount of throttle to carve a perfect turn. The strong wind blew against his helmet as he accelerated. It was an exhilarating feeling. He felt totally alive and free on his Ducati, the world rotating around him and his bike.

A new shipment of drugs had come in tonight from a new connect. Even with that happening, he still couldn't forget his lust and affection for Aoki. Earlier, he had sent her a text message, the fourth today, followed by repeated attempts to contact her by calling, but he still hadn't received an answer all night.

He was worried about her, but then he started to feel like she was disrespecting him by purposely ignoring his calls and texts. Now that he had cut Brandi off completely, his attention and effort were exacted on Aoki. He wanted her all to himself. He wanted Aoki to choose him.

At first, he thought perhaps he should have finished what he started, which was to kill AZ. Then he wouldn't have to worry about Aoki sliding back AZ's way. But then he thought if anything happened to AZ, Aoki would blame him. There was something special about her, and he didn't want to lose her. B Scientific knew the bitch had to have some platinum pussy for him to even allow his competition to breathe.

He hurried toward an area in Red Hook, Brooklyn, jumped his bike onto the sidewalk, and came to a stop in front of an unassuming building on Carroll Street. He killed the engine and climbed off, removing his helmet and tucking his gun into his waistband. The block, adjacent to an industrial area of Brooklyn near the busy docks, was quiet.

Always observant, he looked around and saw the black Escalade parked in front of the building. His right-hand man, Marcus, was already on location and handling their business. Before he walked to the door, he pulled out his cell phone and dialed Marcus. It rang several times before he picked up.

"Yo!"

"I'm outside. Everything okay inside?" he asked Marcus.

"Yo, we good like church on Sunday."

"Open the door," B Scientific said.

"A'ight!"

B Scientific hung up, placed his phone back into his pocket, and walked toward the reinforced steel door, which Marcus swung open. B Scientific climbed the short stairs into the three-story building and gave Marcus dap.

Marcus glanced at the Ducati leaning against the kickstand on the sidewalk and said, "I see you decided to bring the bike out tonight."

"Needed to think about some things."

"You okay?"

"Copacetic!"

B Scientific walked through the dim hallway into the kitchen in the back with Marcus right behind him. Security cameras and armed goons were positioned in the stash house. There was too much money and drugs going in and out of the building for them not to be extra cautious. If anything moved wrong, their men wouldn't hesitate to gun it down.

Entering the kitchen, B Scientific smiled at what he felt was the most beautiful thing in the world—fifty kilos of cocaine spread out across the kitchen table. It had arrived directly from Mexico via hidden compartments of various vehicles, from a tractor-trailer out of Zacatecas across the borders into El Paso, and onto the freeway east, where it was transferred to a minivan with a soccer mom driving. Marcus and one of their lieutenants were at the meeting point to extract their part of the five hundred kilos brought into the United States.

"Damn! This is like Christmas morning," B Scientific said gleefully. "I think I'm getting an erection."

Marcus laughed.

"Everything went cool?" he asked Marcus.

"No issues. This new connect is on point. They definitely about their shit."

B Scientific nodded. "And the purity?"

"We about to test it now."

Marcus nodded toward one of the workers in the stash house, and the young man lifted his ass from off the kitchen chair and grabbed a product purity kit. The worker took a seat at the table and pulled out a small knife. He cut a small slit into one of the packaged kilos and removed about 20mg of cocaine. He then placed it into the ampoule with clear liquid and stirred it up a little. B Scientific and Marcus focused on the outcome of the test, watching the liquid change colors. Quickly, the bottom layer was almost like coffee, indicating their product was 90% pure.

Both men smiled. What they had was worth more than gold. This connect had better quality for a better price. Fifty kilos was worth tens of millions on the streets.

"Yo, let's start getting some of this shit street-ready," Marcus said.

The workers went into action, processing part of the cocaine into crack. The remaining kilos were to be shipped for wholesale to upstate New York.

B Scientific lit a cigarette and inhaled. He walked out of the kitchen, enjoying the rush of nicotine entering his system, and went into the next room.

Marcus followed him. "We gonna have some of the best shit in town and make a shitload of money. Hey, you lookin' like a bitch gave you some disease. What you thinkin' about, my dude? A bitch didn't give you an STD, right?"

"Nah, I'm good."

"'Cuz we kill bitches for that shit. You got Brandi on your mind?"

"Man, fuck her! She dead to me," B Scientific replied.

"You know I can make that become literal."

"No need to waste your time or bullets on that bitch. Let that bitch be poor and homeless. I already almost beat her to death. Shit! I made that bitch who she is today."

"I know you did. You a good dude, B. So what else got you looking like this? I know it ain't over some street shit. Most of our enemies are dead." Marcus laughed. "It gotta be over some pussy, right?"

B Scientific didn't answer him. He stared out the living room window, looking at his motorcycle. He continued to smoke his cigarette, seeming distant from the conversation with Marcus.

"It's the other one then. What's her name . . . Aoki?"

B Scientific turned around and looked at his friend. "I don't get this bitch. She hard to read, yo. I don't know if I wanna put a bullet in her fuckin' head or put this dick in her and make her wifey. I've been trying to reach this bitch all day, and it feels like she's ignoring me. Like, why the fuck do I like this bitch so much?"

"She's different, and you always liked different," Marcus answered for him. "You sure she didn't put a spell on you?"

Marcus moved closer to his friend. He stood six two and looked like a powerhouse fighter that could kick ass in the UFC ring. Like B Scientific, he was well built and intimidating with his strapping physique, black beard, gleaming bald head, and eyes darker than a black hole.

B Scientific said reflectively, "I shoulda killed that nigga AZ."

"Why didn't you?"

"It was a mistake . . . a mistake made over some pussy."

"Yo, truth to power, we can't be making stupid mistakes over some pussy. You feel me, my dude? We making too much money out here to be fuckin' up."

B Scientific nodded, unable to pull himself away from thinking about what Aoki was doing that she wasn't answering or responding to any of his texts or phone calls.

"Hey, all you need to do is give the word, and I can make them go away. However you want it, my nigga."

"Nah, we all good now," B Scientific replied. "I made a promise."

"To her? And we made promises to get these ki's to our distributors on time. Business, my nigga, business! You always been smart and on point. And we got too much money in that room to fuck it up, B. You feel me?"

"Yeah, I feel you."

"You know what? After we finish shit up in here, let's go down to Platinum Plus in Jersey, fuck wit' some big-booty hoes. Get you a blowjob to get your mind off this bitch."

B Scientific managed to smile. "Let me think about it."

"You do that, my nigga. In the meantime, I'm gonna go back into this kitchen and make myself feel like Scrooge McDuck." Marcus left the room.

B Scientific remained in the living room still pondering about his future with Aoki. In a way, he felt himself unraveling around her, acting like a pushover for love and giving her slack he would never give any other bitch. He'd heard everything Marcus said to him, but it wasn't registering.

Alone in the living room, B Scientific pulled out his cell phone and tried again to call Aoki. This time, she picked up.

"Hello?"

"I've been trying to call you."

"I've been busy."

"You at the hospital with him?" he asked, a trace of jealousy in his tone.

"Yes, and him still in a coma."

"I wanna see you, Aoki. I'm not talkin' about just to fuck, I wanna take you out."

"B Scientific, now not a good time," she told him.

"You serious?"

"Me just wanna wait till everything blows over. Dating you right now is not ah good idea."

"I need you, Aoki. I miss you, and I don't miss anyone. I can be discreet with you, like before. You still owe me. AZ's in the hospital instead of the morgue because I allowed it. I helped save his life."

"Me ain't forget."

"So don't fuckin' play me!"

His statement put Aoki into a tight spot. But he was right, she did owe him. Now that she knew from Heavy Pop that B Scientific had tried to kill her and AZ over some manufactured lies, she wanted to be sure that if someone lied on her again, that he would come to her first. She needed B Scientific to trust her again.

"Me will meet you," she said.

"When and where?"

"Sunday night, at de usual hotel."

"Okay, and, Aoki, don't let me down. I really wanna see you," he said, ecstatic inside, but playing it cool on the phone. He could already taste her pussy in his mouth and feel her wet walls pulsating against his thick erection.

Aoki hung up.

Standing by the window, B Scientific took in a deep breath. He thought about how good he was going to make love to her, to convince her that he was the man for her. He was ready to wine and dine her. If AZ pulled through from his injuries and decided to make problems for him, then he would put Marcus on his ass. Then, there would be no more problems.

CHAPTER 10

Aoki stepped off the elevator carrying the usual bagels and coffee for the nurses on AZ's floor. It was late morning. She planned on checking on AZ for a moment and then leaving. She walked to the nurses' station with a smile and handed them breakfast.

Nurse Childs looked at Aoki with an unsettled gaze as she took a bagel and a hot cup of coffee. From the expressions on the nurses' faces, Aoki knew something wasn't right.

"What's wrong?" Aoki asked, fearing the worst.

Nurse Childs looked at her. "We almost lost him last night," she said.

"Ya kiddin' me! What happened?" she hollered.

"We don't know what happened, but his heart rate started to drop tremendously, and he went into a seizure," Nurse Childs explained.

Aoki was scared to hear the details. She hurried to AZ's room.

AZ's condition had been stabilized again, but he was still on shaky ground, fighting for his life every single day. The bullets had done a lot of damage to his body, and he had to be treated with antibiotics to prevent lung and wound infections. He was on a ventilator and had a chest tube in place, a flexible plastic tube inserted through his chest wall and slipped into the space between the wall of his chest and his lung. The tubes were attached to a suction device used to vacate air and any residual blood or fluid from his chest cavity. The doctors needed to keep his lungs inflated.

Aoki stared into AZ's closed eyes and stood wordlessly over him. She felt herself filling up with a great concern. She couldn't have him die on her and allow so many questions to go unanswered.

"Ya live!" she said to him. "Ya need to live!" She took his motionless hand into hers and squeezed it gently. She placed her butt into the chair next to his bed.

Her phone vibrated, and she saw a text from Emilio. She hadn't seen or spoken to him in several days. She missed him, but now wasn't the time.

Aoki sat for over an hour with AZ, staring up at the TV, watching a few silly daytime talk shows. She was never big on television, since the streets always had her attention. She watched Whoopi Goldberg and some other bitches on *The View* and didn't think much of them. *They wouldn't last in my world one day, catty fuckin' hoes,* she thought. She yawned as they talked about politics and the day's events.

She turned to stare at AZ for a moment, but nothing had changed. It was like she'd expected some kind of miracle to surface during the hour she'd been sitting with him.

There was a knock at the door, and Aoki quickly looked to see who was about to walk into the room. She wasn't expecting a threat but was still armed with a .380, because in her world, you never knew when or where your enemies would come for you.

The door opened, and into the room walked Lisa, AZ's baby's mother. Aoki was shocked to see her. She didn't like that bitch. She always felt Lisa got pregnant by him purposely so he could be her personal ATM.

Lisa walked into the room, looking ghetto-fabulous in a pair of coochie-cutting shorts and heels. Her heavy make-up was flawless, and she was sporting a pair of diamond earrings and a weave so long, she looked like a black Rapunzel.

Lisa cut her eyes at Aoki and said, "Oh, I didn't know you were here, but it figures. You his side-bitch, right?"

Aoki tightened her face. "What make ya come now, huh? Ya can't cash de insurance policy 'cuz him not dead."

"Cute." Lisa smirked. "I didn't come for any money. I came because I care about the father of my child."

"So ya care now, huh? Him been in here ah weeks, and ya come now?"

"Aoki, I didn't come here to argue with you. I came to see the father of my daughter." Lisa walked closer to AZ's bed and stared at him. "What did the doctors say? What happened to him?" she asked, concern in her voice.

"What ya think happened? Him was shot!"

"Why?"

"Is there ever ah why in what people do, huh?" Aoki spoke in riddles.

Lisa shrugged her off, hating the accent, and continued staring at AZ. She gently kissed him on the forehead, and a few tears trickled from her eyes. She then turned and looked Aoki's way.

"No matter what you think of me, Aoki, I love him. He's the father of my daughter, and I can't stand to see him like this."

"Lies. Ya never cared fo' him. Me think ya always put on a good show, because that's what bitches like y'all do—give him a little pum-pum to get ya way! Ya only dealt wit' him and got pregnant 'cuz ya know him was a drug dealer."

"Bitch, you sit there and judge me, like you some saint! You think I don't know about you too? What, you loved him more than me 'cuz y'all grew up together and were best friends? He's your man now? Y'all fucking, right? But you also out there whoring yourself to B Scientific! Yet you supposedly love my baby father? Bitch, you fake!"

Aoki had to stand up. She glared at Lisa. "Me never fake! And, bitch, ya don't know me!"

"And you don't fuckin' know me, bitch!" Lisa shouted. "I'm tired of your shit, Aoki! You need to stop coming at me. I ain't fuckin' scared of you like all these other stupid bitches you try to intimidate. I ain't the fuckin' one, bitch!"

"Ya ah bloodclaat leech, bitch! And ya need to be scared, cunt!"

Aoki felt she needed to protect his best interest against hoes and thots like Lisa, and Lisa felt Aoki was a bully and a poser. It became a tense shouting match inside the room with Lisa and Aoki scowling at one another.

Nurse Childs came into the room and shot a sharp look at both ladies. "Listen, y'all two gonna have to keep the noise down in here or leave the room now. This is a hospital, not the streets. We have other patients on this floor too."

Both girls looked at Nurse Childs, her arms folded across her chest and looking intensely at them.

Lisa and Aoki stood in silence, embarrassed.

"I'm sorry," Lisa said to Nurse Childs. Then she added with attitude, "I'm leaving!" She grabbed her purse and marched toward the door. Before she left, she cut her eyes at Aoki. "Fuck you, bitch! I'll see you when I see you!"

"Him don't need ya! Ya cracker jack ho!"

Lisa slung her purse over her shoulder and stormed out of the room, smacking her protruding butt, indicating for Aoki to kiss her black ass.

Nurse Childs asked, "What was all that about anyway?"

"We just had ah simple misunderstanding."

"Well, y'all keep the misunderstandings out this room and out of this hospital."

"Me will. Sorry."

Nurse Childs turned and left the room, and Aoki closed the door behind her. She sighed heavily as she took her seat again next to AZ. She looked at him and said, "Why ya just didn't let me kill dat bitch? She need to go!"

CHAPTER 11

The stress from the hospital and the streets was taking its toll on Aoki. She had been doing so much, she'd completely forgotten about AZ's place in downtown, Brooklyn, which was left abandoned after he was shot. AZ was a meticulous person who liked to keep his home and business in order. She knew that someone needed to take care of his home, and with Heavy Pop still in the hospital, it was up to her to check things out. Besides, Aoki felt that she needed a place to get away from the neighborhood and clear her head. Too many people knew where she lived, but AZ's place was like the Batcave—secluded, unknown, and secure.

First, she drove home to collect a few things of her own. She hit Linden Boulevard in her Yukon, constantly checking her rearview mirror to make sure she wasn't being followed.

She came to a stop in front of her home, but decided to linger in her truck for a moment. The block was shadowy, and it was late. Looking at the bloodstained concrete near her home was a haunting reminder of how she'd almost lost her life at the hands of a friend.

The house was dark—maybe a little too dark. Everything looked copacetic, but one never knew what was lurking on the other side of those doors.

Aoki removed her pistol from under the seat and kept it close. Along with her gun, she had her sharp, six-inch blade hidden on her person. She opened the door and climbed out of the truck. She proceeded toward the home and inside, her pistol gripped in her hand, and made sure to check every room in the place. Paranoia was her best friend.

Once she was sure the entire place was clear, she started to breathe a little easier. She wasn't about to become a victim again. She closed every curtain and blind in the house and marched into her bedroom to pack a few things.

She swung open her closet door and started removing clothes, tossing them on the bed. Next were the drawers. It was time for her to stay someplace else—at AZ's downtown, Brooklyn place.

As she was packing a few duffel bags, her cell phone rang. She looked at the caller ID and saw it was Emilio calling. She hadn't forgotten about him, but things were just too crazy on her side of the world. She hesitated in answering. She wanted to talk to him, but she was also in a rush to leave her house.

The phone rang again, and she decided to answer. "Hey!"

"Hey, beautiful. I've been trying to call. I was worried about you. You okay?"

"Me fine, just been busy."

"I miss you."

"Me miss ya too."

"Where are you? Home?"

"For de moment."

"I wanna come over."

Aoki quickly replied, "It's late."

"And? That's never stopped me before."

"Emilio, now not ah good time, ya hear?"

"Aoki, you sure you're okay? You sound a little distant. What's going on? What's on your mind? Is it AZ?"

Aoki was about to answer when she saw a black Denali with deep dish rims idling outside her front door, headlights still on. Perched by her bedroom window, her curtains slightly pulled back, her attention was fixed on the vehicle.

"Emilio, me gon' have to call ya back."

"Wait! You sure everything's okay? I can be over there in a half hour."

She hung up on him.

He called right back, but she sent him to voice mail.

She continued staring at the truck outside, this time with her pistol in hand, cocked back and ready for anything. She wondered who was inside and how many of them there were. Were they there to kill her? If so, who sent them?

Emilio called her back a third time, but she refused to answer. Her life could be on the line.

Aoki would pretend she wasn't home, but her Yukon was parked on the block, right near her front door. *But do they know my truck?* In the hood, everyone did, but were these muthafuckas from the hood?

The driver and passenger door opened up, and two nicely-suited men dressed in black exited the Denali. They both looked serious.

The feds, Aoki thought. But when did the feds start driving high-end SUVs with deep-dish rims? Besides, they had *mobsters* written all over them.

She watched them approach her home. There were no guns visible, though. They walked up the stairs and rang the bell.

"Killers and hit men don't ring doorbells," she whispered to herself.

Carefully, she crept downstairs into the darkness. She could hear them prancing around outside on her porch. She took a deep breath and aimed the .380 at the front door. If they came charging in, they would get the surprise of their lives.

She kept extremely quiet and still, her eyes focused on the front door, ready to explode on the two mysterious men.

They continued ringing the bell, but she wasn't about to answer.

Finally, they gave up, and she could hear them walking off.

Aoki made her way toward the window and looked outside. She could see them getting back into their vehicle. They drove off without incident.

Aoki exhaled. Whoever they were, she wasn't interested in meeting them. She had a bad feeling about them. She went back upstairs into her bedroom and continued packing the things she needed. Every so often, she would walk to the window and look outside, making sure the two men didn't return to catch her slipping.

With everything she needed packed into her bags, including a few guns and knives, Aoki grabbed two bags in each hand, slung one over her shoulder, and hobbled downstairs. She decided to exit out the back door instead.

She carefully walked outside with her gun in hand and looked around. It was quiet and clear. Warily, she proceeded toward her truck and hurried inside. She started the ignition and drove away.

While she drove, Aoki's eyes stayed in all her mirrors, once again making sure that she wasn't being followed.

In no time, Aoki was in downtown, Brooklyn, coming to a stop in front of AZ's place on State Street, a tranquil part of town. She breathed out, feeling somewhat relieved she'd made it there in one piece. She figured her troubles, though not left behind, were put on hold for tonight.

She used the spare key AZ had given her a while back and sauntered inside like she owned the place. She flicked on the lights and did a once-over on the place. It needed some cleaning, but it was late and she was too tired to clean anything tonight. She went into the master bedroom and plopped down on AZ's queen bed and fell asleep.

The next morning, the bright morning sun percolated through the bedroom windows, and the sunrays urged Aoki awake. She had slept in her clothes, like a baby. She removed herself from the comfy bed and went into the bathroom to wash her ass and brush her teeth.

After the bathroom, she started to make herself at home. The place was spacious with parquet flooring, a big living room, two bedrooms, and flat-screens in every room. AZ's apartment was furnished with Italian leather, historical black paintings on the walls, and African artwork. AZ definitely had taste, from his home, to his clothes, to his music and his car.

Aoki started to clean up, though there wasn't too much to clean. AZ's place was neat and well put-together. She washed a few dishes, vacuumed, and put a few things in order.

In the backyard, there was a small rose garden, and although it had clearly once been carefully planned and nurtured, it was now riddled with weeds. She liked to garden. There was still a lot about AZ that Aoki didn't know. It was the reason why she wanted him to live. They needed to have a serious talk.

The remainder of Aoki's day was spent watching movies and enjoying her solitude, like she was on vacation. Her phone buzzed and rang, with various text messages coming in from Emilio, Ri-Ri, and B Scientific. She decided to ignore them all for the moment, especially B Scientific. She had already promised to meet him at the hotel Sunday night. She wasn't in the frame of mind to talk. She planned on giving him what he wanted—some pussy—and then move on.

While Aoki was in the kitchen making herself a snack, AZ's cell phone buzzed on the countertop, indicating that it was about to die soon. It'd been in Aoki's possession since the day he was shot, but she'd never looked into it or answered any of his incoming calls. But today something told her to do so. Maybe there was a text message or something that could clear the clouds that had been forming since that hectic day. It was time to try and brighten things up.

She plugged his cell phone into the wall charger and had to wait a few minutes for it to power back on.

He had like a zillion messages and unopened voice messages. Aoki couldn't check the voice mail because she didn't have the password, but she could see the text messages. The majority of them were from dealers wondering where he was and wanting to link up about business. She wondered how they could not know about his condition.

Some of the messages were serious. They wanted either their product or their money back. AZ and Heavy Pop were down and out, but the world continued to turn, lives went on, and people still yearned to get rich or die trying.

If she didn't do something, AZ could lose everything he had worked so hard to build. She started texting back all of his customers, explaining the situation and trying to micromanage things from her end. Some were sorry to hear about the shooting, others didn't give a fuck. Some of his customers had already moved on and copped from someone else when they didn't hear back from AZ or Pop.

She had a plan. She knew a majority of his customers because she and her crew used to run drugs for AZ all over town. What she needed to do was locate his stash and continue what they used to do. But this time, they would be in charge.

Aoki decided to call Ri-Ri. With her phone to her ear, she stepped outside into the backyard waiting for Ri-Ri to pick up.

"Hey, what's up, girl?" Ri-Ri answered.

"Me need ya help."

"You okay?"

"Just meet me quickly," she said.

"Where?"

"Me at AZ's place, in downtown, Brooklyn."

"Downtown, Brooklyn? I didn't even know AZ had a place out there."

"No one was supposed to know."

"Just give me the address, and I'll catch a cab ASAP."

Aoki gave her the address, and Ri-Ri promised to be there soon.

While she waited, Aoki decided to search the place, knowing AZ trusted this location to stash drugs and cash. She didn't come across anything unusual or out of place when she was cleaning or scoping out the place, but her gut instincts told her he had something hidden somewhere inside the residence.

She blew out of her mouth and decided to start looking in the bedroom and work her way from room to room.

When Ri-Ri arrived, she joined in on the search. They went through the entire house painstakingly. Two hours and six rooms later, still nothing.

The girls were in the master bedroom on the bed.

"You sure he had it here?" Ri-Ri asked.

Aoki nodded.

"Well, we went through this whole house, and we came up with nothing, Aoki. Maybe you didn't know AZ as well as you thought you did."

But she did. His customers were calling for their re-up, and AZ was always on time and on point with shipment. Aoki knew he kept it somewhere in the brownstone. It was somewhere cunning and naked to the human eye. Frustrated, she jumped up and kicked the base of the bed. The sound it made struck her as kind of odd.

"What's up, girl? What you thinkin' about?"

"Get up," Aoki said.

"What?"

"Just get up."

Ri-Ri stood up from the bed.

Aoki looked transfixed by the bed all of a sudden.

"Why you lookin' at his bed like that?"

Aoki didn't answer her. She removed the thick mattress from the bed. An armored bed bunker with combination vault doors was under it. The bed bunker was designed to replace the box spring under the queen size mattress and was compatible with the bed frame. If she hadn't been paying close attention, she would've missed it. Aoki knew AZ had to have paid a pretty penny for it.

"No way!" Ri-Ri uttered, looking dumbfounded.

Aoki smiled.

"Tell me you know the combination," Ri-Ri said.

The combination. Now that was the tricky part. Though AZ was smart, he could also be predictable.

Aoki crouched near the safe and thought before she started punching in any numbers. She had to think. What would be the expected combination for him to put in? They grew up as best friends, and their friendship transitioned into a relationship. He loved her. Did he love her that much that the combination would be something connected to her?

Aoki crossed her fingers and decided to punch in numbers that she felt were related to him, like his birthday, some numbers from his social security number, the day they met, but nothing!

"We ain't gonna ever get this thing open!" Ri-Ri complained.

Aoki ignored her complaint. She had to focus. She sighed and continued trying her luck. What about her information? Maybe her birthday? It was farfetched to think that, but she had to try something. She punched in the numbers to her birthday and crossed her fingers. Lo and behold, it opened.

"Oh shit, you did it!" Ri-Ri exclaimed.

Aoki lifted the thick doors to the bunker inside, and she and Ri-Ri peered at the contents. A broad smile emerged on their faces.

"Wow! Ohmygod!" Ri-Ri said in amazement.

Aoki was speechless. Inside the safe was fifteen kilos of cocaine, bundles of cash, and quite a few guns. It was a beautiful thing to see. AZ had definitely come up. He was on his way to becoming the biggest gangster in New York before he was shot down.

"Yo, your boy was living large, fo' real," Ri-Ri said.

"Him was," Aoki replied.

Ri-Ri went for the bundles of cash, and Aoki removed the kilos.

Ri-Ri looked like she was about to have an orgasm as she clutched the cash and leafed through the bills. It was all hundreds in ten-thousand-dollar stacks, so many of them. "What we gonna do, Aoki?"

"Continue him business like nothing happened."

"You serious? Yo, we could take this money and drugs and run, leave the city, and start somewhere else. Besides, didn't he try to kill you?"

"Me don't know nowhere else but here. Besides, me have a plan."

"A plan? What plan?"

"Just trust me."

CHAPTER 12

Less than a week later, Aoki and Ri-Ri started to measure out the cocaine per customer. They'd learned the business really well through AZ. Aoki planned on continuing where AZ had left off. He had transactions to fulfill throughout the city.

It was just the two of them, seated in the kitchen with kilos of cocaine and his business book on the table and making phone calls to his customers. They felt it was their duty; they didn't have a choice, especially after the phone call from Oscar the previous day.

Aoki looked at the caller ID, and it was an unknown number. Although she was hesitant, she answered anyway. "Hello?"

"I apologize. I had the impression that this was AZ's number," Oscar said coolly.

Aoki recognized his voice immediately. They'd done business together. Whoever he wanted dead, she wouldn't hesitate to kill for him.

"This is. Him ah incapacitated at de moment."

Oscar appeared to recognize her Jamaican accent immediately. "Aoki?"

"This is she."

"It's been a while."

"It has."

"Unfortunately, this is not a social call. AZ has a payment due to me for a large quantity on consignment. I called to inform him that I will be in the States in two weeks to collect my money. I do hope he has my money."

"Him in de hospital. He was shot; Heavy Pop too."

"I'm saddened by the news, but I'm still coming to collect what he owes me. We had an agreement, and an agreement with me still continues despite circumstances. A predecessor falls, but there's always the successor," Oscar said, finality in his tone.

"Me understand."

Oscar hung up, leaving Aoki with a bad taste in her mouth. She liked and respected the man, but she didn't like how he ended their conversation. It felt like he was threatening her.

❧

"This is a lot of shit. You sure we gonna be able to move it all by ourselves?" Ri-Ri asked.

Overnight, it appeared as if the two girls had become drug lords.

"We gon' be okay," Aoki assured her.

"I hope so. Usually a load like this comes wit' muscles."

"Ri-Ri, we are de muscles—did ya forget?"

They continued dividing the kilos and going over the business details in the kitchen. AZ's records were immaculate; he kept track of everything.

They had a few trips to make to Queens, New Jersey, and Staten Island, where they'd killed Peanut and a few of his men brazenly in public a few months earlier.

But that didn't mean business stopped in that location. Peanut's lieutenant, Hex, took over. The girls had never met him, because they went from being AZ's transporter to his personal killers.

"I'm not tryin' to see that fuckin' borough," Ri-Ri complained of Staten Island.

"Ya don't need to worry; this ah business, Ri-Ri." Aoki was determined to do what she needed to do to keep AZ's business afloat.

Ri-Ri sighed. She felt they should take everything and run. If AZ was about to kill Aoki, then why go through all this? Though they were killers themselves, it was a risk going out into the streets to meet with men. Then there were the nosy detectives trying to investigate them.

"Ri-Ri, ya know me always gon' have ya back," Aoki told her.

"I know, but I wanna be careful and not rush into things."

"Oscar wants his money."

"From AZ. We don't owe him, really," Ri-Ri said.

"Ya think him gon' want to hear that excuse? We run off wit' AZ's supply and money, who ya think him gon' come after? Us! We don't need them type of problems."

"Then let's do this," Ri-Ri said with confidence.

CHAPTER 13

The nurse wheeled Heavy Pop into AZ's hospital room, and the moment he set his eyes on his friend, his emotions took over. A few tears trickled down his face. They said thugs don't cry, but it was a lie. It was Heavy's first time seeing AZ in his condition, and he didn't know what to think, feeling anger, sadness, and betrayal.

The nurse wheeled him closer to the bed. He was temporarily confined to a wheelchair. Though he was able to walk around, the nurses didn't advise it. Heavy Pop was going to be discharged in a few days. He checked out fine, was lucky to alive and able to leave, but he couldn't say the same thing for his friend. Yes, AZ was alive, but was this living? He was comatose, fucked up from head to toe, and connected to machines like a car battery on juice.

Heavy Pop looked up at his nurse. "Can you leave me alone with him for a few minutes?"

She nodded and left the room, closing the door behind her.

Heavy Pop groaned with dismay. There was a war against them, and he had no explanation of why they were being attacked. B Scientific said their beef with him was squashed, but what issues did they even have with him? Heavy Pop was puzzled by B's words passed to him via Aoki. In fact, where was she? Heavy Pop had seen her once, and then she didn't come around anymore. It was strange of her.

"Yo, you gonna be okay, my nigga," Heavy Pop said to AZ. "We gonna get through this and continue doing us, you hear me, AZ? This ain't gonna stop you and me. We gonna continue building our empire, and one day—just stay with me, my nigga! You do that!" He wiped the tears and turned from his friend.

He called out for the nurse. He needed to leave. He was becoming too emotional. Before he left the room, he glanced back at AZ. "I'm gonna find out who did this to you, and I'm gonna make them pay. I promise you that, my nigga!" And he left the room with the purpose of implementing his vow to his friend.

CHAPTER 14

B Scientific and Marcus rode quietly in the backseat of the luxurious Escalade as the driver cruised through Brooklyn late in the evening. It was a chilly, cloudy night with rain in the forecast, but there wasn't a drop in the sky. They were on their way to another one of their stash houses in the city. This time they had a large shipment of heroin arriving from Culiacán, Mexico, an area controlled by the Sinaloa cartel. B Scientific's cocaine business was profitable, but the bulk of his money came from heroin sales.

Heroin had made a comeback in the city in the past ten years, with the number of users doubling in every borough. B Scientific took advantage of the spike. He had so much money coming in, it was becoming harder and harder to launder and hide it from the feds and the IRS. He had invested in a string of businesses to wash his drug money, from laundromats, car washes, real estate and a string of cash-intensive businesses. He was a rich man, but he felt that he was missing something.

On the way to their next stash house in Brooklyn, B Scientific's cell buzzed from his hip.

Marcus glanced at him as he answered the phone.

"Yo!" B Scientific answered.

"It's me, Nome. I'm just letting you know that Heavy Pop is being released from the hospital in a few days."

"A'ight," B Scientific replied indifferently. "And what about AZ?"

"Ain't no change in him so far. Nigga is still all fucked up and shit," Nome replied.

"A'ight, just keep me updated," B Scientific said before hanging up.

"You keeping tabs on them niggas?" Marcus asked.

"I'm not taking any chances. Better safe than sorry, right?"

"You think they might come at you?"

"I had Aoki relay the message—they let it go, I let it go; let bygones be bygones."

Marcus shook his head. "And you think they gonna let it go? You shot the nigga, B. I wouldn't let that shit go!"

"They don't want a war with us."

"But you still fuckin' AZ's bitch, right?"

B Scientific didn't answer.

"He comes out his coma, hear you dicking his bitch down, how you think the nigga gonna take it? Shit, any nigga gonna flip out over some pussy if it's as good as you say. Why don't you just take care of them niggas now, while they're vulnerable? You said no more mistakes, right?"

B Scientific still didn't reply.

"What, because you made a promise to some bitch?" Marcus answered for him roughly. "And you trust her?"

"I still made a promise."

"And we made a promise to the cartel that we would be able to move close to a hundred kilos a month. I don't need you getting distracted, yo."

"I'm good, Marcus. I'm focused."

"I hope so, because the last thing we need is problems with the Sinaloa cartel."

The Escalade traveled on Atlantic Avenue and then turned off on Nostrand Avenue and took it until they reached Marcy Houses. The driver parked in front of the project building and killed the engine.

B Scientific and Marcus climbed out of the SUV on Park Avenue and walked toward the nearest project building. It was a dangerous neighborhood, but the two men were like gods in the area, and not to be fucked with. They walked into the building, strutted through the grubby-looking lobby, stepped into the pissy elevator, and took it to the sixth floor.

Marcus knocked on apartment 6b, and a rectangular slot in the door slid back for the occupants to see who was knocking. The reinforced steel door opened, and B Scientific and Marcus walked inside.

Inside the two-bedroom apartment were serious-looking armed men. Each man had *killer* written all over his face. They greeted B Scientific and Marcus with respect, but B Scientific and Marcus were only concerned with the large shipment of heroin, and they wanted to know if there were any problems. The owner/manager of the apartment, Manny, assured them that everything had gone down okay.

"All money, y'all. I'm always on point when it comes to moving in weight like this," Manny said.

"Where is it?" B Scientific asked.

"Everything's in the bedroom, boss," Manny said.

B Scientific went into the bedroom and saw seventy kilograms of heroin on the floor, valued at $50 million. The apartment also contained three million in cash and a few firearms. The Marcy stash house was B Scientific's most prized one. It was heavily guarded with security cameras and armed thugs. They even had the apartment two doors down from the primary apartment, and that one also occupied several thugs for backup, in case someone stupid tried to rob the stash. B Scientific also had lookouts on the building rooftops to alert his men via walkie-talkie of any police raids, because cell phones could easily be tapped.

Seventy rectangular-shaped kilogram packages of heroin branded "Brooklyn's Finest" had arrived in a hidden compartment under the floor of a van. B Scientific tested the batch and was satisfied with the results. It was A-grade quality, and the users couldn't get enough of it.

"They know what to do. Y'all niggas get to work," B Scientific ordered his crew.

B Scientific went into the second bedroom, closed the door, and went to the safe that held over three million in cash. He put in the combination and removed ten bundles of the money, totaling a hundred thousand dollars, and placed them into the bag he carried.

Marcus walked into the room while he was placing the last bundle into the bag. "What? You making a withdrawal?"

"Only a hundred stacks."

"For what reason?" Marcus asked.

"Personal shit."

It was his money, and B Scientific felt he didn't have to explain himself to anyone, even his right-hand man. He closed the bag and walked past his friend.

Marcus shrugged and walked behind B Scientific out of the bedroom. He just hoped that the withdrawal didn't cost them deeply. They had always been smart when it came to trying to make every dollar matter and cooking their books just a little so no red flags would be raised.

The very next day, the black Escalade came to a stop in front of the Audemars Piguet boutique on 57th Street. B Scientific climbed out of the truck, and so did Marcus. B Scientific wanted to come alone, but Marcus insisted on coming too. B had nothing to hide and wasn't ashamed about what he was going to do. He carried the hundred thousand with him.

Marcus was somewhat flabbergasted by his friend's choice. "Yo, you really here, *B*? For who? Her? What, you trying to be nice?"

B Scientific wasn't in the mood for Marcus' antics. He was focused on doing one thing—buying the Audemars Piguet watch for ladies.

The men were greeted by one of the well-dressed saleswomen in the store. "Good afternoon, gentlemen.

What can I help y'all with?" the lady asked them politely with her pearly-white smile.

Marcus pointed to his friend. "He the one pussy-whipped."

The woman kept her demeanor.

"Never mind him. He was dropped on his head as an infant. I'm looking for a specific watch for a lady friend," B Scientific said to her.

"Lady friend. That's cute," Marcus teased.

"Of course, I can help in that department," the woman said. "Do you have a certain collection?"

"Royal Oak," B Scientific told her.

"Expensive taste."

"I'm not worried about the cost," he said.

Hearing that, the saleswoman knew he was paid. "Follow me, gentlemen," she said.

They followed her to an exclusive collection of expensive watches displayed behind a thick, security glass case. B Scientific set his eyes on the perfect watch for Aoki—a piece of class and time all in one. The Audemars Piguet Royal Oak for ladies was beautiful and expensive—white gold, 276 brilliant-cut diamonds, pave dial with black counters.

B Scientific told the lady, "I'll take that one."

She smiled. "You have great taste. She'll love it."

Marcus shook his head in disbelief. The price tag on the watch was a nice house or a luxury car, and it was going to be around a bitch's wrist. He looked at B Scientific with uncertainty. "Yo, maybe I need to fuck that bitch too, because she must have that new and improved pussy. Let me see what the bitch might have me buying her, if her pussy is that good."

B Scientific cut his eyes at Marcus.

Marcus read his look and quickly apologized. "My bad, *B*. You in love then you in love. Do you, my nigga."

B Scientific planned on wooing Aoki until she fell on her knees in front of him and only wanted him. His ego was way above the stratosphere, and there was no bringing him down. The watch was just a testament to his love for her.

CHAPTER 15

Aoki and Ri-Ri sat in front of Jump and Rhino in their Jamaica, Queens apartment trying to discuss business. Jump controlled the majority of the projects and corners in that part of town, and Rhino was his trusted lieutenant. The girls regularly delivered to Jump when working for AZ, so they'd developed a relationship with him. In fact Jump was at the top of their list of customers to drop off work to. He wanted five kilos from AZ.

"Yo, I heard about AZ," Jump said. "Sorry to hear about my dude. He was good peoples."

"Him not dead!" Aoki quickly corrected.

"Yeah, but I heard he ain't in such good shape either."

"Listen, ya don't need to be worried 'bout AZ. Him will pull through. We just here to correct this misunderstanding between ya and his organization."

Jump said, "I know y'all tryin' to keep his business alive, right? But here's my thing—y'all gotta come down on them prices."

"Come down? What fool do ya think me am?" Aoki spat. "Dem de prices ya been payin' for a ki."

"Yeah, but with AZ in the hospital and then y'all got some beef goin' on with this nigga named B Scientific. Plus, I heard y'all muthafuckas are under investigation because of the shooting. Fuckin' with y'all right now is risky business."

"Ya believe everything ya hear, Jump?" Aoki replied.

"Yo, the streets are talking, and right now Brooklyn is hot. Makes it a good day to be a Queens nigga. Right, my dude?" Jump said to Rhino.

Rhino gave his friend dap. "Fo' sure, my nigga."

"Jump, don't be a fool, ya hear?" Aoki said.

"Me, the fool? What makes you think that?"

"Ya ever hear de sayin', if it ain't broke, don't fix it? Why ya tryin' to fix our business when it ain't broke? Huh? Ya and your peoples been doing business with AZ and me for a moment, and everything always went smoothly. Ya wan' go and test de waters, gwan and do so, but when ya drown because ya dealin' with a fool, don't come runnin' back to us. Me no lifeguard. Ya need to be smart, ya hear? This incident, it won't break us, and me nothin' to play wit. We been loyal to each other since day one."

"Loyalty ain't much these days. Niggas just out here tryin' to get rich and don't give a fuck who they step over to make that money," Jump said.

"Ya not loyal, Jump? 'Cuz me and me crew is. We stand tall for ours, and if ya ain't with us, then ya against us."

"So, you tryin' to come up in my crib and threaten me? Bitch, you crazy?" Jump exclaimed.

"Me not threatenin' you. Me come to talk rational and to come to a mutual agreement. Me respect ya business, me respect ya, and me want the same respect in return. Ya understand, bredren?"

"Yeah, I understand. So what you getting at, Aoki? You talking, but I ain't really hearing what you saying to me."

"Since me like ya, me gon' go down on de price a thousand."

"Just a thousand?"

"Me go any lower, me cut me own throat."

"But I got better offers elsewhere. No disrespect to you, beautiful, but I gotta live too."

"Me understand that."

"And you want me to stay connected with a crumbling empire? That's like believing the Titanic ain't sinking once it hit that iceberg."

"Me don't know 'bout de Titanic, but me know we ain't sinking, and we still strong. One hand washes de other, right?"

"Yeah, I would love to wash you, ma," Rhino chimed at Aoki. "Take my time wit' that too."

Aoki cut her eyes at Rhino, giving him a deathly stare. She was there for Jump, not him. Rhino was always a pervert, and she'd never been fond of him. She had no time to entertain his foolishness

"What you getting at?" Jump said.

"Ya ever heard a group call de Killer Dolls?" Aoki asked.

"Yeah, them those crazy bitches running around executing muthafuckas in public and shit. Them bitches got balls, for real," Jump said, sounding like he was impressed by their resume. "What that got to do with us here?"

"Ya stay with us, and me promise you, if ya ever need a problem taken care of, then ya can call on outside help."

"What you mean? You connected with them bitches?"

"Ya can't be in dis kind of business without killers to call, ya hear?"

"Yeah, I feel you. So what you sayin'? A thousand less on the ki, and if I need assistance with some trouble, I got these bitches on my side?"

"For de right price, of course."

"Yeah, it's about that money, right?"

Aoki nodded.

Jump sat across from her, pondering his options.

"I'll stay, for now," he said.

"Ya made de right choice."

"We'll see. I'm gonna hold you to your word, Aoki."

"Me always keep me word," she returned.

Ri-Ri sat in the background, listening to Aoki talk like a professional negotiator. She had never seen Aoki go hard with negotiations before. Her friend had transformed into something major. Aoki refused to be thrown down; she was taking the bull by its horns and taking control. Ri-Ri was impressed that she was able to keep Jump onboard. It took guts and brains.

Aoki stood up and shook hands with Jump.

As they were about to leave the apartment, Rhino asked, "Yo, where's your other girl at? Tisa? Why she ain't around?"

"She just not," Ri-Ri said.

"Damn! I'm saying, I liked her. She owes me a date. I know she wanted to fuck. Tell her Rhino say, 'Hi.' A'ight?"

"You tell herself when you see her. We don't fuck with her anymore," Ri-Ri said.

"What?" Rhino uttered. "So what's up with you, Ri-Ri?"

Aoki and Ri-Ri weren't about to entertain Rhino. They scowled at him and left the apartment. The girls walked out of the project building on 160th Street and moved toward Aoki's Yukon.

Once inside the vehicle, Ri-Ri asked, "Where to now?"

"Staten Island."

"Seriously?"

Aoki nodded. She wasn't about to be deterred because they'd killed Peanut. There was money to be made out there, and Aoki knew they needed to be a part of it. She started her truck and drove off.

※

Aoki and Ri-Ri were seated together in a bland room, waiting for Hex, the man of the neighborhood. Aoki was far from nervous, though Hex's goons had patted them down from head to toe. She took it lightly and wasn't nervous.

Ri-Ri, however, was a different story. "This is crazy, Aoki. Why are we here?" she whispered into Aoki's ear.

"They gon' listen to what makes sense," Aoki replied.

"What makes sense is we leave now. Fuck these Staten Island niggas!"

Aoki wasn't budging. AZ had mentioned Hex to her before he got shot up. He'd told her that Hex was Peanut's successor, and within a few weeks Hex had expanded his crew's territory. That meant that Hex needed a good supplier, and AZ wanted to mend fences and repair the fractured business relationship.

Aoki was determined to land this account. She wanted to tell Hex something he wanted to hear. The past was the past, and now it was time to focus on the future. Staten Island was a major territory they needed to move the ki's. It was independent territory away from B Scientific and other major drug dealers that ruled the other boroughs. It was the reason AZ had reached out. He felt it was an untapped market, being across the bridge and mostly Mafia-controlled. There were some black neighborhoods in the borough that wanted a piece of the pie.

Hex walked into the room, accompanied by a few of his men.

Both girls stared at the man who'd succeeded Peanut. He was a large man, well over six feet tall and most likely weighing over three hundred. He was neat and well put together, for a man his size. He wore black slacks and a button-down shirt with gold cufflinks. He had short, dark hair and a thick goatee. Hex was an intimidating-looking man, totally the opposite of Peanut in looks and in character. He chose to run his neighborhood like a don, not like a two-bit thug. How a man of his size and intellect worked under Peanut was a mystery to Aoki and Ri-Ri.

He stared deadpan at Aoki and Ri-Ri for a moment, pulling smoke from his cigar, not saying a word.

They wondered what he was thinking.

He took one final puff from the cigar and finally spoke. "Y'all two ladies came a long way across the bridge for this meeting," he said civilly.

"We did," Aoki said.

"I know you. You deal with AZ, right?" Hex asked, staring at Aoki.

"Yes."

"So what brings you here after what happened to Peanut? You think I don't know your boy had something to do with that hit?"

"Peanut, him was a fool, but lookin' at ya, me know ya no fool."

"Damn right, I'm no fool."

"So let's talk respectfully and make a brighter future for us," she said.

He chuckled. "You want a bright future, huh. What the fuck y'all bitches got to offer, besides some pussy? And what makes you think I won't have my niggas here kill y'all pretty bitches and throw y'all bodies into the sea?"

Aoki wasn't laughing. "Us dead doesn't put money in ya pockets. That would be stupid, and ya look like a smart man. Ya not Peanut."

"You damn right, I'm not Peanut. He was stupid and sloppy," Hex said. "That nigga was a fuckin' fool, bringing this crew down with his grimy ways, not paying his debts, robbing his suppliers, and just pissing off the fuckin' world."

"Well, ya de one in charge now, so make it count."

"You know, you got balls coming into the forgotten borough to talk to us, but I like that," Hex said coolly. "You got something in you that most these niggas on these streets don't have. So what y'all bitches wanna talk about?"

"How to continue making some money together," she replied.

"A'ight, I'm listening. Let's talk."

Aoki smiled at him. "Yes, let's talk."

She pitched her proposal. She would continue supplying what he needed. She set a reasonable price. Hex was a businessman, and if it made dollars, then it made sense. Fortunately for Aoki, he was in search for a good supplier and he knew AZ was fair until Peanut turned stupid and wanted to bite the hand that was feeding him.

A half hour later, Aoki and Ri-Ri were riding in her Yukon, approaching the Verrazano Bridge. Things had gone well with Hex. Two down, and a few more places to go. Aoki was on a roll, becoming the head bitch in charge.

CHAPTER 16

From her bedroom window, Tisa observed Ri-Ri strutting through the projects and climbing into Aoki's truck, the truck that used to be AZ's. She smoked her Newport as she stood near the window in her panties and bra. She frowned from above, hating her sister and Aoki with a huge passion.

"Stupid bitch! How she gonna put Aoki before family?" Tisa cursed out loud.

Tisa couldn't help but to burn with rage and revenge. She took a few more drags from her cigarette and then flicked it out the window.

As a crew, they'd always gotten their respect and had each other's back. Now, Aoki and Ri-Ri were at odds with her, for reasons she didn't know. Aoki's name was ringing out in the hood. Some folks were saying she had gone from being AZ's girl and drug mule to making a few power moves of her own.

Tisa removed herself from the window and continued to walk around the bedroom. She was dizzying herself with frustration and resentment. Feeling alone, with no boyfriend and no friends, she plopped down on her bed, closed her eyes, and tried to come up with a million and one ways to get back at everyone.

Tisa continued to sulk on the bed. *They think I'm not like them. They must think a bitch is weak, because I didn't kill anyone.*

She got up and went into the dresser and removed a snub-nosed .357 from the top drawer. It belonged to Ri-Ri, but she never took it out of the apartment. Tisa inspected the gun, a beautiful, petite piece that fit just right in her hand. It was a tool of death, but yet, she loved holding it and wanted to fire it. She felt that she deserved a second chance.

She looked at her sexy image in the mirror. Then she pointed the gun at herself.

"Damn! I look so fuckin' hot with this in my hand." She continued to play with it.

Tisa wondered if her sister had ever killed anyone with the gun. Ri-Ri had changed so much. The look in her eyes was a lot more devious and coldhearted. At times, Tisa didn't recognize her own family. Ri-Ri was always on the go with Aoki. The two of them had their own special thing happening, and they continued to exclude her.

Tisa remembered the days when they were just hood chicks, moving drugs for AZ, fighting bitches in the projects, gaining their respect, hanging out with the hustlers, and having sex with the cute ones. But since they'd become the Killer Dolls, all that changed. Their lives became a lot more serious.

"Maybe I should start my own fuckin' crew." Tisa continued to stare at her image in the mirror. "Them bitches

ain't better than me. I know I can do this better than them."
She huffed and frowned.

She continued to toy with the gun and then decided
to open it. It was fully loaded, six bullets lodged in the
chamber. Of course, Ri-Ri would keep a loaded gun in the
bedroom. Why wouldn't she?

Tisa placed the gun back into the drawer and closed it.
She was still sulking. She wanted to be a part of something,
and the feeling of being left out was killing her.

"Fuck this!"

She stormed out of the bedroom and hollered, "Ma!"

Lately, Tisa had been sharing her issues and her
problems with Gena, but Gena vaguely listened to her
daughter's quandaries. Gena didn't care about those young
bitches; she had a life of her own. She wanted to come up
too. She wanted a fine, paid, big-dick nigga to take care of
her. She wanted a better life for herself out of the ghetto,
even if she had to fuck and suck her way out. She wanted
to prove to her daughters that she wasn't down and out yet.

Tisa marched into her mother's bedroom without
knocking.

Gena had just gotten out of the shower and was
wrapped in a towel, sitting on her bed with her leg propped
up and giving herself a pedicure. "Bitch, you don't know
how to knock!" Gena barked.

"I'm sorry. I just wanted to talk to you, Ma."

"About what? Your sister and Aoki again? I'm gettin'
ready to go out tonight."

"Where to and with who?"

"Bitch, why you in my business?"

Tisa sighed. "Whatever!"

"Bitch, you standing lookin' fuckin' pathetic, like someone ran over your fuckin' puppy! You just need to go out and get a life, get you some fuckin' dick, like I'm tryin' to do."

"I just got a lot on my mind, Ma!"

"Like what? Your sister and Aoki? Tisa, get over that shit! Them bitches is fake! Yes, I said it about ya sister! Why you wanna be friends with Aoki anyway? I don't trust that bitch. Never did!"

Gena removed herself from the bed, dropping the towel to the floor. For a woman in her late thirties, she still had a nice body—suckable tits, nice butt, and clean-shaven pussy, smelling like roses. She wasn't shy walking around naked in front of her daughter.

"You ain't got no shame," Tisa said.

"Why should I? I look damn good for my age, naked and clothed, and I can still put this good pussy on a nigga and make him my bitch. Shit, a bitch needs a few dollars in her pockets and some new fuckin' shoes."

Gena went into her closet and pulled out a few outfits for her date tonight. The man she was going to see wasn't B Scientific, though she wished it was. It was some twenty-nine-year-old hustler named Mills, who pursued her while she was in the streets.

She hadn't heard from B Scientific lately, but she wasn't giving up on him, knowing he was a busy man. And she kept their relationship a secret. She wanted to prove to him that he could trust her. With Aoki out of the way, she presumed, her man wouldn't have a choice but to come running back to her and sweep her off her feet. In the meantime, she had to continue living, and that meant using other niggas to get what she needed out of life.

Mills wasn't B Scientific, but he was somewhere in the ballpark. He was a young drug dealer pushing a Lexus and trying to lock down a few blocks in town, making his money pushing dope and building a strong crew. He was cute, tall, and just the type to keep her distracted from the true love of her life.

Gena continued getting ready while preaching to Tisa.

"Look, bitch, you just need to step your fuckin' game up. You definitely got my genes inside of you. The only way to get these bitches' pressure up is to be the baddest bitch in town. Get yourself a fuckin' baller, simple as that. Get you a fine-ass, big-dick nigga to take care of you. Upgrade your status. Period!"

Tisa was listening, knowing her mother was speaking some truth. She was too focused on Aoki and her sister that she was starting to look like a hater, like a weak bitch desperate for their friendship.

"Tisa, I know you got some good pussy for these niggas," her mother exclaimed.

"What?"

"Take what I gave you in life and put that pussy on a nigga and get yours, Tisa! Get a nigga to take care of you. You need to become that bitch! And once you become that bitch, Aoki and Ri-Ri will kiss your black ass. You understand me?

You and Ri-Ri are my daughters, but you got what it takes to get you a nigga to take care of you. Like I told you, fuck and suck a nigga like a professional ho should, and you can get anything you want out of him."

Gena knew that out of her two daughters, Tisa was more cunning and prettier, and they clicked together like Lego blocks. However, Ri-Ri was smarter, gutsier, more headstrong, and a savage in the streets, and that's why she and Aoki clicked.

CHAPTER 17

Aoki and Ri-Ri moved every last kilo they'd found in AZ's house and collected what was owed to him. They were at his place now, sitting on the bed, which was covered in money. The new counting machine they'd purchased was on the dresser nearby.

Ri-Ri just wanted to lay naked across the money. "Yo, I can't believe we did this," she said.

Aoki felt proud of herself. "Believe it. Me told ya to trust me. There's a lot more to come if we stick together and continue standing strong."

"What now?" Ri-Ri asked.

"Call Oscar, tell him we got his money," she said.

She sighed heavily. "Damn, it hurts to give up so much of it to him."

"Him de connect. We gon' need him."

"I know. I still wish we could just disappear and lose ourselves—the Caribbean maybe."

Aoki didn't respond to her foolish idea. She was about handling her business and building a strong name for herself.

The girls counted out the money owed to Oscar and then put aside their share, taking exactly what AZ would have paid them. It was more cash for them, since they'd cut Tisa off from their crew. The rest was re-up money. They needed more kilos to push. The clientele was hungry. Aoki had made promises to several men that she planned on keeping. Oscar was their link. They had to establish a good relationship with him to stay in business.

The girls separated the cash, putting a chunk of it into a small duffel bag for Oscar; another chunk of it went into another bag for a re-up, and the rest it was theirs, to do whatever they pleased with it.

It was Sunday night, and they had to meet with Oscar the next evening to make the drop. Aoki was positive he would see things her way. With AZ and Heavy Pop out of commission for a moment, there was no one else strong and smart enough to replace him.

It gave Aoki such a high, dealing with certain men in risky neighborhoods and talking that shit that they wanted to hear. It was almost better than sex and killing. Almost.

She had sewn up areas in Staten Island, Jamaica, Queens, Newark, and Plainfield, New Jersey, and a few off-brand areas in Queens and Long Island. She did lots of traveling, lots of talking, and lots of convincing. Oscar had to let her rock. There was no plan B.

Aoki removed herself from the bed and started to peel away her clothing.

Ri-Ri looked at her. "What you about to do?"

"Take a shower. Me have someplace to be."

"On a Sunday night?"

Aoki nodded.

"What is it? Business or personal?"

"Damn, Ri-Ri! Why ya all in me business?"

"Because I thought we were partners in this, Aoki. No secrets, right?"

"Well, if ya need to know, it's personal."

"A guy?"

"Ya don't need to know him name."

"Will you be out long?"

"Just chill until I get back."

Aoki wasn't about to tell her it was B Scientific. She already had enough drama in her life and didn't need Ri-Ri judging her. She didn't want to meet with him, but she had made a promise, and B Scientific was someone you didn't break a promise with. She needed to stay inside his circle and get him to trust her again. She simply needed to stay on his good side. Especially now.

Aoki went into the bathroom and turned on the shower and allowed it to get hot. She loved taking hot showers. She stepped into the shower as the steam filled the bathroom. The water poured down on her, cascading on her tight, brown body. It was her moment of solitude, closing her eyes and allowing her mind to fade into serenity as the sensation of the steamy water on her skin calmed her nerves. She started to bathe, soaping her body from head to toe.

She thought about Emilio. She missed him. She yearned for his touch, missed his lips kissing on her and his erection inside of her, bringing her to a point of climax from his wicked lovemaking. She slipped her hands between her thighs, touched her clit, and started to massage herself. Her eyes closed, she pleasured herself while imagining it was Emilio touching her.

Minutes later, she came back to reality. She pulled back the shower curtain, stepped out of the tub, and started to towel off. It was getting late, and she had to be at the hotel in an hour to meet with B Scientific. Aoki planned on looking her best. Although Emilio had her heart, B Scientific was the significant man at the moment.

She got dressed in a pair of tight jeans that accentuated her stunning figure, a halter-top under her Mackage fall jacket, and a pair of heels. Her long hair flowed down to her shoulders. She looked like she could do a rap video and be the center of attention.

She strutted out of AZ's place and into her Yukon. The hotel was twenty minutes away, and it wasn't a good idea to keep B Scientific waiting.

Forty minutes later, Aoki pulled into the parking lot of the Marriott Hotel in Brooklyn and parked her truck. She checked her image in the visor and made a few touchups to her makeup. She was slaying tonight.

She climbed out of her truck, entered the trendy lobby, stepped into the elevator, and strutted toward the room number B Scientific gave her. He was in room 5B. She knocked, and it didn't take long for him to answer. He was shirtless, looking handsome with his chiseled/muscular physique exhibiting his sexiness, his baldhead gleaming and his goatee neatly trimmed.

B Scientific smiled from ear to ear. "You look beautiful, Aoki," he said to her.

"Thank ya," she said.

He stepped aside, allowing her to slide into the cozy room with a queen size bed, rose petals spread across it, five dozen roses scattered throughout the room. The room was beautifully up-to-date with all the modern amenities, and a bottle of Cristal champagne on ice, waiting to be opened. He had made the place look like a honeymoon suite and they were newlyweds.

Aoki was floored. "Wow!" she managed to utter.

"You like it? I went all out just for you."

"Ya didn't have to go through all dis."

"I did. I wanted tonight to be special. Just you and me, alone, together, no interruptions."

Aoki didn't know what to think. In her eyes, it was a little too much.

"I got rid of that bitch, Brandi," he told her.

"Ya killed her?"

"Nah, I didn't. I should have, though. But I'm done with her."

Aoki remembered him saying it in the text he'd sent her a few days back. She had no remorse for his ex-girlfriend. She'd lied on her and almost gotten her killed. She deserved what she got. Aoki wished she could have seen B Scientific fuck up her world in person.

As she stood in the room, he approached her from behind and gently wrapped his arms around her slim waist and pulled her closer to his half-naked frame. He kissed the side of her neck affectionately, touching her breasts hungrily. The muscles in his chest flexed against her back. His breath was hot against her skin.

"Damn, I missed you!" he whispered into her ear.

He continued kissing the side of her long, slim neck and touching her in areas that were arousing. She allowed him to engage in his indecent behavior.

As he held her in his arms, he asked, "How is he doing?"

"Who?"

"AZ."

She was shocked he asked about AZ, but she kept her cool and simply answered, "Him fine."

"I'm pulling for him to come through."

So was she. "Heavy Pop is coming home."

"He is, huh?"

"Yes."

"Did you relay my message to him? Are we good?"

"Him good wit' ya. Ya have no need to fret."

"Believe me, I'm not fretting about it. It's for their benefit, not mine," B Scientific coolly explained to her.

He continued loving on her, removing her clothing. His stiff dick poked her in the rear. He couldn't wait to be inside of her. He smoothly spun her around to face her. "Damn, you're gorgeous," he said.

He couldn't take his eyes off of Aoki. Her look was hypnotic. She smelled of fresh roses and cherries. Having her in his grasp felt like he had paradise in his arms. Everything about her was perfect. AZ was a lucky man to have her in his life, but tonight she belonged to him.

They kissed passionately. B was always a good kisser, making Aoki cream in her panties as he swiveled his tongue inside of her mouth. Aoki got lost in the kiss, but the last thing she needed was to forget who he was and what he was about. She had a game plan, and it didn't involve him. This romantic moment inside the hotel room was leading to something. She felt it. Maybe it was something big, or maybe it wasn't. But it was something.

B Scientific scooped Aoki into his strong arms, causing her to straddle him in the air. He cupped her butt and carried her to the bed, dropped her on her back smoothly, and continued tonguing her down.

When they finally came up for air, Aoki asked, "Why de special moment?"

"What? A nigga can't show the woman he loves a romantic time?" he said. "You don't like it?"

"Ya love me?" she asked, looking at him skeptical.

"Aoki, you know I do. I want you, just you and me," he announced clearly.

Why is he making shit so complicated? She wanted some dick, and the muthafucka wanted to fall in love. She wanted to hustle, and B wanted to tie her down. What if Emilio wasn't in her life? Would she feel different about B Scientific?

He continued kissing her and removing her clothing and what was left of his, both of them becoming butt naked and entwined in each other's arms on the cushioned bed.

Unexpectedly, he pulled away from her, his dick hard like concrete and asked, "You want some champagne?"

Damn, is he toying with me? Aoki thought.

His kisses and touch had gotten her all hot and bothered, and now he wanted to stop and drink champagne. What kind of game was he playing?

He walked toward the champagne on ice and poured two glasses. He handed the second to Aoki. He locked eyes with her and said, "I wanna give a toast. To you and me, to our future. I want you to become my rock, Aoki. Are you down wit' me?"

Aoki didn't know how to reply to his toast. Getting into a relationship with him after everything that'd happened wasn't a wise choice.

"Ya crazy," she replied.

"I am. I'm crazy for you," he countered. The look in his eyes showed everything, how he felt about her. "And later on, I'm gonna show you just how serious I am about this."

He downed his drink and she followed. Then they got back into sexing each other. He pushed her against the bed and was ready to have some fun. He continued kissing her body and licking her flesh. He placed her tits into his mouth and sucked on her nipples, and then he climbed between her legs and impaled her with his thick, black dick.

B Scientific began to piston his dick in and out of her, and Aoki let loose a grunt at his motion. She could feel him thrusting deep inside her, causing her hands to tense into fists, feeling her entire body taken over by his heavy-duty sexual healing.

She wrapped her legs around him and groaned as he stayed deep inside her.

"You feel so good, baby. Ugh! Ah shit, your pussy feels

so good," he moaned with his eyes closed as he pushed into her more and more. "Oh shit! Damn!"

Aoki opened her mouth and continued to moan in pleasure. She arched her body beneath him, swimming in pleasure and feeling his dick rooted so deep inside of her, she almost felt pregnant.

"Oh, fuck me!" she cried out.

They twisted into position after position, doggy-style, cowgirl, sideways. B Scientific hit it in multiple positions like they were shooting a porno, and he was enjoying every second of her. He wanted to make the experience last. He repeatedly tongued her down whenever his face neared hers, and licked her body like it was a lollipop as he fucked her.

"I'm gonna fuckin' come!" he announced.

Her pussy continued to milk his dick, and they both felt an orgasm rousing up inside them. B Scientific pounded himself inside of her, sometimes rough, sometimes smooth. She was so wet, he was so hard; it was the perfect combination.

"Come for me," she demanded in anticipation.

"I'm gonna fuckin' come in your tight pussy," he said breathlessly.

And when he came, she came, their bodies vibrant like disco lights inside a nightclub.

He panted with Aoki lying on top of him feeling complete and satisfied. B Scientific was a skilled lover. He knew how to work her body. From his lips and his touch to how he worked his dick inside of her, he was magic.

"Damn, what you be doing to me?" he joked.

"Ya do it to yaself," she said.

B Scientific huffed lightly, collecting his sanity, and then removed himself from Aoki's grasp. He stood up butt naked, his dick swinging between his legs like a snake. Even when flaccid, it still looked remarkable. He smiled at Aoki.

Inside the hotel room, he was far from the thug he portrayed in the streets. This man standing in front of Aoki was so much kinder and gentler. He was a man in love.

Aoki's eyes followed him across the room. She was cautious, watching his every movement. He stood at the desk with his back turned to her and went digging for something.

She lifted herself from the bed. "What ya doin' over there suh?"

"I got something special for you."

Aoki had come armed with a .380 inside her bag, and she was ready to get it in a hurry. She started to think everything was a ruse, and B Scientific just wanted some pussy before he killed her. Maybe he changed his mind. Saw her, AZ, and Heavy Pop as a threat and decided to eradicate them. She felt so stupid. She was ready to fight for her life.

However B Scientific turned back around to face her with a black watchcase in his hand.

Aoki looked confused. "What's that?"

"I got this for you," he said, handing her the case.

She took it, still looking skeptically at B Scientific and the case. When she opened it and saw the watch inside, she was speechless. It was too expensive. And she didn't need a watch. B Scientific done lost his mind. "What?" she uttered, looking at the damn thing like it was alien.

"It's Audemars Piguet. Cost me a pretty penny."

"B Scientific, me didn't ask fah this."

"I know you didn't, but it's yours. A gift from me."

She wanted to give it back, but he was adamant that she keep it. It was an elegant piece. It was way too much for a jump-off. If she took it, what would it mean? Would it mean more trouble for her?

As she held the watch in her hand, she looked B Scientific squarely in his eyes and asked, "Does it come wit' any strings attached?"

"I got it for you because I was thinking about you. I owe you," he said.

"Ya owe me what?"

"I was stupid to believe that you would pawn my rosary and cause Brandi to have a miscarriage. People were lying on you, and I was quick to believe it. I'm sorry, Aoki, and this is a small token of my apology."

She stood there in silence.

"Try it on." B Scientific took the watch from her hands and placed it around her wrist. It was the only thing she had on. "There you go. Perfect fit. It looks nice on you, Aoki. You wear it well."

She looked at the watch and then up at him. "Me still wid AZ, nuh matter what, and me nah leave him, ya understand?"

B Scientific, with a straight face, looked right back at her, and replied evenly, "Yeah, I understand. It doesn't mean you and me can't still have a good time and see each other, right?"

Aoki nodded vaguely.

"That's my girl. Now c'mon, the night's still young, and I got this room for twenty-four hours. Let's enjoy ourselves. Let's make a baby tonight."

Aoki frowned. She didn't see the humor.

Picking up on her sour look, B Scientific quickly said, "I was just joking, baby."

CHAPTER 18

It was Monday morning. Aoki felt she'd wasted too much of her time with B Scientific. But he didn't want her to leave and insisted that she stay the night. Reluctantly, she did. She woke up early and hurried to get dressed and depart. B Scientific was sleeping off the champagne and some good pussy. He was lying in the bed, butt naked, looking dead to the world. She threw on her shoes and collected her things.

As she was about to exit, she saw the watch on the table. *Should I take it or not?* she asked herself. It was lovely, and it did look good around her wrist. *Fuck it.* She snatched the watch from the table and left the room.

She got in her truck and hurried back to downtown, Brooklyn, knowing once there, Ri-Ri was going to be all up in her shit, asking questions about where she was all night, like they were a lesbian couple.

Tonight, however, was their meeting with Oscar, and Aoki had to get ready today, run some errands, and make some moves. It was a major move for her on the chessboard. Aoki was no longer anyone's pawn. She was becoming a major centerpiece in the game, trying to become the queen. The queen was able to move any number of squares vertically, horizontally or diagonally, and Aoki was about to become that bitch.

As she drove, her cell phone rang. She glanced at the caller ID and saw that it was Emilio. She immediately answered. "Hey!"

"Hey, beautiful. Where are you?"

"On me way to de house. It's been a rough couple of days."

"I feel you, beautiful. I got term papers to write and exams to pass," he said.

"Poor, baby. Ya need a hug?" she teased.

"I need more than a hug. I need you. I miss you. I want to see you, Aoki."

She smiled. She'd missed him terribly too. He was busy with school, and she was busy with the streets.

"Can I see you today?" he asked. "And please don't say no. I'm dying here without you."

She chuckled. "Sure. Me come to ya."

"I can't wait, baby. I'm free this afternoon until five. I'll be in my dorm, okay?"

"Okay."

She hung up and hurried toward downtown, Brooklyn. So much was on Aoki's mind, from love to war, she felt like she was starring in a never-ending movie with drama, horror, romance, violence. Her life felt like a blockbuster hit. Maybe she could write a tell-all novel, from her beginnings to now. But how would her story end? One thing was for sure. It was definitely a page-turner.

She pulled up to the house and removed herself from the Yukon, looking exhausted. When she walked inside, she saw Ri-Ri in the kitchen making breakfast. Her friend spun around and uttered, "What? Late night?"

Aoki ignored her. She needed a shower, some coffee, and some rest. She walked by Ri-Ri like she was invisible.

"So you just gonna walk in here and not let me know anything? Who you fuckin', Aoki? I know you got some dick last night." Ri-Ri walked closer to Aoki and smelled her. "You smell like fuckin' sex! Was you wit' B Scientific?"

Aoki cut her eyes at Ri-Ri and spat, "Just mind ya fuckin' business!"

"Aoki, c'mon, tell me it wasn't him you was with."

"Wasn't him," she lied.

"We got that thing tonight with Oscar."

"Ya think me forget? Me know!"

"Don't make our situation any worse, Aoki."

"Ri-Ri, me know what me doin'. Ya don't need to fret."

Ri-Ri released a frustrated sigh and shook her head in disgust.

Aoki removed herself from the room and went to get cleaned up. With her clothes spread out across the bathroom floor, she stepped into the tub to take a long shower. With her arms outstretched and her hands flat against the shower wall, her head down, the rushing water cascading down on her lowered head, she closed her eyes and exhaled.

She needed to wash away B Scientific's scent from her body. He was all over her last night; not a part of her body was untouched. From top to bottom, B had his way with her. He was a beast. But now it was time for her to forget about him and last night, and focus on today. She wanted to go see Emilio, spend some time with the man she was actually in love with, and then later, it was business with Oscar.

Aoki lingered in the shower for a half-hour, collecting her thoughts and getting herself ready. She stepped out of the shower and toweled off. She wiped the fog from the mirror and looked at her naked reflection. The body of excellence stared back at her. Her wet, long, black hair and soaked skin made her look exotic. Men wanted to be with her. They wanted Aoki all to themselves. Her Jamaican accent was enticing, her attitude was intriguing, and her sexuality was alluring. She was like poison ivy, a plant so beautiful to look at, but once you get too close, you start to feel the effects of it.

Aoki knotted the towel around her and left the bathroom. The time was flying by, and she had to get dressed and then go see Emilio. She locked herself in AZ's bedroom, wanting to be alone. She wasn't in the mood to be bothered.

Aoki knocked on the dorm room door twice, and it opened up immediately. Clad in gray sweatpants, a wife-beater, and tube socks, Emilio smiled widely at her. He looked her up and down and was ecstatic. He couldn't contain his composure, nor could she. They hugged each other tightly while standing in the doorway, and then he pressed his lips against hers and they started to kiss fervently.

Their mouths and tongues connected for what felt like an eternity. It looked like they were about to get busy in the hallway.

Aoki had to pull away from him and say, "Ya gon' let me inside?"

"I'm sorry. I just got so carried away. You know I missed you."

Emilio stepped to the side and allowed her into the dorm room. His roommate wasn't there. The place was neat with both beds made, free of any clutter, and smelling nice. Emilio had a few of this textbooks opened up on the desk near his window and the chair pushed back.

"I was just studying for this exam coming up," he said.

"How is dat comin' along?"

"Hard!"

"Ya smart. Ya gon' pass."

"Always encouraging and uplifting, one of the many things I love about you."

"One of de many things, huh?" she said, approaching him intimately, smiling.

"Yup!"

They kissed passionately again. Emilio couldn't keep his hands off her. She was too beautiful, and so different.

He was different too. He was so smart and impressive. And he was cute, polished, but yet masculine. He had an edge—an educated thug that drove her crazy. When she was with him, she was happy.

Aoki pulled away from Emilio's captivating lips and his appealing hold around her, and took a deep breath. She walked toward his desk and picked up one of his textbooks, a thick and heavy political science book. She held it up. "Ya readin' dis?"

"Unfortunately, yeah."

She saw the price tag on the book. *Sixty-nine dollars!* "Wow! College is expensive."

"Yes, it is. Textbooks alone can cost anywhere up to five hundred dollars."

"Me see why ya need to hustle."

"Exactly."

Aoki opened the book and flipped through the pages, not understanding the material inside. *Political science.* She had no idea what that was, or what it meant. She was street smart, not book smart. But she pondered what it would be like to pursue a legit career in the world. What if her chips had landed differently in life, where would she be right now? But they hadn't, and this was her—a drug dealer and killer all rolled into one devious, pretty bitch!

"Political science," Aoki uttered. "It don't make sense to me." How could politics and science meet?

"The government doesn't make sense to anyone," Emilio joked. "But it's a branch of knowledge that deals with systems of government."

Aoki still looked dumbfounded by his answer.

He smiled and added, "It's pretty much the analysis of political activity and behavior, you know, like studying why the government is so fucked up!"

"Ya so smart, Emilio."

"I just read and study a lot."

"And it's what makes me love ya so much."

She kissed him. And then they played around with each other, tickling each other and laughing. She was always able to escape with Emilio, feeling like a young girl with a high-school crush.

"You hungry?" he asked her.

She nodded.

"How does pizza sound?"

"It sounds fantastic!"

He smiled and then got on his phone to order a large pizza from the pizzeria a few blocks away from the school.

Aoki sat on his twin bed, and instead of sex for the moment, she wanted to study with him. She wanted to learn more about political science. The subject piqued her interest.

Forty minutes later, their pizza came, and the two of them dined on some official, hand-tossed pepperoni pizza and downed some Pepsi. They continued studying political science together, and Aoki was surely learning from him.

As they sat together on his twin bed, Aoki smiled his way, feeling her pussy getting wet and her heart fluttering with desire and lust for him.

But then, out of the blue, Emilio looked at her and asked, "How is AZ?"

Why would he ask that? He was the one who'd shot him. If she hadn't stopped him, he would have shot AZ point-blank in the face and killed him. "Him hasn't woken up yet," she said. "Why ya so concern wit' him condition?"

"Aoki, look, I gotta know. Why are you still so worried about him when he wanted to kill you?"

"Ya don't know that!"

"Open your eyes! He had a gun pointed directly at you that night!"

She huffed. Suddenly, their special time together was transitioning into an argument about AZ. "We been best friends for a long time," she said.

"And?"

Aoki sucked her teeth and added, "We grew up together. Me still tink it was a misunderstanding wit' him. Once him wake up, me will get the full story."

"Misunderstanding? Seriously, you wanna believe that," he replied gruffly. "And what if he wakes up and says nothing? What if he wakes up and tries to have you killed again? Huh? You can't trust him, Aoki."

"Ya don't know him," she countered weakly.

"I know with my own eyes what I saw that night, and I saved your life. No matter what you think about AZ, I see a snake in him, and I don't trust him."

Despite everything, Aoki still didn't believe AZ was a killer. She did all of his dirty work and got her hands bloody because of him. She had enough dirt on AZ to destroy him. She knew who he was exactly, never mind what he portrayed to others in the streets. But she did find it endearing that Emilio was so concerned about her.

Emilio exhaled loudly and looked at Aoki with a softer stare. "Look, I'm sorry that I got loud with you. It's just that I love you a lot, and I don't want to see anything happen to you."

"Nothin' gon' happen to me," she assured him.

"That's because I'm gonna be there to protect you."

Aoki smiled.

As good as B Scientific had fucked her last night, she still wanted some of Emilio's Puerto Rican dick. He leaned closer to her, and they locked lips tightly like magnets. Their clothes became memories, and she straddled Emilio on his twin bed, lowering herself onto his hard dick, overwhelming him with pleasure.

He leaned forward to kiss Aoki, tasting her precious lips while feeling her insides.

She slowly started to ride him, making him groan and quiver lightly beneath her. He leaned forward again and latched his lips onto her nearest breast and sucked on it, while she continued consuming him with her slippery walls.

Her legs draped around him as he pushed deeper into her, she groaned as he worked her clit, thrusting in and out of her fervently in the missionary position, impaling her with his lust, groping her breasts, and pulling at her nipples.

Both of them let out passionate moans of pleasure.

"You gonna make me come!" he exclaimed.

"Ugh! Ya gon' make me come too!" she announced excitedly.

Her pussy continued to tighten around his dick, and their mouths continued to hungrily devour each other. She sucked on his tongue while pulling in his erection. Aoki's long and passionate kisses while they fucked were melting Emilio' heart, just as her pussy had started to melt his mind.

"Ummm, shit! You feel so good, baby! Ugh! Oh shit! you gonna make me come!" he uttered once more. With each deep penetration into her, Emilio felt his ejaculation bubbling more and more.

Aoki cooed beneath him, her pussy pulsing nonstop around him. She felt her orgasm brewing. He was pressed into her, thrusting and thrusting, their flesh catching fire, their bodies glistening with sweat and desire. The dick was so good, it had her eyes half-open. Aoki looked like she was in a sexual trance, her pupils gleaming with deeply devoted love.

Soon, Emilio released his seed deep into Aoki, and she came along with him, letting out a weeping scream of elation as her body shook electrically under him. It felt like she had taken off like a rocket, and her body was slowly coming back down to Earth.

Emilio lay perfectly still against her, huffing and catching his breath and letting his girl ride out the orgasm on her own. He felt delighted that she was pleased.

"Dat was fun," Aoki said.

They both laughed.

"It was!"

"Ya ready fah round two?"

"Damn! You ain't gonna let me catch my breath."

"Nuh, 'cause me miss ya and me can't get enough."

They kissed again and started another round of sex. They fucked their brains out until he had to go to class at five p.m., which was cultural history. But before they parted ways, Emilio promised to come to her house sometime next week to finish up her deck, which he had started.

Aoki left his dorm feeling like she was on cloud nine. B Scientific who? She left the building on a natural high.

Already, she was missing Emilio. Could they really have a life together? She was hoping so.

Climbing into the driver's seat of her Yukon, she momentarily looked at herself in the rearview mirror. Playtime was over; now it was back to business. She had a meeting with Oscar in a few short hours.

As she was about to pull off, she spotted them again—the men in black, looking like federal agents blended with that mobster touch. This time they were in a black Dodge Charger and parked across the street from where she was parked. They looked like the same men that had come to her house the other day and were wandering around the front entrance.

Were they trying to be inconspicuous or bold? Aoki wasn't sure. And if they were the feds, what did they have on her, and what were they waiting for? She stared at them, not sure of her game plan. Did they follow her? How did they find her in the city?

She was ready to confront them, but then just like that, the men drove away. No hassle, no explanation. It spooked Aoki, and she didn't spook easily.

CHAPTER 19

Aoki and Ri-Ri entered the 48-story high-rise with reinforced concrete and glass wall façade in Jersey City. They coolly walked through the large, elegant lobby and stepped into the elevator. Aoki pushed for the top floor. It was the penthouse. They were just moments away from their meeting with Oscar. Both girls rode the elevator in silence. Aoki carried the bag of cash, which contained close to half a million dollars, money owed to Oscar and money for their re-up. Ri-Ri carried the gun, although they figured they would be searched before they stepped foot near Oscar. Aoki was the only one who had laid eyes on him. She had carried out a successful hit for him, so she felt she was in good graces with the drug kingpin.

Reaching the top floor, the girls stepped into the carpeted hallway, trying not to look apprehensive. This was a big moment for them, and they didn't want to mess things up. They wanted to be taken seriously. Both girls were dressed in dark pantsuits and heels, and their hair was styled into buns.

"Ya ready?" Aoki asked Ri-Ri in a whisper.

Ri-Ri nodded.

They approached the door to the penthouse, where one of Oscar's suited henchmen stood guard outside. He stared at the girls and asked roughly, "What y'all business here?"

"We here to see Oscar. Him expecting us," Aoki told him.

He scowled a little.

Aoki and Ri-Ri could see the holstered Glock showing to some extent from underneath his black jacket. He was a mammoth man, towering over the young girls, and looked extremely dangerous.

He stared at them and then got on his handheld radio. "Yeah, two females out here saying they here to see Oscar," he said.

Quickly, a voice crackled through his hand-held radio. "He's expecting them. Send them inside."

"Okay."

The man looked at Aoki first and said, "I need to search y'all."

"To let you know, big man, I'm the one packing," Ri-Ri told him.

"Give up the weapon then. Let's not make this difficult."

Ri-Ri removed the 9 mm from her person and handed it over to the guard, who went on to search them both thoroughly. When he saw that they were clean, he punched in a code to the door and allowed the girls to walk into the penthouse.

Oscar's security was tight. He had cameras everywhere and guards posted throughout the building. Some of his men were so inconspicuous, it was hard to tell they were armed thugs.

Aoki and Ri-Ri stepped inside the lavish room with floor-to-ceiling glass exterior walls offering skyline views of Hudson River, New York Harbor, Manhattan, Jersey City, and Hoboken. The room they stood in was tastefully decorated in white furnishings and detailed with a modern, minimalist approach.

They were told to wait in the room by one of Oscar's men. Aoki took deep breaths, as she and Ri-Ri waited.

After about ten minutes, Oscar walked into the room clad in a white linen suit. He looked like a model. He was very handsome, well dressed, and his smile could light up a blackout. It was hard to believe he was part of the murderous Gulf cartel.

They called him "the Smiley man" for a reason. He smiled at the girls, showing off his pretty white teeth that looked like pearls in his mouth. His smile was wide and contagious.

He extended his hand toward Aoki. "It is a pleasure meeting you again, Aoki."

"Likewise," she replied.

"You being here tells me you have my money," he said.

"Me do." Aoki placed the bag filled with cash on the floor, in front of him.

He looked down at the bag, but he wasn't the one who picked it up. One of his men grabbed the bag from the floor and placed it on the table nearby. He opened it, and the bundle of money looked like a bag full of gold.

"It's all there," Aoki said.

Oscar smiled. "Impressive."

"Me a hustler."

"I see you have many talents," he said, referring to her being a contract killer. "You never cease to amaze me."

Ri-Ri stood silently next to her friend. Being in the presence of a notorious cartel figure had her feeling a bit apprehensive. This was a man high up on the food chain, boss of all bosses. Men like AZ and B Scientific couldn't even compare to him. She was almost star-struck by Oscar. Aoki had spoken about him, and Ri-Ri knew they had done a job for him, but their business relationship didn't go beyond one hit.

"We ready to move some mo' product," Aoki said.

"Ambitious and beautiful, and yet wasted in an area such as Brooklyn," Oscar said.

"It's our home!" Ri-Ri chimed.

"I understand. Would y'all ladies like a drink?"

"We just want to get back to business," Aoki said.

"Business, yes, business. The purpose of a business is to create a customer who creates customers," he stated. "And you, Aoki, definitely know how to create customers. I like you. You're not scared to take risks. You've gone out there and connected with some very dangerous men from all over the city."

"Me did what me had to do."

"To save your boyfriend's organization. Question though, when AZ wakes from his coma, you think he'll be grateful for what you've done? Or will he feel threatened by you? I mean, you are a very smart woman, and one not to be messed with. Am I correct?"

Aoki didn't answer him. It was a question she'd never pondered. In her mind, there were so many things threatening her relationship and friendship with AZ. But would he continue to go after her if he ever woke up from his coma? Would he feel threatened by her? She looked at a loss for a moment.

"The look on your face tells me what I need to know," Oscar said, walking to his mini-bar to prepare himself a drink. He poured himself a shot of tequila and insisted the girls have a drink with him.

Aoki and Ri-Ri took a quick shot of tequila, and it felt like a storm was crashing in their mouths.

"Wow!" Ri-Ri uttered.

"I appreciate anyone that can have a drink with me. But you two came to talk business, so let's talk some business." Oscar removed himself from the bar and approached the young women with a strong gaze. He gestured to the chair behind them and said, "Sit and let's talk!"

The girls sat in the club chairs across from Oscar. He sat with a drink in his hand, a cigar in the other, his legs crossed. He took a sip from his glass and focused his attention on the girls.

Oscar's personal assistant and advisor, Enrique, stood closely by with a stoic look. He wore wire-rimmed glass, was clean-shaven, and he was dressed handsomely in white slacks and a button-down shirt, and he was not to be underestimated by his looks.

Aoki went into business mode. "Me ready to move at least thirty kilos a month for ya," she said.

"Thirty kilos? That's all?" Oscar laughed.

Oscar had men moving hundreds of kilos a month for him in New York, Atlanta, Charlotte, DC, and Philadelphia. In his eyes Aoki was talking about mere peanuts.

"Ya had AZ movin' 'bout that much," she said.

"Yeah, I know, but he was different."

"How him different from me?"

"You're a woman."

"That's fuckin' sexist!" Ri-Ri chimed.

Oscar chuckled. "It's life, my dear."

Aoki wasn't backing down, though. She didn't bust her ass on the streets and risk her life, only to be turned away. She knew Oscar had an angle, and she was going to find it. She didn't think he was sexist, but a businessman. He was smart enough to know a good thing when he saw one.

Aoki asked, "What it gon' take to make we both happy?"

Oscar smiled at her and then downed the rest of his drink. Then he lit his cigar and took a few puffs from it. He locked eyes with Aoki and said, "You're determined. I tell you what. I need a favor, and it's a major one."

"A contract hit?" she asked.

Oscar nodded. He took another puff from his cigar and then nodded Enrique's way.

Enrique left the room and came back with a manila folder, which he placed in Oscar's hand. Oscar placed it on the hexagonal coffee table between him and the girls.

Aoki looked down at the folder. "What's dis?"

"Like I said, a job," Oscar replied. "I feel your talents are wasted as a drug dealer, Aoki. You make a great killer. But there's no reason why a woman can't multi-task, right? I tell you what—You carry out this contract for me, and we're in business together. I'll give you your thirty kilos a month, and plus, just to show you that I'm a fair man, I'm willing to pay a quarter of a million for the job."

"Damn!" Ri-Ri uttered.

Aoki leaned forward and opened the folder, revealing a glossy 8x10 photo of a young woman. She was beautiful with long, black hair and blue eyes. The photo of her was taken from a short distance, and she looked unaware of it.

"Who she?" Aoki asked.

"She, Aoki, is Rosario, the ex-girlfriend of one of my associates. And our huge dilemma with her is that she's turning state's evidence."

"The bitch is a snitch, huh?"

Oscar ignored Ri-Ri's comment and continued with, "If things go to trial and she testifies against my associate, then she could bring down several cartels. So she must die, and die very soon. I need a female killer like you, Aoki, who is skilled and quick. The window of opportunity on this job is very slim. One week from today will be the last day before she's transferred to a secure location in WITSEC. I've paid handsomely for accurate information on her.

"Rosario likes to keep up her appearance. She likes to look nice. She and a federal agent named Elizabeth frequent a nail salon in downtown Manhattan, a place on Chambers Street called Acute Nails. But the feds sweep the place first, and they're always around, always with her, standing outside, watching and are very protective of her. I need you and your crew to quietly take out Rosario and Elizabeth, and not get caught.

"If Rosario makes it to the WITSEC program, then it means I will have to kill my associate. Doing this will most likely bring about a full-scale war with other cartels. And my associate is more valuable to me alive than dead. I don't want to kill him. So Rosario must be silenced. You do this for me, and I'll show you my gratitude perpetually."

Aoki was hesitant to take the job. It was too risky. She had to deal with federal agents, and that part of the city was always congested with people and traffic. And they only had a week to carry it out. She didn't know if she and Ri-Ri could pull it off, now that they were two instead of three.

"We can do it, Oscar," Ri-Ri spoke out.

"Good," Oscar said, looking in good spirits.

Aoki cut her eyes at Ri-Ri. Who gave her the authority to speak for her? But she kept silent. It was too late; she was already condemned to a chancy contract.

Oscar looked at Enrique again and spoke to him with his eyes. Enrique already knew what to do. He left the room once more and came back carrying two briefcases, which he placed on the coffee table. He opened one, containing fifteen kilos. The second had $125,000 in cash.

Aoki and Ri-Ri were in awe.

"I trust that you two will not let me down," Oscar said. "When the job is complete, I'll give you another fifteen kilos and the remainder of your fee."

"We won't let you down," Ri-Ri assured him.

"We won't," Aoki added.

"Ladies, our business here has concluded. Enrique will escort you out." Oscar stood up, looked at the girls one last time, and made his exit from the room.

Aoki and Ri-Ri stood up. Aoki grabbed the briefcase with the drugs, and Ri-Ri grabbed the cash. They followed Enrique toward the door.

Enrique was the strong, silent type. Aoki felt that if she ever had to go up against him, it would be a long, painful battle.

The girls left the penthouse and then exited the building.

"Ya fucked us, Ri-Ri!"

"How?"

"How we gon' do dis job in ah week?"

"Aoki, we went against harder shit and pulled it off, just me and you, doing what we do best."

Aoki sighed heavily. They had no choice. Rosario had to die, and they had to be the ones to kill her. They needed to get to work and start surveillance, gather information, and scope out the nail salon on Chambers Street.

Ri-Ri looked at her friend and smiled. She said, "Yo, let's just go shopping tomorrow. Let's have some fun for once. We've been stressed out since AZ got shot. Let's do us."

Aoki wasn't sure, but she did want a new pair of shoes, and she did need to get her mind off things.

The girls climbed into the Yukon, and Aoki headed back to the city, going through the Holland Tunnel and then crossing over the Brooklyn Bridge.

CHAPTER 20

The next day it was the life of luxury for Aoki and Ri-Ri. Earlier, they had gotten their hair done at one of the top beauticians in the city at a salon in Midtown Manhattan that celebrities frequented. Afterward, they went shopping on 5th Avenue for shoes and clothes. Now, it was manicures and pedicures, and girl talk as the Korean ladies worked meticulously on their feet and toes.

Aoki sat back and closed her eyes. If only every day was like today. She felt like she was in a different world. She was able to breathe and feel some peace in her life. She loved being pampered. She deserved it. Ri-Ri had the right idea to do them for a day.

"After this, let's get a drink and something to eat. I'm starving, girl," Ri-Ri said.

Aoki nodded.

The diamonds and stars on Aoki's toes were coming out perfectly, colorful and intricate. She smiled at it. Ri-Ri decided to go with hot flames, representing her hotness.

An hour later, the girls stepped out of the nail salon with their fingers freshly painted with gel polish. They went into a bar and grill and ordered two strawberry daiquiris and took a seat in a corner booth to talk.

"You have any suggestions on how to carry out this hit?" Ri-Ri asked quietly.

"Ya de one that got us into it. Ya ain't got a plan?"

"That's always been your department, Aoki."

Aoki smirked. She knew Ri-Ri got this far only because of her. "We need to come up wit' somethin' in a week. Oscar is a man ya don't want to let down."

"I kind of figured that. I'm nervous."

"We gon' be okay."

Ri-Ri took a sip from her drink and sighed heavily. She had put her trust in Aoki, knowing her friend would come up with a game plan to execute this bitch while she was getting her nails done. They had a small window, and it needed to count. Both girls felt that once they pulled this contract off for Oscar, then they would be in his favor for a very long time.

"Me gon' think of somethin'."

Aoki wasn't nervous, only determined to succeed. There was no reward without risks, and so far their risks were paying off.

First things first, they had to scope out the nail salon and the area around it, look for escape routes, and monitor the folks coming and going from the place. The planning was the tedious part of a job. They already had Rosario's photo; now it was time to learn about her life, so they could end it.

The girls talked and drank, but their time in the city was winding down. The day was passing by, and it was time to head back to Brooklyn. They ordered a few more drinks, had a nice dinner of lobster, crab legs, fried shrimp, and French fries, and left.

Aoki and Ri-Ri deliberately arrived at the projects with a few shopping bags filled with goodies. They were feeling nice and wanted to go and fuck with Tisa and Gena. In their eyes, both were haters. Aoki walked with Ri-Ri toward her mother's apartment, laughing and talking. Aoki needed a laugh. Laughter and good times were becoming rare in her life.

Both girls strutted through the projects in their new shoes and fabulous hairstyles. They turned heads, and the neighborhood goons salivated over them like hungry slaves over some soul food. The attention felt good, but the girls continued walking, ignoring the catcalls.

"Girl, I think I'm gonna need some tonight." Ri-Ri giggled.

"What ya mean?"

"You know what I mean—some dick."

Aoki laughed. "When was de last time ya had some dick?"

"Shit, we been so fuckin' busy and so much shit been goin' on, I haven't even been thinkin' about it. But I'm so horny."

Aoki continued laughing. "Hey, me hope ya nah lookin' at me fah help."

"No, stupid." Ri-Ri laughed. "You know I don't get down like that."

"Ya never know today."

"Please, I'm strictly dickly."

"Mmm-hmm. Ya ain't never stepped out and try some pum-pum?"

"No. You?"

"Me love dick too much," Aoki replied lightheartedly.

"I feel you, girl." Ri-Ri slapped Aoki a high-five.

The girls stepped into the elevator and rode it to Ri-Ri's floor. They stepped out into the hallway where the smell of burning weed inundated the air. Ri-Ri figured the smell was coming from her apartment; either her mother or her sister was burning some strong kush.

They walked into the apartment with their shopping bags. Ri-Ri wasn't in the mood to deal with her mother, so she and Aoki made a beeline to the bedroom. They planned to go clubbing in the city and wanted to try on their outfits.

The moment they walked into the bedroom, there was Tisa, sitting on the bed chatting on her cell phone and smoking a cigarette. The moment she saw her sister and Aoki come in, she cut her eyes at them and caught a stink attitude.

Ri-Ri snickered, knowing it was about to be some bullshit with her sister.

Tisa looked down at the shopping bags the girls were carrying, and instantly, jealousy and anger consumed her. "So y'all bitches went on a shopping spree?"

Ri-Ri cut her eyes at her sister. "How is this your business?!"

"Yo, I'm gonna call you back," Tisa said into her cell phone. She then jumped up from the bed looking like she wanted to start some trouble. The bags Ri-Ri and Aoki carried were from high-end stores in Manhattan, and Tisa felt left out.

"Yo, y'all some grimy bitches, fo' real. Y'all out there gettin' money without me? Fuck y'all!"

"Tisa, ya need to relax," Aoki said calmly.

"No, fuck you, Aoki! Don't fuckin' tell me to relax. You been throwing shade on me since AZ got shot! And I ain't done shit to you!"

"Didn't I tell you my sister be trippin'?" Ri-Ri said, chuckling.

"I ain't fuckin' trippin'! Y'all bitches is trippin'!" Tisa screamed.

"Tisa, don't fuck wit' me. Me givin' ya a warning. Chill, ya hear!"

"Aoki, you can kiss my fuckin' ass! Ya hear that, bitch!"

Aoki frowned so heavily, her face almost sagged to the floor. Tisa was crossing the line.

Ri-Ri shouted, "Bitch, that's why we don't fuck wit' you anymore, because you're stupid and disrespectful!"

"Bitch, you the stupid ho! You and that stupid-talkin' bitch behind you! Y'all the ones wit' blood on y'all hands, not me!"

"Tisa, ya need to shut up," Aoki said.

"Fuck you, bitch! 'Cause you know what? I know every fuckin' thing about y'all. Yeah, try me, bitch! Y'all out there gettin' money without me? Okay, bet. But I guarantee I can stop that shit real quick if I start talkin' to the right ones and get y'all locked up! Yeah, police gonna be wanting to know about some unsolved murders out there! Bet. I'll talk and tell everything. I ain't kill anybody! Y'all bitches are killers, not me."

Aoki and Ri-Ri scowled so hard, they looked like they were chewing on concrete.

"Bitch, you snitch, you die!" Ri-Ri warned her.

"You think I'm scared of you, bitch?"

"You know what? Enough!" Ri-Ri shouted. "This shit is all about you fuckin' stealing what didn't belong to you!"

Tisa feigned shock. "Steal what?"

"Me chain dat I had 'pon my neck. *You* took it!"

"Ain't nobody steal shit!" Tisa barked. "I told y'all what happened!"

"Ya lie!" Aoki shouted. "Ya took it!"

"Y'all some stupid bitches!" Tisa shouted. "I said I ain't steal shit!"

Ri-Ri stepped closer to Tisa, but Tisa wasn't backing down. She continued to threaten the girls.

Aoki, her blood boiling, already had her fists clenched, and she was locked in on Tisa. At the moment, Tisa and her wild threats were enemy number one. The sisters were ranting and screaming so loud, their voices could have knocked down walls in the bedroom.

Ri-Ri called Tisa a snake bitch, and Tisa flicked her lit cigarette in her sister's face, slightly burning her.

Ri-Ri reacted without thinking. She punched Tisa in the face so hard, the girl went flying off her feet and crashing into the wall, looking like Superman had hit her. But Tisa refused to go down without a fight. She fought back, striking her sister in the head with a TV remote and smashing it.

Aoki quickly intervened and two-pieced Tisa with a right then left. Tisa stumbled, but she grabbed Aoki roughly and the two tussled violently inside the bedroom. The fight was real, and Tisa felt she was trying to survive in her own home. Ri-Ri and Aoki tossed her around like a rag doll.

Aoki punched Tisa in the face with a right hook then Ri-Ri kicked her in the stomach, and Tisa went flying across the bed and crashing against the floor.

Both girls snapped. The threat of Tisa snitching to police transformed them into demonic creatures, and they lost themselves in pure rage.

They continued to beat Tisa mercilessly.

Aoki pulled out her sharp blade and placed it against Tisa's face. "Ya better keep ya fuckin' mouth shut, ya hear!"

"And if you run to Gena about this, we'll fuck you up again!"

Pinned to the floor and unable to move, Tisa was crying. She could taste her own blood. It felt like they had broken her nose, and her left eye was swollen. She gazed up at Ri-Ri with a broken and bleeding stare. "I'm your own flesh and blood," she cried out to her.

"You ain't shit to me, bitch! You a fuckin' snitch! You always been fuckin' weak, bitch!" Ri-Ri rebuked.

Tisa started to cry like a baby. Her sister's words cut her deep. It hurt her more than her physical wounds. The way they looked down on her tore her apart.

Ri-Ri continued cursing her sister out. She made it clear that she didn't want anything to do with her. They made it clearly known that they were going to kill her if she opened her mouth and started talking.

Aoki removed the blade from Tisa's face and backed off. She scowled at Tisa and cursed her some more.

"Ya lucky me don't kill ya for stealing me chain!"

Tisa was glued to the floor, lying in the fetal position. "I didn't do it," she sobbed.

Aoki and Ri-Ri picked up their shopping bags and fled, leaving behind a busted and broken Tisa and a bedroom that looked like a hurricane had gone through it. The girls hurried away from the apartment, jumped back into the Yukon, and they were gone.

CHAPTER 21

Did you see her face when I mentioned the chain?"

"She guilty."

"Of course, she's guilty. Grimy bitch is so stupid!"

"Ya think she gon' talk?" Aoki asked Ri-Ri.

"That bitch ain't stupid. She knows to keep her mouth shut. She knows we're crazy. I don't give a fuck if she is my sister, she violated."

"Ya mudda violated too."

"Aoki, please, let's not go there again. She's my mother, and at the end of the day B Scientific got his chain back and no harm came to you. I know it was fucked up and Gena is a grimy bitch but I just can't put my paws on my moms, or worse, like you did."

Aoki was offended. "I told ya what happened wit' me fadda. It was self defense."

"So you've said."

"Me loved me parents, Ri-Ri."

"Um-hmm."

Aoki didn't like the implication. She knew that Ri-Ri had just taken a dig and tried to make her feel like she was cold and heartless. "Me hope you and me don't have a problem, Ri-Ri. Me really do hope dat I don't start ta feel threatened by you too."

The tone in Aoki's voice sent a chill down her spine. "Wait, what? Aoki, you know me. I would never, ever threaten you. I love you, girl, you know that right?"

Aoki shrugged.

Ri-Ri continued with, "I just beat the shit outta my sister for what she did to you. All's I'm askin' is that we don't confront Gena. But, if you can't sleep at night and need to say something then I have your back."

The two rode in silence for a few awkward moments. Aoki heard the plea in Ri-Ri's voice and tried to put herself in her shoes. Ri-Ri always had her back no matter what. When Aoki swung on a bitch, Ri-Ri swung too. When she plunged her dagger into Greasy Dee, Ri-Ri had her back. Aoki felt that she could do this one solid for her best friend. Gena would be spared a beat down.

"Nah, we cool. Me gonna let it ride. Fighting wit' Tisa today and all her threats put me in a bad mood. And ya know Gena ain't got love for me. But she ya mudda and me respect dat. Me promise still stands. Gena is off limits."

Ri-Ri could only nod her approval.

Stealing a chain was one infraction, threatening to snitch was on another level. Aoki didn't want to do the unthinkable if Tisa decided to run her mouth off, but if push came to shove, she was willing to kill her. Tisa had enough dirt on her that could put her away for life.

Aoki glanced at Ri-Ri and wondered if she was all smoke and no fire. Was she serious? If the day came that Tisa became a threat to them, would Ri-Ri have the courage to help kill her own sister? That concept plagued Aoki's head, but she didn't say anything. She continued toward AZ's place, feeling her place still wasn't the place to be.

The moment the girls came up to AZ's brownstone, Aoki knew something was off. They had company. The silver S-Class sedan parked nearby belonged to Connor.

Aoki noticed him inside the vehicle. She sighed heavily as she and Ri-Ri exited the vehicle. She glared at Connor's silhouette as she approached the Benz.

Ri-Ri was clueless. "Girl, where you goin'? Who car is that?"

Aoki ignored her, marching toward the Benz.

Connor stepped out, looking at Aoki like he had the right to be there, trying to be fearless. "You had me barred from his room?"

Aoki shouted, "Ya shouldn't be here!"

"Why not? Huh? Who you think you is, bitch? I care for him more than you ever will!"

"Connor, now ah nah de time! Just leave!"

"Speak English, bitch. I'm tired of your stupid fuckin' accent!"

"Me told ya that me not de bitch to keep fucking wit'," she shouted through gritted teeth.

Ri-Ri looked at the sudden commotion not too far from her. She was confused. Who was the thin, neatly dressed man? It was easily seen that he was gay, but she couldn't place his reason to argue with Aoki. She approached the argument ready to have Aoki's back if needed. In her eyes, the man didn't look threatening.

"Aoki, who this nigga?" Ri-Ri asked roughly.

Connor cut his eyes at Ri-Ri. "Oh, y'all bitches think I'm supposed to be scared! You brought your pitbull-looking friend to fight your battles! Fuck y'all!"

Aoki and Ri-Ri both scowled at him, and Connor continued going on with his insults and threats.

Aoki shouted, "Ya need to turn ya bitch ass around an' go home, ya hear? Me warnin' ya once."

"Fuck you! I love—"

Aoki pushed him before he could finish, and he stumbled backwards but quickly caught his balance.

Then he did the unbelievable. He slapped her across her face, like a pimp disciplining one of his hoes on the street. He quickly realized he'd made a mistake.

Rapidly, her fists went slamming into his face, and Connor went stumbling backwards again, but once again, he caught his footing.

Ri-Ri quickly jumped into it, kicking Connor in his side and then trying to hit him with a garbage can lid as Aoki went blow for blow with him.

Connor swung wildly at his attackers, striking them like a strong female, but Aoki and Ri-Ri were experienced fighters. They tore into him from both sides.

Aoki threw her weight into her punches, nearly knocking him out with an uppercut that drew blood from his mouth, but for a thin, gay man, he was stronger than he looked.

"Ya must be stupid and crazy!" Aoki hollered.

Ri-Ri, unrelenting, repeatedly attacked him with the garbage can lid, trying to knock him in the head with it.

Connor collapsed on his knees against the concrete, and the vicious attack continued. They stomped him out on the ground like he was a bug.

Aoki growled, "What now, bitch? Me warned ya!"

Connor started to gag and tremble. He held his hands up in surrender, begging for them to stop. "I'm sorry! I'm sorry! Stop, stop, please!" he hollered at the top of his lungs.

Aoki thought briefly about cutting him, but for the sake of AZ, she didn't. She spat on him.

Ri-Ri kicked him in the butt. "Get the fuck outta here, nigga!" she shouted.

Connor peeled himself from off the street beaten and bruised. With his tail tucked between his legs, he retreated toward his car looking like a broken man. He sped away like a scared bitch, screaming threats and all kinds of obscenities at the girls.

"Stupid bitch!"

Ri-Ri couldn't stop laughing. "Fuckin' faggots! I hate them niggas!"

They went into the house to discuss business, but Ri-Ri was still curious about Connor. Why was a faggot like him showing up at AZ's place, raising hell? It didn't make any sense. She wondered something but quickly shrugged it off as foolishness.

Aoki warned Ri-Ri to leave the situation alone. Aoki reminded her that they had more important things to talk about, like the contract they had to implement in less than a week. They needed to strategize on how to get away with killing a federal witness.

CHAPTER 22

Tisa licked her wounds and accepted her defeat for the moment, but she wasn't down and out. A strong aggression had been created inside of her. She hated Aoki and Ri-Ri with a passion. They'd beaten her badly, and her face was proof. When she looked in the mirror, she would cry and cringe. She felt vulnerable and hated it.

She sat in her bedroom, smoking a cigarette and trying to formulate her revenge on two people she once trusted. And to top it off, it was all Gena's fault. That bitch had stolen the chain she had stolen. What irony! And Gena had pawned the chain and didn't give her any money.

Tisa wanted revenge on everyone. First, she'd deal with Ri-Ri and Aoki, then Gena.

She armed herself with a blade and a pistol. If she couldn't kill anyone before, she now thought differently. Aoki and Ri-Ri had probably beaten that unwillingness to kill out of her. Now it was about her survival.

Unbeknownst to Aoki and Rihanna, Tisa had befriended one of their rivals. For years, Penny and her crew—Stephanie, Kim, and Lady—fought Aoki, Tisa, and Ri-Ri for territory and respect. But overnight, Tisa and Penny had become close friends, smoking together, drinking, laughing, and behaving more like sisters than former enemies.

Tisa ran into Penny on the streets, and the foul looks at each other transitioned into small talk and then chitchat. Soon the chitchat turned into gossip, and both girls let bygones be bygones and started to hang out, going out to eat, going to the movies, and chilling.

Tisa quickly got dressed and headed to Penny's apartment. When she got there the house was already full. Penny's crew was salivating, waiting to hear the dirt. Tisa lit a cigarette and shared her pain with her new crew, omitting that Aoki and Ri-Ri were contract killers for hire. She let it all out to Penny, about her sudden beef with Aoki and Ri-Ri, how they beat her down in her own bedroom, how Aoki was constantly throwing shade on her, and how they accused her of stealing a chain.

Of course, Penny put in her two cents. "Yo, that's fucked up. I would never betray my own flesh-and-blood sister, especially for that bitch Aoki. I ain't ever liked that ugly bitch anyway. She think she's so fucking cute too!"

"Straight up! She a foul bitch," Kim chimed.

"I told you that bitch was foul," Penny said to her crew.

"That bitch turned my own sister against me. I'm ready to kill that fuckin' bitch," Tisa complained. "What kind of name is Aoki anyway? Bitch sound like some Japanese reject out of a bad Godzilla movie, and the bitch supposed to be Jamaican. Yo, you know her parents were fucked up."

The girls laughed.

Penny shared a blunt with the girls, seated and gathered around the small coffee table in her dirty living room. It was a quiet night in the projects. With all the bad things happening in their hood, there was some positive news traveling around the way. Word was out that Heavy Pop was coming home soon. Though Tisa once had her differences with Penny, they both had a mutual love and respect for Heavy Pop.

Tisa got high and laughed with her newfound crew. She was tempted to tell Penny everything that had been going on, from the murders to the drugs, but decided to keep her mouth shut. The weed was making her talkative, and her high was taking her to the stratosphere. She didn't want to come down, and she felt she was in good company around Penny and others.

"Yo, I got the fuckin' munchies, fo' real," Kim said.

"Me too," Stephanie said.

"Yo, I can eat a farm animal right now. What y'all put in this shit?" Tisa took another pull from the blunt. "I'm like fucked up off the first pull."

Penny laughed. "This that 'Blue Cookie.' Some potent shit!"

"Blue Cookie?" Tisa asked.

"Yo, if you ain't a seasoned smoker, then you can't fuck wit' this," Penny said. "This shit will put you on your ass and make you feel like a cripple."

"Shit, call me the cookie monster then," Tisa joked.

The girls laughed.

"I still got the munchies," Kim said.

"I can easily fix that. I got a fridge full of food at my place. Y'all know my moms be burning her ass off in the kitchen," Tisa said.

"Word?" Lady uttered.

"Oh yeah?" Kim said.

Penny nodded. "We down."

"Fuck it!" Tisa laughed. "Party back at my place."

The girls removed themselves off the couch and headed for Tisa's place. Tisa led the charge. She felt uplifted by the company following her. She didn't care who thought otherwise. If they had something to say, let them say it, but she wasn't going to lose a fight again.

The girls marched into the apartment, and everyone went into the kitchen. They raided the fridge and pantries and took whatever looked yummy. With their snacks in hands, all the girls piled into Tisa's bedroom to munch on the good stuff and smoke another blunt.

Tisa wanted to piss off her sister. She wanted to make a statement. She couldn't wait until Ri-Ri and Aoki found out that she found a new crew to have her back and treat her with the respect she deserved. She wasn't going to continue to be an outcast in her own neighborhood, and definitely not in her own home.

Ri-Ri had been gone for days in downtown, Brooklyn with Aoki. When she walked into the apartment and heard the noise and music coming from her bedroom the moment she stepped into the living room, she frowned. It sounded like a party had invaded the house. She didn't recognize the voices. Ri-Ri became suspicious and marched toward the back, arming herself with a knife. She stormed into the room and caught the shock of her life.

There was Tisa fraternizing with Penny and her crew, in her own damn bedroom. Penny was sitting on her bed, smoking a cigarette and flipping through a magazine. Everyone looked at Ri-Ri like she was the elephant in the room.

Tisa smirked her sister's way. Their eyes locked. Tisa had that look on her face that said, "Yeah, bitch, what?"

It was awkward for everyone, especially Ri-Ri. Her first reaction was to flip out and go to war with every last bitch in her room for violating her things and her space. It was disrespectful, and the fact that Tisa brought them there clearly showed her ignorance. She was playing herself at a high speed.

Ri-Ri glared at Tisa.

No one said a word. Everyone looked at Ri-Ri, and she looked fiercely right back at them. She was clearly outflanked, and her sister was clearly provoking her.

"What, you came for somethin'? 'Cuz you see I got company," Tisa said.

Ri-Ri didn't respond to Tisa's comment. All eyes were on her. If she reacted, then her bedroom was going to be transformed into World War III. Ri-Ri decided to take a different approach. She chose not to indulge in her sister's ignorance.

She released her frown and somewhat smiled. "Nah, I'm good. How you been, Penny?"

Ri-Ri's cordial reaction to everything, even Penny, threw Tisa for a loop.

Tisa became secretly pissed, but continued to wear a fake smile in front of everyone. She wanted Ri-Ri to make a scene, so she and her crew could beat her down like she'd been beaten the other day.

"You okay, sis?" Ri-Ri asked coolly.

"I'm fine," Tisa replied dryly.

"Okay, as long as you're good, I'm good. Enjoy your company. Aoki and I are about to hit the club tonight. We got VIP at Cream. I just came to get a pair of shoes out the closet."

Tisa didn't want to hear that. Cream was an upscale club in midtown that hosted a variety of celebrities, athletes and shot-callers. VIP meant bottle service, and each bottle ranged anywhere from $800 to $1,800. It was obvious that Ri-Ri and Aoki were balling out of control, partying like rock stars, and making money and connections. And there Tisa was, in her bedroom getting high with Penny and her tired crew. Tisa's plan had backfired, and she didn't like it.

Ri-Ri went to her closet, got her shoes, and exited the bedroom without incident. She was in the company of sworn enemies from around the way, and she handled herself like a professional. She didn't break a sweat, and she didn't lose her cool.

Tisa face was tight with jealousy. As Ri-Ri was about to leave the apartment, she jumped up and hollered, "Ma!"

Ri-Ri laughed. Her sister was a petty bitch, and she didn't have time to entertain her nonsense.

Tisa went around the apartment looking for Gena, who she found in her own bedroom, dressed like a hoochie momma with tight clothing and heavy makeup. She was about to go out on a date. In actuality, it was a booty call.

When Tisa came bursting into her bedroom, Gena frowned and cursed, "Bitch, don't you ever fuckin' knock!"

"Mama—"

"Tisa, I ain't got time to hear your bullshit! I'm 'bout to go out, and you need to get the fuck out my room! Besides, don't you have company?"

Tisa pouted, spun around, and marched out of the bedroom like a two-year old. Once again, it looked like her sister was winning, and she didn't like it at all.

CHAPTER 23

B Scientific took a pull from his Black & Mild. Business was good. His dope was moving like burgers at McDonald's. The cartel was pleased with him. He was becoming one of their main guys in New York City. He was having things his way—power, money, and pussy. It's what kept him focused.

He thought about Aoki and the night he had with her in the hotel. It was phenomenal. He was a little upset, though, that she'd walked out on him while he was still sleeping. He wanted to continue the fun.

Though things were going good in his life for now, he still had some unfinished business. He hadn't forgotten about Gena. She'd deceived him, making him believe that Aoki had pawned off his prized rosary when she was the culprit all along. It was time for him to return the favor the B Scientific way.

He finished off his Black & Mild and picked up his cell phone. He dialed Gena's number, and it rang several times before she picked up.

"Hello!" Gena's voice was elevated into excitement.

"Hey, gorgeous. How you been?"

"What you think? Missing the hell outta you!"

"You miss me, huh?"

"Baby, I do. I want to see you. I wanna do things to you that will make you go crazy. But I heard shit's been crazy. Is everything okay wit' you?"

"I'm fine, handling my business. But let's link up. I wanna see you."

"Okay." Gena couldn't blurt it out fast enough. "When? Tonight?"

"Nah, tomorrow night. Come meet me."

"You want me to wear something sexy with easy access?"

"Wear what you want," he replied nonchalantly.

"I'm gonna look nice for you, baby. I can't wait to see you."

"Cool. I'm gonna have a special surprise for you."

"Oh, baby, I can't wait."

It was a nice, but breezy night in Brooklyn. The sky above was freckled with a few stars, and it was a full moon. Gena walked out of her building, knowing she was looking fabulous in drop-waist double button pants, a sequin tube top under a light jacket, and wedge heels. She was all smiles. Her boo had finally called.

She walked toward the waiting cab on the street. Her pussy was already pulsating. She couldn't wait to taste him and feel him inside of her. Plus, she needed the break—Tisa and Ri-Ri were driving her crazy. She was tired of dealing with the fights, the jealousy, the drama between them.

Gena figured neither of her daughters was getting any good dick. If they were, then there wouldn't be so much hostility between them.

She climbed into the backseat of the idling cab. She told the driver she was going to Queens. She smelled of sweet candy. She had on no panties, and she was cleanly shaven below. Everything about her was fresh and clean for her boo. She was grinning from ear to ear as the driver headed toward Queens. Gena figured that B Scientific had finally come to his senses and realized that she was the right bitch for him, his ride-or-die chick. Fuck Aoki and his other hoes! It was about time he cut them whores off and made it official with her.

The cab made it to Queens, exiting the Belt Parkway and going toward a large housing complex called Rochdale. Gena was no fan of Queens, nor was she familiar with the suburban neighborhood. Brooklyn had always been her home.

The cab driver pulled into the parking lot of the housing complex and stopped. Gena searched around for B Scientific's truck and saw it parked at the far end of the parking lot. His black Escalade brought a huge smile on her face. She quickly paid the cab driver and leaped from the cab breathlessly and hurried toward her lover with a sense of urgency.

B Scientific was seated behind the steering wheel, alone and smoking a cigarette. He let off a deadpan stare. He was dressed immaculately and sported his rosary.

He saw Gena coming his way. She was coming toward his truck, glowing and lit up like a light bulb.

She opened the passenger door and hopped inside. The minute she laid eyes on the rosary around his neck, she was flushed with apprehension. For a moment, she was speechless. How did he get it? Did he know it was her who took it from Aoki and pawned it in her name?

B Scientific threw her off guard when he leaned forward and landed a plump kiss against her full lips. He rubbed her legs and was in good spirits.

Gena nearly melted in front of him. She didn't want him to stop kissing her. Her pussy throbbed, and her heart raced. She figured he didn't have a clue. His kiss was strong, long, and deep, as he almost carved his tongue inside of her mouth.

B Scientific pulled himself away from her. He looked at her and said, "So, you miss me, huh?"

"I do, baby. Don't ever disappear from me again. And she misses you too," Gena said, touching between her legs provocatively, rubbing her kitty kat through her pants.

He smiled. "You know I got a surprise for you."

"You told me. What is it?"

"I'll show it to you later."

"You know I'm impatient, baby, and it's hard for me to wait."

"You gonna have to."

Gena playfully pouted, but she didn't mind waiting for her gift. As long as she was with him, her entire world stood still and nothing else mattered. In fact, the only thing that mattered to her was his touching her more, kissing her mouth, fondling her breasts, and blessing her with some dick.

They stayed in the parking lot for a moment. The two of them chatted, and Gena began to relax more. She wanted to taste him.

He looked at her with an impish smile. "Yo, you know what I miss and what I need right now?"

"What's that, baby?"

"You already know," he said, unbuttoning his pants and unzipping his jeans. B Scientific's tinted windows gave them some privacy.

Gena smiled. She had no problem doing what he asked. She loved him deeply, and she hoped he loved her too. She bent forward into his lap and wrapped her full lips around his hard dick. She then swallowed him down into the depths of her throat, her suction long and deep.

B Scientific began to moan, grabbing a fist full of her hair and forcing her to deep-throat more of his length. Like always, Gena's blowjobs were impeccable. She took on his big dick like an anaconda devouring its prey. It caused B Scientific to lose himself and almost forget what he was there to do. She sucked him so hard, it felt like she was about to pull the skin off his dick.

"Oh shit!" he groaned. "You definitely know how to do a nigga right."

Gena sucked and sucked until he came in her mouth.

B Scientific looked deflated in his seat, trying to collect himself.

Gena rose up and wiped his fluids from her mouth. "You always taste so good to me."

"I'm glad I do."

After a minute, B Scientific started the vehicle and backed out of the parking spot.

"Where are we goin'?" Gena asked.

"To your surprise."

B Scientific exited the parking lot and headed toward the project buildings on Guy R. Brewer Boulevard. Gena sat still and quiet. So far, her night was going perfectly. This is what she wanted; some time with B and to be treated with respect. He drove in silence and then turned toward the project buildings and into another parking lot.

Gena, once again, started to get nervous. "What are we doin' here?" she asked.

"I just need to meet wit' someone. It's just business. Just relax, baby."

The parking lot was dimly lit. It was late, not many people around, and the lot was dense with empty parked cars. B Scientific came to a stop near a dark brown van.

Gena looked around nervously. This wasn't her cup of tea. Was it a coincidence that he parked next to a creepy-looking brown van or not?

He killed the ignition and looked her way, playing with the rosary around his neck.

"Everything okay, baby?" Gena started looking around.

He grinned. "Yeah, everything's okay."

The doors to his Escalade unlocked, and suddenly the side door of the van next to them slid open, and three men leaped from the vehicle and charged toward the passenger side of B's truck. The door flung open forcefully, and several hands reached for Gena.

Gena looked at B Scientific for his help, or his mercy, but he sat in his seat coolly with no reaction. She screamed and tried to fight them off her, but they roughly dragged her out of the truck, with her kicking and screaming, and pulled her into the van. She continued to scream, punch and kick, but these three men were brutes.

One punched Gena in the face so hard, blood spewed everywhere.

"B Scientific, help me! Please!" she screamed at the top of her lungs.

He sat there like she was invisible to him. He lit a cigarette and smirked. He continued to amuse himself with his rosary. She had gotten the hint.

Once the van door shut and Gena was beaten and subdued, one of her assailants pulled out a 9 mm with a silencer at the end and pointed it at her head. Gena was wide-eyed and terrified. She continued to plead for her life, but the pleas fell on deaf ears. Within a minute or two of being thrown into the van, she was shot point-blank in the head, and her body lay face down on the floor of the van.

B Scientific started his truck and drove off. It had to be done.

CHAPTER 24

The morning sun was fresh in the sky, the large glowing ball shining down brightly on a brand-new day. The wind from the ocean blew calmly, and the vivid blue ocean stretched out in every direction to meet the horizon. The water crashed against the shore, and the early morning sun sparkled off the rippling water.

A father and son duo trekked toward the rocky shore near the Canarsie pier. The boy was twelve years old and carried a long fishing pole, some clam bait, and his excitement. His father walked behind him, carrying a small cooler filled with ice.

It was the perfect morning to go fishing. As folks were rising up to be greeted with rush hour, the two looked forward to a morning of sitting in tent chairs, drinking sodas, eating sandwiches made by Mom, catching fish, and bonding as father and son.

The boy ran ahead of his father, his eyes fixated on the ocean. As he neared the ocean, something strange in the distance caught his attention. It was lying in the sand.

He spun around and called out to his dad, "Dad, I see something!"

"What is it, Jason?"

The boy started to run in the direction of what he saw. It was small and unrecognizable from afar, but he was sure he saw it move. He continued running toward the object, his father following right behind him. "Dad! Hurry up! I think it's moving! It might be a seal, or a small whale, I think."

"Jason, stop! Wait for me!" his father cried out.

But the boy continued running. When he finally reached it, he screamed in horror.

Upon hearing his son's scream, Jason's father dropped everything and ran full sprint toward his son and the object lying on the sand. When the father came near, he too was shocked.

It was the body of a naked woman. She looked dead, but to their surprise, she was still barely alive.

"We have to call 911!" the father exclaimed.

"Daddy, what happened to her?"

"I don't know, but don't go near her." The father quickly pulled out his cell phone and dialed 911. Their fishing trip together had abruptly turned into a crime scene.

An hour later, the beach and the shore were flooded with police and detectives. They had the entire area roped off, combing for any evidence. The woman was barely alive, shot once in the head and left for dead. EMS rushed her to the nearest hospital, while the detectives stayed behind and questioned the father and son.

At Brookdale Hospital, Gena was hurried into surgery and was in critical condition. Doctors thought it was a miracle she survived the gunshot to her head after being left for dead. Two detectives wanted to talk to her, but she was in no condition to answer any questions. She was too busy fighting for her life.

CHAPTER 25

The black E-Class Benz came to a stop on Stanley Avenue and the passenger door opened. Slowly, Heavy Pop, clutching a cane, emerged with the help of a few friends. He looked around. The crowd around the Benz made it look like a celebrity was in their neighborhood.

The entire hood was buzzing about Heavy Pop finally being released from the hospital. But he wasn't so heavy anymore. He had lost a lot of weight. Being shot was like his SlimFast. He looked good, though, and folks stood around him, welcoming his return and in his ear about this and that. His goons had to clear a path for him to walk.

Heavy moved slowly, but surely. He walked toward his grandmother's building. He couldn't wait to see her again. His grandmother was a nurturing and praying woman, and she was sure going to nurse her grandson back to health and take good care of him.

Heavy Pop walked into the building, stepped into the project elevator, and rode it up to the third floor to his grandmother's place, his small entourage helping him.

The minute he got to the aged brown door, his grandmother opened it and greeted her grandson with a huge smile and open arms. "Welcome home, grandson!" she said excitedly.

Heavy Pop hugged his grandmother lovingly. She was a petite, dark-complexioned woman in her late sixties clad in a flowered housecoat and slippers. She wrapped her arms around him tightly, and it was hard for her to let him go. She'd almost lost him, but she thanked God that he was still alive.

"God gave you a second chance, Henry," she said to him. "You take advantage of it and thank Him."

"I will, Grandma," he replied.

She finally released her grandchild from her loving hold, and he walked into the apartment, where he got the surprise of his life. There were over a dozen people gathered in his grandmother's living room, and the minute he stepped foot into it, everyone started to congratulate him and show him support. There was a cake, and on it read: Welcome Home Heavy Pop.

Heavy Pop was a popular man in the neighborhood. Though he was a drug dealer, he was a kind, caring man. And he was smart and motivated. Heavy Pop was all smiles. He knew everybody and was shocked that they'd all come out to see him home.

As he talked and laughed with them, there was a tinge of guilt inside of him. He thought about AZ and wished his best friend was right beside him enjoying the benefit of being home and conscious. He worried about AZ being in a coma but tried to think positive. Sure, he was going to wake up and rejoin him in building their empire.

Nine approached Heavy Pop in the kitchen. "Yo, it's good to see you home, my dude, fo' real. We got one back; now we waitin' for AZ to get good, and we gonna make them niggas pay!" Nine growled.

"Make who pay, Nine?" Heavy Pop asked. "B Scientific?"

"He the nigga that shot you, right? So give the word, and I'll return the fuckin' favor." Nine lifted his shirt to reveal the gun tucked in his waistband.

"Nine, we at my grandmother's house, and I just got out the hospital."

"My bad, my nigga. No disrespect to ya grandma. I'm just a cautious nigga out here, ya feel me?"

"Yeah, I feel you. But tonight, let's chill, a'ight? I'm tired."

"A'ight. Welcome home, Heavy."

The two hugged, and Nine went on to help himself to some apple pie and snacks.

The party had food and drinks, laughter, storytelling, and friends encouraging Heavy Pop's rehabilitation. They wanted to see him healthy. But Heavy Pop was still aching in a few places as he moved around his grandmother's apartment little by little.

After the guests left, he locked himself into his old room to relax and think. Sitting on his bed, he stared at an old photo of him and AZ. They both were fourteen, looking like two wannabe street kids in their hand-me-down clothing. He smiled at the picture, feeling nostalgic.

Then he suddenly broke down as he reflected on his life, tears trickling down his cheeks.

Heavy Pop was in a predicament. B Scientific had almost taken his life, and if he didn't react, then his reputation would suffer in the streets, and would set off an invitation for more wolves to come at them. And if he did react, it would start a war, and going against B Scientific was like a small village going to war with Rome.

As the tears continued to fall, he couldn't get the question out of his mind, *What am I going to do?*

CHAPTER 26

The hood was shocked to hear that Gena had been shot in the head and found near some beach off the Belt Parkway. They were even more shocked to hear that she was still alive and in critical condition. She was a tough bitch! A survivor! Everyone wanted to know who did it, and why? What was going on in their neighborhood? Everyone was getting shot. It was chaos. It was bloodshed.

Aoki and Ri-Ri raced to the hospital the moment they heard the news about Gena. Ri-Ri was a basket case. Aoki pushed her feet down on the accelerator and pushed the Yukon to eighty on the highway, swerving in and out of traffic. She didn't care about a speeding ticket. Her friend's mom had been shot, and getting to the hospital was the only thing that mattered. Though Aoki couldn't give a fuck about Gena, she never wanted to see her friend without a parent.

Aoki came to a stop in front of the hospital, never mind parking, and both girls leaped from the vehicle. They ran into the emergency room, and Ri-Ri started spitting out, "I need to see my moms! She's been shot! Where the fuck is she?"

The ER staff looked at her oddly. It was a busy night, and the emergency room was swamped with patients coming in for everything, from gunshot wounds to stabbings, heart conditions, and food poisoning.

Ri-Ri traveled deeper into the ER, frowning tightly, her eyes moist with tears and determined to be heard. She shouted, "Where the fuck is my moms? I need to see her!" She looked like she was about to break down with worry and grief.

Aoki stood behind her friend. She was ready to be supportive. Whatever it took, they were about to get answers and results.

Security quickly intervened, as Aoki and Ri-Ri were becoming a disturbance to the emergency room staff.

"Ladies, what's going on?" the security officer asked them.

"My mother is in here. She was found shot in the head."

"Okay, calm down. What's her name?" he asked.

"Gena."

"I'm gonna need her full name," he said.

Ri-Ri couldn't think straight. She was frantic and angry. Who had the audacity to shoot her moms? Gena wasn't a saint. She was a whore and a gold digger, but like everyone else in the hood, she was only trying to come up and survive the only way she knew how.

Aoki had to step in and give the security guard the information he needed. He directed them to a nurse and instructed that she would be better suited to assist them. Once Ri-Ri gave the woman the information, the nurse told her that her mother was in very bad shape and her situation was touch and go.

A doctor came to speak with Ri-Ri, and told her Gena had swelling in the brain and had lost a lot of blood. The bullet had done a lot of damage, and though it was too soon to tell, there might be some brain damage. The doctor told Ri-Ri that it would take a miracle for her mother to pull through.

As Ri-Ri was talking to the doctor, Tisa came charging into the hospital. Like her sister, she was overwhelmed with grief and concern.

For a short moment, they looked at each other, Aoki standing between them. But then, both sisters put their issues with each other aside and decided to come together for their mother's sake.

Ri-Ri and Tisa talked to the primary surgeon who had been operating on their mother. They were inconsolable. The doctors were doing everything they could for her, working around the clock. But it was going to be a long night for everyone, and it would be some time before Gena was out of surgery and they could see her.

Meanwhile, Aoki slipped away to answer a phone call from Emilio. She stood to the side and answered, "Hey."

"Hey, baby. Is everything okay?" he asked.

"Why ya ask that?"

"I got this feeling that something is wrong. And I needed to call you. I want to see you, baby. I've been thinking about you, and I miss you."

"Now not a good time, Emilio. Me at de hospital."

"What? Why? What happened?"

"Me friend moms was shot. She in critical condition."

"What hospital? I'm coming to see you now."

"No, that's not a good idea."

"Aoki, I want to be there for you, not half-ass, but a hundred percent. I want you to be my girl. I want you in my life, and I don't care who knows about it. Maybe everyone needs to know about us."

Aoki sighed. Now wasn't the time, but she felt the same about him. "In due time," she replied.

"When? I don't care about you and AZ's relationship. He doesn't deserve you, I do. I want you, baby."

"Emilio, me gon' have to call ya back."

Emilio wanted to stay on the phone with her, to hear her voice, but she insisted that she'd call him back. She hung up on Emilio pleading with her to meet up.

Aoki had to make another call. She disappeared into the stairway and dialed his cell phone number.

It didn't take long for B Scientific to pick up. He answered, "Hey, beautiful."

"Hey."

"So when am I gonna see you again?"

"Now's not ah good time, B. Me need to ask ya somethin'. Did ya know me friend's mom? She name Gena?"

"Gena? From where?"

"Pink Houses projects."

"That old bitch, Gena. Yeah, I know her. She's always beggin' any nigga that come through for a cigarette. Why?"

"She's been shot in de head."

"Gena? Word? That shit is fucked up! Why somebody wanna do that shit to that old broad?"

"Ya tellin' me yah didn't do this?"

"Me? Aoki, I don't know what you're talkin' about. I had no part of that, I swear on that. Why would I do some shit like that?"

"Ya chain."

"My chain?" B Scientific began to raise his voice. "Yo, you buggin'! What the fuck is going on? What she have to do wit' my chain?"

Aoki felt she had made a huge mistake. The man in the pawnshop had only described Gena, but he didn't call her by name. The description fit a million women. She took a huge leap thinking he had made the connection.

"Me thought she might be the one who pawned ya rosary."

"Did she?"

Aoki had enough on her plate. It was a moot discussion. He had his chain back, she didn't get murdered behind it, and Gena was lying face up with a bullet in her head fighting for her life. What good would kicking dirt on her do?

"No. But me thought that's what ya thought and shot her."

"Not at all. That bitch isn't even on my radar. You have my word on that, Aoki. It wasn't me or any of my peoples."

Aoki somewhat believed him, but it still didn't add up. She sighed.

"You said *shot*, Aoki. You mean she's still alive?" B Scientific asked.

"Yes. Barely though."

B Scientific couldn't believe it. How could the men he'd hired fuck up an easy hit like that? "I'll send her some flowers and I wish her the best," he said.

"Me gotta go."

"Aoki, wait. When am I gonna see you again?"

"Me don't know. Got a lot goin' on."

"I hate the way you left me in that hotel, stepping out on me so early. I woke up thinkin' you would still be there."

"Like me said before, me got a lot goin' on."

"I know that. But what's going on wit' us?"

"Me don't know that either."

"I hate this back and forth shit wit' us. I love you, and I want you in my life, Aoki. You understand that? Fuck AZ! I want you to be mine. I hated that I spared his life for you." B Scientific couldn't hold it in any longer. She was special, and he wanted and needed her in his life, no matter who was against it.

"Me talk to ya later," she simply replied to his emotional rant. She hung up and took a seat on the stairway, contemplating her next move.

B Scientific called her right back, but she refused to answer his call. She needed some time away from him.

After a moment in the stairway, she tried to collect herself. She stood up and left, knowing who she needed to see next. She walked into AZ's room, and he was still the same. She felt that his condition would never change. He was a vegetable, though the doctors had said he was coming along fine, and his vital signs were stable.

Aoki took a seat in the chair in AZ's room and sat there alone, staring at him and wondering what was next in her life, or who would be the next one to die in her life. Would it be her? She'd made enemies, and she'd made mistakes. She wondered if the man lying in a coma next to her was one of her mistakes.

CHAPTER 27

Aoki fell asleep in the hospital room while watching over AZ that night. She was snuggled up in the chair with a blanket and a pillow. She didn't want to go home, or to his house. She felt lazy and more secure in the hospital room. She was exhausted. She was so tired that her body felt paralyzed by fatigue. She'd just closed her eyes and the hours went by.

❧

She woke up hours later, yawned, rotated her head toward AZ and froze in utter shock. There he was, awake, sitting upright and gazing at her. She couldn't believe it. Aoki jumped out of her seat and stared at him. He looked at Aoki impassively, like he was in some kind of trance.

"AZ, ya awake! How do ya feel?" she asked him.

He didn't answer. He just sat there, erect and looking at her like she was transparent. Was something wrong? It was like he didn't know who she was at all.

"Me gon' call ya a nurse."

Aoki felt ambivalent seeing him awake. Was it in her favor, or would it stir up much more trouble? He looked weird, lost, and completely out of it. It was natural for a coma patient to be disoriented and silent, but it was creeping her out. AZ's eyes were icy-cold and black. It looked like he no longer had a soul in his body and was just a piece of mindless flesh gazing at her.

"Ya were shot," she said.

Still, he was silent.

Aoki took a step closer to him, but then he reacted, completely catching her off guard. He brandished a gun and aimed it at her.

Aoki was shocked and frozen with fear. She locked eyes with him, gasping and then sputtering out, "AZ! Wh-what ya doin'?"

He finally spoke. "I wanted to kill you. Now is my chance."

He aimed for her head and pulled the trigger. The blast was loud, like dynamite exploding, and Aoki jumped awake from the nightmare she was having.

Aoki found herself still in the chair and looked over at AZ. He was still in a coma and not a threat to her at all. She was wheezing from the bad dream. She stood up, deciding it was time for her to leave. Was her nightmare trying to tell her something? Was it a prediction of her future?

It'd been two days since Gena was found shot. They had her on life support. Ri-Ri was constantly by her bedside, as was Tisa. For the sake of their mother, their battle had ceased, and they focused on Gena.

Aoki was there too, going back and forth between hospital rooms, and still continuing with her life. She was beat and stressed out.

The girls sat in Gena's hospital room, and everyone was quiet, each exploring their individual thoughts. The streets had been put on pause for a minute.

Aoki had to think and regroup. She needed to carry out a major hit, and she still didn't have a handle on things. Her life was spinning out of control. Two niggas constantly calling for her pussy, one dude laid up in the hospital, and now this. Gena's shooting was a huge obstacle. She needed Ri-Ri.

They still hadn't scoped the nail salon. In fact, the only thing they'd done since agreeing to the hit was spend the money. And there was less than twenty-four hours to execute the contract.

Quietly, she slipped out of the hospital room and drove to the nail salon. It was too little, too late. The salon was closed, and all she could do was look for cameras and an escape route. Aoki knew from the gate that this hit was way over their heads. The murder wasn't going to be the hard part. She knew she could get close enough to plunge her dagger into the victim's heart. The kicker would be getting away with it.

She sat in the front seat of her Yukon until the sun came up. Her heart told her that a storm was brewing. Reluctantly she drove back to the hospital to check up on Ri-Ri. There was only one thing to do, and that was move forward and try to fulfill the contract. She had to at least try. If she didn't, then she was dead. If she tried and failed, then she would make sure that the feds killed her. No way was she doing jail time.

❦

The doctors and nurses were in and out of the room around the clock, checking everything, jotting down Gena's vitals, changing bandages and IVs, poking her with needles, extracting and injecting, and making sure their patient was being treated fairly and given every chance to live, though things looked bleak. She would need more surgery, and she would need a lot of rehabilitation. Still, survival was a long shot.

The gunshot was so close, the powder had burned her flesh. During impact, her brain shifted and tissue damage occurred, and there was still heavy swelling in crucial areas of her brain.

Ri-Ri held onto her mother's still hand. Dejected and transfixed with grief and concern, she'd never stopped crying.

Aoki sat in the corner for hours, dozing in and out of sleep. Mentally and physically she was drained. Her cell phone rang.

The moment she picked up, a voice said, "You let me down. You disappoint me, Aoki."

It was Oscar. Aoki's heart began to palpitate. She'd overslept!

Aoki removed herself from the room to talk to Oscar somewhere in private. She hurried toward the nearest stairwell, her heart racing. She knew she had fucked up. "Oscar, let me explain—"

"What is there to explain? I gave you a contract, and it hasn't been fulfilled."

Her heart dropped. How could she be so stupid?

"Me sorry, a lot has happened. Ri-Ri's mom been shot in de head an' it's been chaos. I'm at de hospital, but I planned to do de hit. I overslept, me swear."

"I do not care about your personal life, Aoki. I contracted you and your crew to do a job. Now it's too late. She's going to testify, and unfortunately my colleague is a dead man. I've come to realize you are nothing but an amateur. I made a mistake, but I'll correct it."

Oscar was too calm, and that worried Aoki even more.

"Oscar, me still can execute de contract!"

"There's no need. Goodbye, Aoki." Oscar hung up, leaving Aoki on edge.

Aoki knew there was trouble coming her way via Oscar. You don't fuck up like she did and get to live. She felt herself falling deeper and deeper into a spiraling nightmare. Not only did she have to worry about B Scientific and AZ, but now Oscar was added to her list.

She exited the stairwell with a calm face. She walked toward the room and decided not to go back inside. There was no need to concern Ri-Ri with the bad news right now. She was already going through enough.

CHAPTER 28

Aoki let the water rain down on her naked flesh with her head lowered. She wished her hot shower could simply wash away all her worries and pain. She didn't want to think about Oscar, B Scientific, AZ, or the streets. Everything was in bad shape.

She'd fucked up on a large scale this time. Not only was she deeply indebted to him, but she had also fucked up her drug connection.

Oscar wasn't the type of man to forget about money or mistakes. She understood that she was a dead woman walking, but not if she could get to him first. Which was virtually impossible.

She hadn't told Ri-Ri about the call from Oscar, but she couldn't keep it a secret for too long, especially since Ri-Ri was the one who'd suggested that they take the contract.

As Aoki soothed herself in the shower, the curtain was pulled back and Emilio joined her. He wrapped his arms around her frame and pulled her closer. He kissed the side of her neck, squeezed one of her tits, and fondled her body like he was a horny little boy.

"What you thinking about?" He was always concerned for her, wanting to please her and take care of her.

"Me just concerned 'bout me friend."

"I feel bad for Ri-Ri. Cops don't have any suspects?"

"None."

"It's a crazy world out there. It's a good thing you got me. I'm not going anywhere, no matter how bad shit gets."

Aoki managed to smile. He squeezed her tightly, their wet skin entangled together under the cascading water from the large showerhead. His touch was riveting.

Aoki sighed a little, trying not to stress her dire situation. She closed her eyes and exhaled. Emilio was touching her tenderly and loving her everywhere. She felt his hand between her legs, and there were more kisses to her wet skin. His chest pressed against her back, she could feel his erection rubbing against her butt.

Emilio turned her around to face him. He looked at her warmly. "Don't worry, baby. Everything is gonna be okay. I'm gonna protect you from everything. I won't let anyone ever harm you, I promise."

Aoki wished he could be her Superman and stop a speeding bullet, or take down an entire cartel with his super strength.

She took his hard dick into her hand and stroked him as they kissed. What she needed was a distraction, something pleasurable to ease her mind, even if it was temporary. Emilio's dick in her fist was the ideal distraction. She jerked him off in the shower, her pussy pulsating, his dick throbbing in her hand.

"I want you," she said.

"I want you too."

They continued to tongue each other down with the water running between their lips. The shower water was invigorating.

Emilio held her by her hips, close and gentle. He spun her around, positioned her away from him, and curved her over under the showerhead with her hands flat against the wall. He penetrated her from behind. He was inside of her, thrusting and moaning. He held her wet hips steady and fucked her nice and slow, in and out, in and out, in and out.

Emilio's eyes started to roll back in his head. He grunted and groaned, wishing the blissful feeling never ended.

After sex in the steamy shower, they toweled off and went into her bedroom. Aoki had been spending a lot of time over AZ's place, so being in her own home again felt somewhat odd. But she was making the best of things.

She and Emilio kissed passionately once more while sitting on her bed. When they came up for air, Emilio stared at her with this look of a warrior. Not averting his eyes from her, his look spoke volumes to her, and once again he made a vow to protect her and Ri-Ri if needed.

"I don't scare easily," he said to her.

"Me know ya don't."

"I can stay here with you, move in, if needed."

Aoki wanted him close, but not that close.

"No need fah dat."

"Why not? You sure you're telling me everything, Aoki? I feel that you're leaving something out."

She didn't want to tell him about her troubles with the cartel. It was her problem, and there was no need to drag him in that deep. "Just hold me," she said.

Emilio draped his arms around her and held her like she wanted him to. Though she was a cold-blooded killer, she still needed affection and some TLC. She realized this was love—when a man never wants to let you go and would do anything for you.

They lay beside each other naked, and she invited him into her body once more, pulling him on top of her. He accepted her sexual invitation, going inside Aoki's pink temple in the missionary position nice and slow.

Emilio continually gave her that out-of-body experience. She came once more, and he erupted inside of her.

Again, she lay nestled against Emilio on her bed. She still kept quiet about the cartel, but did mention her problems with B Scientific.

With a straight face, Emilio growled, "Yo, I'll execute that muthafucka if I have to."

It felt good to hear he had her back.

"You know what? You and Ri-Ri can stay at the dorm."

"What?"

"I'm serious. My roommate gonna be out of town for a minute. He had a death in the family. So if you and her need to get away, come there. It'll be fine, I promise you."

It was a generous offer, and Aoki was contemplating taking it. It would be nice spending some quality time with Emilio, even with Ri-Ri around.

For the next couple of days, Aoki kept Ri-Ri close by her side like her own ribs. Wherever she went, she brought Ri-Ri with her. They couldn't take any chances. It was better to be together than apart. Aoki had to tell her about the phone call from Oscar.

Ri-Ri looked white as a ghost when she heard the news.

"I took the contract without even talkin' to you, Aoki. I got greedy. I fucked up! I'm sorry."

"Nuh need cryin' over spilled milk. What's done is done!"

Together, they stayed armed and dangerous. Staying in Emilio's dorm was cool, but things got cramped and weird the three days they were there.

Emilio had classes, so the girls tried to fit in like they were students. Emilio even got them fake student IDs, but it wasn't their cup of tea.

They decided to leave town for a while, until things cooled down.

Aoki had a friend in Philly who owed her a favor. They had met years earlier when they both went to a free summer camp for underprivileged kids. For years they kept in touch with sporadic long distance telephone calls until they lost touch. Last year they reconnected on Facebook. Aoki made the call, and Melody said they could stay with her for a while. The girls packed their bags for the ride to Philly, but first Ri-Ri had to go see her mom.

Ri-Ri and Aoki stepped off the elevator into the hospital corridor. They walked toward Gena's room armed with concealed pistols, not taking any chances with their lives. It felt like they had gone from being the hunters to the hunted, and it was time to get out of Dodge for a minute.

First, they had to check up on Gena. The closer they got to her room, the more they could hear a bunch of catty bitches. When they entered, the girls were shocked to see Tisa seated by their mother and being consoled by Penny, Stephanie, Kim, and Lady.

"What the fuck!" Ri-Ri looked at everyone like they were out of their mind. "Why are y'all here?"

"We here for Tisa," Penny said, a snarl in her tone.

"Oh, so now y'all here for Tisa," Ri-Ri said.

Scowls and glares cut across the room like knives.

Aoki wanted to carve her knife in their eyes and faces. She hated them. Her frown was stern. Her eyes hooked on Penny, the main bitch she wanted to go after. Tisa had the audacity to bring their enemies to Gena's room. It was the ultimate disrespect.

"We don't want any trouble, Ri-Ri," Tisa said.

"You don't want any trouble? Are you out your fuckin' mind, Tisa? Having them here is trouble."

The words coming out of Tisa's mouth were fueling Aoki's anger. She wanted to snap and pull Tisa apart.

Penny stood up. She wasn't about to be caught slipping and seated, and looking vulnerable in front of Aoki. She knew that bitch was serious and that at any moment, shit could pop off.

Both parties kept their cool and remained calm. They were in a public hospital, with Gena right there clinging to life. She looked even more terrible than before.

"We're leaving," Penny announced.

"Bye!" Ri-Ri exclaimed.

Aoki didn't divert her hard stare from Penny. Her hands were closed into tight fists, her face was contorted with resentment, and her nostrils were flaring. She was like a volcano ready to explode, and she was ready to spew her hot lava everywhere and destroy everything in its way.

Penny, Stephanie, Lady, and Kim walked by Aoki and Ri-Ri slowly.

Aoki locked eyes with every last one of them. She dared them to say something smart, but they didn't. They walked away and left Tisa with her sister and Aoki.

"Cunt bitches," Aoki said under her breath.

Ri-Ri cut her eyes at Tisa. "What is wrong wit' you?"

"Nothing! They're just friends checking up on me. Is there something wrong wit' that?"

"Everything."

"Y'all don't fuck wit' me anymore. So I moved on."

"To them?"

"Why you care?"

"You just being stupid, Tisa," Ri-Ri said.

"You know what, Ri-Ri? Fuck you!"

"Typical you—fuckin' ignorant!"

Aoki snorted slightly, looking at Tisa like she was a fuckin' fool, a clown in tight clothing and dumb makeup. The naïve bitch just didn't get it at all.

Tisa said, "You got somethin' you wanna say to me, Aoki?"

Aoki smirked. "Ya need to stay in ya place, little girl!"

"This little girl will fuck you up!"

"Not even on me worst day."

Aoki wasn't in the mood to waste time with Tisa. Her card had already been pulled. She wasn't a threat to anyone, but one day, Aoki was going to hurt her really bad. But today wasn't that day. She had more important issues to deal with than a spoiled, dumb bitch.

Ri-Ri had a few more things to say to her sister, and they weren't pretty. After that, they left the hospital. Ri-Ri wiped the few tears from her eyes. She hated to leave town while her mother was in critical condition, but she felt like she didn't have a choice.

From fucking things up with Oscar to two detectives prying into their lives, harassing them, and Aoki running into mysterious men in black, routines had to change. They needed to withdraw from their lives temporarily. How long? Maybe a month or longer.

The girls climbed into Aoki's Yukon and drove toward the Belt Parkway. After crossing over the Verrazano Bridge and merging onto the New Jersey Turnpike, they were on the road to Philadelphia, one hundred miles from New York City.

CHAPTER 29

Three weeks later

AZ could hear voices, but he couldn't understand what was being said. When he opened his eyes, there were blurry faces gazing down at him and moving away, and then the darkness came again. He was coming through slowly but surely, fading in and out of consciousness. It was hard for him to tell if he was dreaming or not. He didn't recognize his surroundings nor the voices talking to him. It was hard for him to move. It was even harder for him to speak. He felt alienated for a moment.

Being unable to move his limbs or raise himself up was terrifying, and his mind was cloudy, like his brain was trapped in a never-ending fog. His body felt like putty. Was he paralyzed?

But progressively things started to become clearer for him, and he was becoming a little bit more aware of his surroundings. He knew he was in a hospital bed and that something had happened to him. How did he get there? He wondered what was wrong with him.

A doctor asked him if he knew his name. He tried to answer him, but it felt like he had rocks in his throat. He knew his first name, but why did it take him so long to recall his last name?

There was a small commotion around him, like he was some kind of miracle. They told him that he was in New York at Brookdale Hospital, and that he had been shot twice and was fortunate to be alive.

Aoki hurried back to New York City after she'd heard the news about AZ awaking from his coma over a week earlier. She had just gotten the news from a friend, who had heard the news through the grapevine. She was upset that she'd heard so late, but she and Ri-Ri packed their bags and left Philadelphia.

Aoki couldn't get back to New York fast enough. She didn't know what to expect when she returned. How would he react toward her? Did he remember that night? Was he still angry at her? And, most important, would he try to kill her again? There were so many questions she wanted to ask him. Aoki had to tread lightly and be aware. Things were changing in her world, and not for the best.

The girls' stay in Philadelphia was a peaceful one. Melody showed them much hospitality. They hid out and kept a low profile at her home, where they tried to come up with a game plan and regroup somehow. It was them against the world, or at least it felt like that. They didn't know what to expect when they returned home.

Aoki arrived in Brooklyn, and her first stop was Brookdale Hospital. She parked a block away, took a deep breath, and armed herself with a .380. With Ri-Ri by her side, they strutted into the hospital, stepped into the elevator, and walked onto the floor that harbored the coma patients. The floor was pristine and quiet, not hectic like the emergency room or other areas of the hospital.

As they marched down the hallway, Ri-Ri asked, "You okay?"

Aoki nodded. "Me fine."

"You know, it might be hard for him to remember that night, Aoki. He has been through a lot—shot, drugged, and in a coma for months."

"Me know."

"I just want you to prepare yourself for whatever happens."

"Ri-Ri, me been ready to speak to him fah a long time now. Me ready fah anything."

The girls walked into his room, and to their surprise, Tisa was sitting next to AZ's bed talking to him. She was dressed in a short skirt, tight top, heels, and her long hair in cornrows.

Immediately, Aoki was irritated by the bitch's presence.

Tisa smirked at her sister and Aoki. Unbeknownst to the two girls, Tisa had been by AZ's side since the day he awoke from his coma, and they'd been talking every day.

Aoki wanted to cut away that stupid fuckin' smirk from her face. If looks could kill, Tisa would have been hacked to pieces like a character in *Friday the 13th*.

Aoki shook her head. "Ya like a cockroach, Tisa! Fuckin' hard to get rid of!"

"Well, look who decided to come back into town," Tisa replied. "I thought y'all bitches woulda stayed gone."

Aoki started to approach her, but Ri-Ri grabbed her by the arm, preventing the attack. "She ain't worth, Aoki. Just chill. We just got back into town," she said.

Aoki grudgingly agreed.

AZ looked at Aoki with no expression. It almost looked like he didn't recognize her at all, even though they'd known each other for years and she had saved his life. He'd lost weight, his face was thinner, and he had grown a beard, but overall, he looked fine. He seemed approachable, but she didn't know what to expect. It wasn't like he was all smiles and looking for a hug from her.

Aoki wondered still, *What was he and Tisa talking about? What kind of lies was she putting in his head?* She held back her tongue and rage to cut the bitch in half. She looked at Tisa and politely asked, "Can ya give me some privacy to talk?"

"Why should I leave, huh? I've been here since he's been awake, not you. And until he tells me to leave, then I'm staying."

"It's okay, Tisa," AZ said faintly. "Give us some privacy to talk."

Tisa didn't like it, but she left. She and Ri-Ri walked into the hallway.

Aoki shut the door behind them. She then pivoted and locked eyes with AZ, who was staring at her stoically, propped up in his bed, looking frail and vulnerable. Today he wasn't a threat, but what about tomorrow?

"How ya feel?" Aoki asked.

"I could be better."

Aoki stepped closer to his bed and looked him up and down. She remembered the nightmare she'd had when he had awoken from his coma and pulled out a gun on her.

"Do ya remember anything 'bout de night ya were shot?"

"I remember."

"Why, huh? Was ya really gon' shoot me?"

"You were the one that betrayed me."

Aoki couldn't believe what she was hearing. "What ya ah talk' 'bout?"

"I'm talkin' about you gettin' B Scientific to shoot me and Heavy Pop."

"What?" What he said almost brought Aoki to her knees. She was bewildered by his words. B Scientific had helped to save his life.

"Your boyfriend, he just came on the block and started shooting. But before he did that, he shouted, 'This is from Aoki.'"

"Him wrong. Me had nothin' to do wit' that night, ya hear?"

"You were fuckin' him!"

"So what? Me would never betray ya. Him was comin' after me!" Aoki sternly replied. "Ya were always like a brother to me."

"A brother?"

It was all adding up to her. Put two and two together and it equaled Gena. She'd pawned B's rosary in Aoki's name, and B Scientific got wind of it and felt Aoki betrayed him. He wanted to kill her. But the truth was revealed a little too late. Gena was in critical condition because of her stupidity, and Aoki was still trying to recover from the aftermath of it.

"I don't know what or who is real anymore. But, yeah, I went to your house with every intention of killing you. I hated you! I felt you betrayed and hurt me. Heavy Pop was almost killed because of you dealing with that nigga. I don't know what y'all were talkin' about, or what y'all had planned, but it backfired. We're still here."

Aoki started to tear up.

AZ looked choked up about something. He looked away from Aoki for a moment and then turned his attention back to her. "I came to your house, knowing you tried to set me up. But when I saw you that night, I realized I couldn't do it. I couldn't take your life. I wanted to hate you, Aoki, but I still loved you."

Emotions were high in the room. Hearing this was good news to Aoki. She still wanted him and needed him as a friend.

"I know who shot me."

"Ya do?"

"Why was Emilio at your house?"

"Him just showed up."

"And you believe that?"

"Me have no reason to doubt him."

"You shouldn't trust him, Aoki."

"Why? Because him shot ya when him was only tryin' to defend me?"

"Defend you?" AZ frowned. "He wasn't there to defend you; he was there to kill you."

"And how ya know dat? Why would him kill me?"

"Aoki, you can't trust him. I barely know him myself. He was just a college nigga from L.A. I sold weight to. You went and fucked the nigga. But who is he? Huh? I find it highly convenient that he was there that night at your place with a gun. That nigga got his own agenda for being there. I don't know what it is, but you need to be careful around him."

Aoki fell into the open chair near his bed, wondering if what AZ was saying was true. She had asked Emilio about that night, and his explanation was that he was simply there to apologize to her, and that he'd only come with a gun because he didn't trust Brooklyn. But Aoki always felt there was more to his story than he was telling. Emilio never came to her home strapped before, but that night he was.

She had finally fallen in love with someone she thought was special, and now she felt betrayed. Once again, she didn't know who to trust—AZ or Emilio. They both could be lying. Was AZ telling her a story because now he was the one vulnerable to her? He said he couldn't go through with it, but it could have still been a lie.

However, her gut was telling her that AZ was telling her the truth. But her heart was still bound to Emilio.

"You gonna stop fuckin' wit' him?" he asked her point-blank.

"It's still me decision."

"So it's like that? After everything I told you about him."

"Ya told me nothin'. Just speculation." Aoki just couldn't break away from Emilio cold turkey, just because AZ didn't trust him. Still, it could have been jealousy speaking from AZ's end.

"And B Scientific? You still fuckin' him?"

She lowered her eyes, which gave AZ the confirmation he needed. He then noticed the diamond watch around her slim wrist and felt disgusted by it. AZ knew it was a gift from B Scientific. How could she still mess with two men who'd tried to kill him? AZ never thought he could hate her, but she was making it easier by breaking his heart again.

CHAPTER 30

Aoki was sprawled out across her bed in her panties and bra, looking like she could be a centerfold for *Playboy*. She was contemplating her talk with AZ. A lot was said the other day, there was still a lot of uneasiness between them, and their friendship was still in bad shape. It was early in the morning and she was alone, and regularly cautious. She slept with a pistol under her pillow, one in the drawer next to her bed, and a loaded shotgun under her bed. If anyone came for her in the night, she would be ready. Everyone was a threat to her. She'd decided to stay away from the Pink Houses and the hood altogether.

Aoki's phone was ringing non-stop. Emilio and B Scientific continuously called her, but she ignored them. She mulled over AZ's words; she was in a triple tug-of-war between all three men. They all wanted her.

She suddenly had a premonition. There was one thing that left her totally exposed to law enforcement. It was something she'd left buried for so long, that it felt naturally safe to have around.

Aoki removed herself from the bed and walked to her bedroom window. She stared at the two large barrels in her backyard, the ones that contained her dead parents. They'd been there for so long that she had grown comfortable with keeping them close. Though she'd despised her parents, the two barrels were a reminder to her that life wasn't to be taking for granted. You're either a whale or a shark. Her father and her mother were a waste of space, two drug addicts that were whales in society. She'd decided long ago that she would become a shark.

The barrels were now a problem. Too many people knew about them. One anonymous phone call to the police could bring cops through her front door. It would be the end of her with such compelling evidence found in her backyard.

She quickly got dressed, drove to the nearest storage facility, and rented out a decent size storage space and small moving van under an alias. With everything paid for and ready, her next stop was to Home Depot to find a few day laborers. Every morning until afternoon, a cluster of immigrants lingered near the store looking to do a hard day's work for some decent pay.

Aoki came to a stop near where a dozen Mexicans stood out front, each one dressed for work in work boots, old jeans and other construction clothing, some men carrying their own tools. She rolled down the passenger window and hollered, "Me need four men."

The men looked at her nonchalantly. No one moved toward the van.

She sighed. "Okay, me gon' try again."

She went into her pocket and pulled out a wad of cash, all hundreds. She dangled the cash in front of the Mexicans and said, "*Cuatro*! Me need men to work!"

The sight of money sent the men running to her van. Before she knew it, her van was swamped with immigrants desperate for work. She had to hurry and pick her four workers for a hundred dollars each. They hopped into the van, and she sped away. The men rode quietly in the back of the van. They barely spoke English, but they understood hard work and a wad of hundreds.

At her house, the Mexicans went straight to work, taking the two heavy barrels and placing them into the van. Then she had them doing yard work, cleaning and mowing the grass, and making sure the area was cleaned thoroughly and there was no indication of where the barrels had been.

After the yard, Aoki drove them to the storage unit, where they carried the barrels into the building and placed them into her storage unit. The Mexicans didn't ask any questions, they did what they were told, and Aoki paid them $100 each. She even bought them lunch before dropping them off where she'd picked them up.

She exhaled. She just felt that it was time to move the bodies until she was able to fully dispose of them properly. She told no one what she was doing. With frayed friendships, she didn't want anything hanging over her head. There were too many snakes out there that wanted to see her downfall, and the last thing she wanted to do was make it easy for them.

AZ slowly climbed out of the money-green Tahoe with Tisa's help and made his way toward his brownstone. He wanted to get back to his old self promptly. Every day he was lying in that coma was money lost and connections gone. Tisa was right by his side to guide him and keep him stable. Overnight, they became a couple. She had been there for him since he came out of his coma, and he was grateful.

It was good to be home. It was great to be alive. However, it felt like AZ had a lot of catching up to do. His steps toward the front door were slow, but solid, whereas before, they were shaky and wobbly.

Still in rehabilitation, he was recuperating fine with the help of therapy and medication. Day by day, he was regaining his strength and his weight.

Heavy Pop had been on top his business in the streets, but they had to rebuild. They needed a new connect. Their relationship with Oscar had dissolved because of Aoki and she wouldn't tell him why. He tried to contact Oscar to hear his side of the story, but all telephone numbers were changed.

AZ had found out that Aoki started to take over his business transactions without his consent, making unauthorized deals with other drug dealers. She had been living in his home. Everything she had done angered him. Behind his back, she'd tried to become the boss, and everything went to shit while she put herself in charge.

As AZ made his way into his home, his cell phone rang. Connor was calling him. He ignored his lover's call because Tisa was right there, and he wasn't in the mood to talk. Connor had been worried about him and missed him deeply, but the reconstruction of his business was more important than some dick right now. He was still on the down low, and his reputation was everything.

He read Connor's text.

BABY, PLEASE DON'T DO ME LIKE THIS. I REALLY WANT TO SEE YOU. I LOVE YOU AND GLAD THAT MY BOO IS BACK HOME. PS, LET ME BE THE ONE TO NURSE YOU BACK TO HEALTH THE RIGHT WAY. :) XOXOXOXOXO!

AZ turned his phone off and let Tisa take care of him. Once they were inside, she drew him a hot bath, helped him remove his clothing, and told him to relax.

"I'm gonna take care of you, baby. You don't need to worry about anything," Tisa said.

"Thanks for everything."

"I'm here for you, AZ. You don't need to be alone when you have a good woman like me willing to take care of you."

He smiled faintly. Tisa was beautiful and supportive in so many areas. Yet he wasn't attracted to her. She was simply a front, a means to expedite his healing. He couldn't tell her he was gay. He did want to see Connor, but at the moment, it was too risky to even go near him.

AZ sat in his bedroom indifferently while Tisa buzzed around. He turned his phone back on and saw there were more texts from Connor. He was thirsty for AZ to contact him. He would in due time. But now, he needed to put a handle on the confusion Aoki had stirred up.

He called Heavy Pop.

The phone rang, and Heavy picked up. "Yo, what's good my dude?"

"Surviving."

"You and me both. It's good to have you back home, AZ."

"You know, it's good to be home. Lying in that hospital, it makes you get a strong grip on life and realize life is too short."

"Tell me about it," Heavy said. "We both were in the same boat, and we both are strong men."

"We need to talk. Can you come by the house tomorrow?"

"I'm there, AZ."

"A'ight. One, my nigga."

"One."

Tisa walked into the bedroom in a sheer robe; her body looked amazing in it. She smiled. "Your bath is ready."

She helped him into the bathroom.

He got naked and submerged himself in the tub, and Tisa soon joined him.

Instead of it being a healing and soothing sitting, she tried to make it into a romantic one with candles and dim lighting. She pulled AZ's naked body to hers and started to massage his shoulders and work her way down, landing her womanly touch on his dick and stroking his flaccid penis under the water while they sat in the tub.

"Let me take care of you, baby," she said in his ear.

AZ closed his eyes and allowed her fondling to continue. It was pleasing, but he wasn't fully into it. There was too much on his mind to enjoy a hand-job. Too much to do to relax and enjoy sex.

Tisa kissed his neck and jerked him off, thinking sex was the perfect healing, but AZ merely remained casual to her sexual gestures.

He closed his eyes and allowed his body to soak.

Tisa's sensitive touch continued. She massaged his limbs, his neck, and his shoulders and gave him the company she felt he needed. She wanted to make love to him, but AZ wasn't in the mood. They hadn't had sex yet, though they were a couple.

"You okay, baby?" she asked him.

"I'm fine."

"You just seem kinda distant. I know you been through a traumatic experience. What can I do to make you feel better?"

"I'm okay, Tisa. I just need some time to think."

"I wanna help."

"I know you do."

"No, I wanna help you, AZ. I want us to become a power couple. I want to make you the man you deserve to be."

The man he deserved to be? And how was she gonna help, besides giving him sex? Which was something he wasn't looking for. What he wanted to be was fiercer and richer. The shooting had him thinking about his future. He needed to change so many things about himself.

Tisa continued to massage him, trying her best to make him relax. She did her best to make him hard so they could have sex, but nothing worked on him. He was still limp like a noodle.

Eventually, AZ stood up and removed himself from the tub. "I need to make a phone call," he said and departed the bathroom.

Tisa sighed. She lowered herself deeper into the tub with her arms folded across her chest, and pouted.

Heavy Pop sat down across from AZ in the living room. Heavy was all smiles, happy to see his ace alive and walking around his home freely, though he moved slow and had a noticeable limp.

They were back in business, but there were issues in their organization.

"Aoki fucked everything up," AZ griped. "I mean, this bitch went behind our backs and tried to take away our clientele and fucked up the connect. You believe that shit?"

"I don't know what to believe anymore," Heavy replied.

"Did you get in contact with that new connect I told you about? Them dudes from DC?"

Heavy Pop nodded. "It went okay."

"What they talkin' about?"

"They're a little pricier than Oscar."

"How much?"

"Five thousand more."

"Shit!"

"I know. But do we have a choice right now?"

"We don't."

"That's why I already set it up," Heavy Pop said.

AZ exhaled noisily. Change was costing him money. But he wasn't about to give up what he'd worked so hard for.

"Their quality is a little bit lower than Oscar's, but I think we can work with it. Have our peoples package it right and wholesale for a little more to our peoples out of state. But the niggas we been working with were already complaining about the prices before, but they couldn't fuss too much because Oscar had the pure quality shit."

"I know. He did. But we can make this work. We came back from worse, my nigga."

"We did," Heavy Pop cosigned.

"Did you meet with Jump and Rhino, tell them the situation? Let them know Aoki fucked us and them?"

"I did."

"And?"

"The way they talking, they're ready to reach out to a new connect, they talking about our house ain't right—shit ain't organized correctly. Jump talkin' like we a sinking ship."

"Fuck that! That nigga owes me a ton of favors, and he ain't smart enough to break away from us like that. And we ain't sinking."

"I tried to talk some sense into his head, but you know how Jump is."

AZ sighed, looking pensive in his chair. He had a lot of cleaning up to do, which meant reaching out to all of his clientele and proposing something reasonable to them.

AZ had the gift of gab, and he knew that he would have to meet with everybody face to face soon to get them to believe that he was still was smart and in charge. There was a shift in the game, but the shake wasn't life-threatening to his organization. At least that's what he wanted to believe.

"I also met with that new nigga in Staten Island, Hex," Heavy brought up.

"And how did that go?"

"Let's just say, he's a whole lot smarter than that fool, Peanut. The new management in that part of town is on point."

"Okay, cool."

AZ walked toward the window and gazed outside. The season was changing. The weather was becoming colder, and so was he. Being shot had stirred something different inside him.

He turned and looked at Heavy. He didn't smile at all. He looked more focused on the game and the street life than ever. Heavy Pop saw something colder and fiercer in his friend's eyes.

"Our thinking before, Heavy—you know that pacifist shit, trying to play this game without any bloodshed, trusting muthafuckas too easily, letting niggas get weight on consignment, being the nice guy—was fuckin' idiotic. Fuck that! We made ourselves look weak out there, even though we were respected. But no more, my nigga! Being shot, it hurts, and I'm not tryin' to get shot again! I'll kill a nigga before he kills me!"

"What, you ready to go all Al Capone?"

"Fuck, yeah!"

"So, we ready to go to war with the game?"

"Nigga, I'm ready to make a change and lay niggas six feet deep."

"Yo, that bullet done changed you."

"It should change you too, my nigga! B Scientific shot you, and I would be ready to kill that nigga right now. Heavy, we gotta let these niggas know we ain't playing. We left ourselves too open. I'm not having it. No more, my nigga."

Heavy Pop observed how AZ went from a fox to a snarling wolf. All morning, they went over every detail that needed to change, every client that might stay or leave, and if they were planning on leaving, then how to prevent it. AZ wanted to micromanage everything in his organization to bring everything up to speed, using violence if needed.

CHAPTER 31

Aoki laughed as Emilio twirled her around on the dance floor. She spun around in her high heels like a top, her white flare dress whirling around sexily and exposing her long, smooth legs, her long hair flowing. Aoki was eye candy inside the Lower Manhattan club. Her smile was radiant, and her attitude was joyous for once as she and Emilio danced in sync to the up-tempo beat of hip-hop. The nightclub was vibrant with revelers from wall to wall, and the DJ was spinning the best music around.

Aoki needed to get away, and though AZ had warned her about Emilio, it was still hard for her see it herself and let him go just because of hearsay, from a man who most likely resented her now.

Emilio was up close on her, running his hands across her body, his feet sliding and stepping on the dance floor.

Aoki smiled at him. "Me impressed, Emilio. Ya got some moves."

He grinned. "Thanks."

He took Aoki by her hand and moved when she moved. They slid left, then right, and she winded her hips against his, throwing her plump butt back against his pelvis, and things went from upbeat to sensual. They didn't care who was watching. It felt like they were alone on the dance floor.

Emilio wrapped his arms around her waist, and the two became entwined sensually.

After the song, they stepped off the dance floor and moved toward the bar. Emilio's hand was against her backside, subtly indicating to those watching from the sidelines that Aoki belonged to him. He saw niggas' eyes looking at Aoki hungrily and probably wondering what this Hispanic muthafucka was doing with a beautiful girl like her. He boldly dared them with his eyes to disrespect him. He was ready for anything.

"You want another drink?" he asked.

She nodded.

The bar was swamped. There was a crowd pushing toward the long countertop like welfare recipients rushing for free food. It was a battle to be served, with the three bartenders desperately trying to keep up with the orders.

Emilio bullied his way toward the bar with Aoki right behind him. He had no time to wait around like a dummy. His woman was thirsty. He lifted his hand in the air, determined to call one of the bartenders over. "Yo, bartender, I need you over here," he shouted with authority in his tone. He pulled out a hundred-dollar bill from his pocket, waving it at the young male near him. "I got a twenty-dollar tip if you take my order now."

Aoki liked the way he moved with confidence. He wasn't afraid to be heard, or what people thought about him.

The man came his way and Emilio asked his queen, "Baby, you want your Cîroc Peach and Sprite?"

"Ya know me." Aoki smiled.

"C'mon, you already know. I always pay attention." He placed the C-note on the countertop, and said to the bartender. "And get me a White Russian."

The man went to fulfill their drink orders.

Emilio smoothly pulled Aoki into his arms and hugged her. He kissed her neck and danced with her a little at the bar. He was happy with her and wasn't afraid to show it.

With their drinks in hand, he made sure to clear a way for his woman. He didn't want the risk of having a drink spilled on her by some drunken or clumsy idiot, ruining her wonderful white outfit. They took seating at one of the tall bar tables in the back of the club and started to converse.

Once again, Emilio glared at the men raping his woman with their foul eyes and made it known that she was with him. His insecurity was steadily seeping into the public eye.

"You are beautiful," he said, complimenting her for the umpteenth time.

"I'm havin' a good time."

"Me too."

"Where ya learn to dance so well?"

"I like the clubs. I like to dance. I love music."

"Me see." Aoki took a sip from her glass. She noticed the attention she was receiving from nearby males. "Ya no need to worry, Emilio. Me wit' ya," she told him, seeing the insecurity developing in his eyes as they sat and drank.

"I just don't want to be disrespected."

"Ya won't."

As the night went on, while she was dancing and drinking with Emilio, B Scientific kept calling her continuously, leaving voice messages and texts. Aoki simply ignored him, not wanting any interruptions.

Around two a.m., Emilio and Aoki exited the club laughing and playing with each other like children in the school yard. She jumped on his back and said, "Carry me to de car, servant!"

"Oh, now I'm your servant now, huh?"

"Yup! Ya gotta do whatever me say."

"Yes, ma'am! Where to?"

"To me chariot."

He laughed and gave her a piggyback while everyone watched them. Emilio was strong, for such a thin man. He carried her on his back like she was a child. Aoki started to lean into him, hunching her back, laughing loudly. Though the liquor had her somewhat tipsy, she was still focused.

As Emilio carried her toward the car, he heard a man say loud enough for them to hear him, "Um, damn, I wouldn't mind having her ride me like that! Shorty got a phat ass! Fuck she wit' that nigga for?"

Emilio cut his eyes at the man spewing the disrespectful comment. The piggyback ride and laughing stopped suddenly. Aoki came down from off his back, and she was scowling too.

"What the fuck you say?" Emilio shouted.

"Yo, you heard me, nigga. What the fuck you gonna do about it?" the man dared Emilio.

Fire sparked in Emilio's eyes. He clenched his fists and marched toward trouble.

Aoki was right behind him. The loudmouth fool had no idea who he was talking shit to. Now it was too late. The bull was out of the barn, and Emilio's horns were ready to impale the sonofabitch.

The man was tall and slim and had *hoodlum* written all over him. Emilio wasn't intimidated by his appearance. He was ready to argue with his fists. They thought he was weak because he was neatly dressed in slacks, a button-down, and wingtips and was doting on his lady. Emilio's temper started to sizzle and was ready to explode on the fool.

"You disrespect me and my woman!" Emilio growled.

"Fuck outta here, you spic muthafucka! Don't get beat down and embarrassed in front of ya fuckin' bitch!"

"Ya need to shut de fuck up! It's gon' be ya who get beat down!" Aoki shouted.

"Yo, ya bitch got mouth too. She fighting your battles, nigga? Fuckin' Bonnie and Clyde here!" The man scowled down at Emilio. He figured because he was taller and had his friend backing him, he could talk to Emilio any kind of way.

Emilio's quick punch to his right jaw was a staggering one. It almost knocked him into Connecticut.

But the attack didn't stop there. Emilio was all over him with several follow-up punches to his gut, folding him over, and another hard punch to his face. And before he knew it, the man's mouth was soaked in the taste of his own blood. He didn't know what hit him.

Emilio stood over his victim, who was on his hands and knees and bleeding profusely, his blood staining the ground. He had been stabbed several times. No one saw the knife in Emilio's hand. It looked like it had come out of nowhere.

Aoki was shocked. Emilio moved like lightning. She stood next to Emilio in awe. The man's friend was no help; he looked tough, but he wasn't about that life.

Emilio shouted, "Fuck with me, muthafucka! You call me a spic and disrespect my woman while I'm standing here!"

"Help me!" the victim cried out.

"Fuck you, muthafucka! Bleed, nigga!"

Aoki knew it was time to depart. There were witnesses. Too many people, too many eyes, and too many problems facing them. "We need to leave," she said. She pulled Emilio by his hand, dragging him away from the incident.

At first he was resistant, but then he came to his senses and fled with Aoki. They hurried toward the car while people were dialing 911. They hopped into her truck, and she sped away before sirens could be heard.

While driving, she turned to Emilio and asked, "What de fuck was dat?"

"I'm sorry. I just got carried away back there. Don't anybody disrespect me or my woman."

Aoki was used to violence, but that definitely caught her off guard. It brought her back to the night he'd shot AZ. He didn't hesitate.

After seeing this side of Emilio, she wondered if she could trust him.

"Baby, I'm sorry. I didn't mean to scare you. I just lost it."

"Ya were stupid back there. Too many people saw ya face. Ya need to lay low."

"It won't happen again. I promise."

She drove, not responding. But it was going to happen again. She knew it. People like her and Emilio were fearless and quick to react. He was sexy and a good/bad boy, but was he right for her?

CHAPTER 32

re you enjoying your meal?" B Scientific asked Aoki.
"I am," she replied.

"Good. I want you to be happy, Aoki."

"Me fine."

B Scientific grinned and took a sip of wine. All he wanted to do was make her happy. They sat opposite each other at the round table draped in white cloth and decorated with flowers. B Scientific wanted to go all out to impress Aoki, so he took her to one of the finest restaurants in the city, Juni, on the upper West Side. The restaurant had dim lighting and live piano music, and the air was thick with the scent of so many different foods.

From her seat, Aoki had a view of the entrance, and only couples were coming in and going out. She allowed herself to soak in the ambiance and the classical music coming from the piano player. She was enjoying her butter chicken and pilaf rice.

Aoki was able to divide her time between B Scientific and Emilio. She was running around Lower Manhattan with Emilio, and running around Brooklyn and the Upper West Side with B Scientific, and fucking them both, and for a moment, things seemed to be going back to normal in her life.

AZ hadn't spoken to her since he was discharged from the hospital. If she needed money, she got it from B Scientific. If she wanted sex, both were willing to provide their services at full throttle, from oral to dick.

B Scientific told her, "You know, your boy is on some different shit since he got out of the hospital."

"Who?"

"AZ. He's been out in the streets, more fierce wit' his shit, grinding hard and making noise. I'm hearing things about him . . . things I don't like. He tryin' to be on some takeover shit."

"Me don't fuck wit' him anymore."

"I know."

"So why bring him up?"

"Just thought I'd bring it to your attention."

"Ya no need to."

"You're right, I don't need to. You're mine now, right? So AZ is history, and you wouldn't care what happens to him."

Aoki remained silent. She knew what he was getting at. He was looking for her approval to murder AZ. Just because she wasn't dealing with AZ anymore, didn't give B Scientific the right to kill him. But he was right. AZ had changed.

"Excuse me. Me need to use de bathroom," she said, pushing her chair back and departing from the table.

B Scientific kept his eyes on Aoki as she walked to the bathroom. He noticed that she had left her clutch on the table.

When she disappeared from his view, he grabbed her bag and opened it, to remove her cell phone. He wanted to know who she'd been calling or texting. Unfortunately for him, it was locked and he needed to know her pass code to unlock it. He cursed under his breath. He placed the device back into her clutch and remained seated, dining on his meal and drinking his wine.

Aoki walked back to the table several minutes later, and B smiled at her. She took her seat, and they continued to eat and talk.

An hour at the restaurant and her cell phone rang. She went into her clutch to see who was calling, all the while B Scientific watching her like a hawk. When it came to her talking to other niggas, he was extremely jealous.

It was Ri-Ri calling. Aoki answered right away. "Hello."

"She's dead!" Ri-Ri said.

Automatically, Aoki knew she was talking about Gena. "When?" Aoki asked.

"Today. This afternoon," Ri-Ri cried out.

Aoki let loose a deep sigh, knowing Ri-Ri was going through a turbulent time in her life. Part of Aoki felt that Gena had brought her death on herself, but at the same time, Gena was her best friend's mother.

"Where ya at?"

"I'm at the hospital."

"Okay, me be there soon." Aoki hung up.

"Who was that?" B Scientific asked her. "And you gonna be where soon?"

"Ri-Ri. Gena just died."

"Damn! My condolences."

Aoki strongly felt that he was the one that had her killed, over a piece of jewelry. "Me need to go."

"I'm going wit' you," he said.

She didn't want him to come, but B Scientific wasn't taking no for an answer. He quickly paid the huge bill, and the two exited the restaurant and walked to the street. Aoki had no choice but to bring B Scientific with her. He was the one driving.

❧

A crowd gathered around the dark walnut casket in Holy Cross Cemetery in Brooklyn, flowers ranging from lavender to roses covering it and arranged to convey a sense of peace and calm. Over three dozen mourners were there to pay their respects to the deceased.

The preacher stood near the casket with his Bible open, ready to have Gena's body lowered into the ground.

Aoki stood next to Ri-Ri, both wearing all black, dark shades covering their eyes. Aoki was silent, but Ri-Ri was crying. Aoki took her friend's hand in hers and kept her close.

Standing on the other side of the casket was Tisa, AZ, and her friends, Penny and the crew. Tisa was clutching a white rose in her hand, her head bowed. She was grieving too, but tried her best to keep her composure. The shades she wore masked the tears leaking from her eyes.

"In the sweat of thy face shalt thou eat bread, till thou return unto the ground; for out of it wast thou taken: for dust thou art, and unto dust shalt thou return," the preacher proclaimed over the casket as it was lowered into the ground.

Overcome with grief, Ri-Ri shrieked loudly and dropped to her knees. Aoki had to help her up.

The cemetery was teeming with Brooklynites, many of them saddened that another one of theirs was murdered. Not surprisingly, the murder was unsolved.

As the casket was lowered, many carrying roses started to toss the flowers onto the casket, decorating the burial site with white and crimson.

Tisa casually approached her mother's casket and tossed her white rose. She stood nonchalant for a moment with Penny and Stephanie standing beside her, and then she pivoted and marched away.

Aoki glanced at Tisa and felt unhinged for a moment. She was with AZ now, and proclaiming it loud and clear everywhere she went. Aoki was a little envious, but she'd moved on from her relationship with AZ. But that didn't give Tisa the right to go and be with him, knowing how she felt about the man. But today was a day of mourning and peace. No violence, and no confrontation.

As the burial wound down, Aoki and Ri-Ri started to walk away. In the distance, Aoki noticed B Scientific's presence. He was in a dark suit, standing with his hands folded in front of him, and his truck parked not far away.

Why is he here? she thought. He wasn't invited to the funeral. Lately, he had been following her everywhere and popping up where he shouldn't be. The man was losing his mind over Aoki.

Aoki and Ri-Ri walked toward the limousine.

B Scientific came her way, a sense of urgency in his steps.

Ri-Ri slid into the limousine, but when Aoki tried to get inside, he grabbed her by the arm and said, "I need to talk to you."

"Now not a good time. I'm at ah funeral!" Aoki yanked away from his grip and got in the limousine. She shut the door on him and turned away.

B Scientific stood by the limousine looking foul. The windows were tinted, so he couldn't get a good look at Aoki. He could have created a scene at the funeral, but he didn't. He knew she was fucking someone else, but he didn't know who.

It truly bothered him that Aoki had another dick in her life. The last time they'd had sex, he could tell that her pussy was sore from another dick. Before he'd fully entered her, she was wincing in pain and asking him to be gentle.

B Scientific stood off to the side and watched the limo drive away with the woman he loved inside. He had no remorse for having Gena murdered. Standing a few feet away from her grave, he didn't even look that way.

CHAPTER 33

AZ surveyed the Brooklyn Streets with a casual gaze as Heavy Pop drove his Dodge Charger with the tinted windows. He took a pull from the Newport he was smoking.

As their Charger cruised through East New York, down Linden Boulevard, on the late weekday night, AZ couldn't help but to think how many niggas' blood had spilled onto the sidewalks. Death was everywhere, and it was 24/7.

He knew he and Heavy Pop were lucky to survive being shot. It was a painful and scary feeling. It was so daunting to AZ, most every night he was having nightmares about his incident. He would wake up in cold sweats, shivering uncontrollably and his eyes wide with fear. His hands would shake, and it would take him a moment to calm down and realize it was only a bad dream.

"Yo, turn left here," AZ said to Heavy.

The truck turned into the Linden Houses, a sprawling project that covered several blocks. Heavy Pop was quiet, focused on getting to their destination.

AZ took a final pull from the cigarette and flicked it out the window.

"Yo, you ever think about death?" he asked Heavy out of the blue.

"That's a crazy question to ask, especially after what we both done been through."

"I know. It's just lately, I got this feeling in me and it won't leave, my nigga."

"What feeling is that?"

"I just can't stop flat-lining, like I'm dying over and over again, and my soul is being ripped away from me and there ain't shit I can do about it. It's like I see this fuckin' shadow every night in my dream, and he keeps coming at me with this huge fuckin' cannon and won't stop until he sees me dead."

"Yo, you been through a traumatic experience, *A*. I know the feeling."

"Yeah, but I don't wanna feel like this, nigga."

"Is your therapy helping?"

"Fuck therapy!"

"So what you tryin' to do about it?"

"Fuck it! Become the big bad wolf, that muthafucka holdin' the cannon. Take shit from no one, strike first, and let these streets know that we ain't fuckin' playin'. Like this muthafucka Mack Ten, he's first on my shit list."

"How much he owe?"

"Twenty-five large, and I'm tired of him dodging us. I know this nigga think we weak."

"So we gonna beat this nigga down, fuck him up?"

"Yeah, Heavy, we gonna beat the shit out this nigga, and I'm gonna break his teeth and then his jaw," AZ said nonchalantly.

Heavy Pop saw the change in his friend. There was rawness in his eyes that showed a transformation. AZ was a caterpillar trapped inside of a cocoon of violence, and his shooting was the beginning of his evolution into an angry, violent beast. To Heavy, AZ appeared angry with life and the world.

Heavy turned onto Wortman, and they came to a stop in front of one of the eight-story project buildings. The surrounding area was quiet.

"You staying or coming?" AZ asked.

"Nigga, and leave you alone to have somethin' happen to you again. Yo, I wouldn't forgive myself."

"I guess you're coming then."

"You guess right," Heavy Pop replied.

AZ reached under his seat and removed the gun and a silencer.

They stepped out of the truck and walked toward the building lobby in the late night, both cloaked in black. Mack Ten was an old head who'd been in and out of jail for many years. He was in his late thirties, trying to get back in the game and reclaim his glory days. AZ had no time to deal with a nigga's nostalgia; he was in the game to make money and build his reputation and his empire.

Inside the lobby, they came across a young, battered looking woman exiting the elevator, crackhead written all over her—sunken face, soulless eyes, and tattered clothing.

AZ's gut told him that she was somehow connected to Mack Ten. He asked, "Hey, you know Mack Ten? You cop from him?"

The woman looked at AZ like he was talking a different language, but he knew what would motivate her to speak. He pulled out a hundred-dollar bill and said to her, "This is yours. Just take me to Mack Ten's apartment. I know you cop from him."

The C-note was gold in the crackhead's eyes. She smiled like a child and was quick to show AZ and Heavy Pop to Mack Ten's new location in the building.

Mack Ten was known for moving from apartment to apartment to throw off cops and stickup kids, but crackheads were always up-to-date on his new location.

They followed the woman up the dim concrete stairway and emerged on the sixth floor. They went down the hallway, and as the woman knocked on the brown door, AZ and Heavy Pop stood off to the side, out of sight from the peephole. AZ removed his pistol and fastened the silencer at the end. They waited.

"Mack, it's me, Tasha!" the woman said, knocking repeatedly.

Just like that, the door opened, and Mack Ten was in the doorway in a tank top and shorts, a cigarette dangling from his lips. "Damn, bitch! You back already?"

AZ sprung toward the door like a jack-in-the-box, shoving the gun in Mack's face and pushing him and Tasha into the apartment. Heavy Pop closed the door behind them. Tasha was startled, and Mack Ten looked at AZ, shouting out, "Yo, what the fuck, nigga!"

"I'm tired of you duckin' me, nigga! You know what this is."

"I got ya money, nigga!"

"You see, this is no longer about the money, but about my fuckin' respect. Y'all niggas need to fuckin' learn." AZ raised the pistol to Mack Ten's head, fleetingly glanced at Heavy Pop like he needed his approval, and then fired one shot.

Pew!

The bullet tore through Mack Ten's frontal lobe and sent his body crashing toward the floor, his blood spraying against the walls and floor.

AZ had done it. He actually killed a man without any hesitation.

Tasha stumbled away with a fearful gaze at the men. "Please, don't kill me," she pleaded. "I'll suck both y'all dicks."

AZ lifted the gun to her thin frame and aimed.

Heavy Pop said, "Yo, AZ, she looks nineteen, nigga."

"She's a witness, man."

"I doubt she'll talk."

"And you think we can chance that? We don't know this bitch!"

"I know, but—"

"Fuck that!"

Pew! Pew!

Two bullets slammed into the poor girl's chest and sent her flying off her feet and to her death.

For a moment AZ was shaky, almost like he was having a seizure. He sort of walked around the room with his hand on his head wondering what he should do. Do they leave the bodies, or make them disappear? He looked at Heavy Pop for an answer.

"That was foul, AZ."

"Yo, it had to happen. I told you, I ain't ever gonna get shot again. You know what; this is a message to the rest of these niggas out here. Fuck 'em! They fuck wit' us, my nigga, and we ain't scared to do this shit." He pointed to Mack Ten's body.

"We need to leave."

AZ nodded.

Heavy Pop was starting to see AZ's way too. It wasn't a joke for hot slugs to pierce your flesh and tear away at your insides. If they wanted to sell drugs, then they had to be realistic. It was all part of the drug game.

CHAPTER 34

AZ and Tisa smoked a blunt and lounged on the couch in their underwear watching the classic movie, *Set It Off*. They were hooked on the scene where the girls were robbing their second bank and T.T. was playing like she was one of the bank hostages, lying on the floor and looking fearful for her life. Then suddenly, she pulled out her gun and got the drop on a plainclothes cop who was slyly trying to react and save the day.

"You see that shit? These bitches didn't play, and they took what they wanted and wasn't scared to take risks. And T.T. stepped up. She went from being a scared bitch to a gangster. I like that shit!" AZ exclaimed energetically. "She shoulda blew that nigga's head off!"

"I know, right!" Tisa laughed. "I would have. Yo, I love them bitches. They were bad. Yo, L.A. ain't no joke."

"Fuck that! I ain't no fuckin' joke! Let me show you how I set it off!" AZ picked up his pistol and flashed it.

Tisa laughed. "Set it off, baby! Set it off!"

"Sometimes, you just gotta set shit off," AZ said.

AZ took a pull from the blunt. His mind went back to

Mack Ten. It was his first murder without Aoki's aid, and he'd definitely set it off that night in that apartment. He refused to hire Aoki because he no longer wanted to look weak. Though he felt a little shaky after the killing, he was happy that he'd done it. Killing that nigga was like his rite of passage. He wanted nothing to do with Aoki. He had cut her and Ri-Ri off from everything, the hits and being drug mules for him.

Tisa was horny, and once again, she tried to please her man. She lowered her head into his lap and pulled out his flaccid dick. She stroked him first, but he wasn't getting hard, so she decided to suck it.

AZ sat there nonchalantly on the couch with his dick in her mouth, not looking the least bit excited.

After minutes of trying, Tisa removed her lips from his cock, looked up at AZ awkwardly, and asked, "What's wrong, baby? I'm not doin' you right?"

"You doin' fine," he replied halfheartedly.

"So why can't you get hard?"

"I just got a lot on my mind."

"I'm tryin' to help you take a lot off your mind."

"I know."

"It's not about her, right?" she asked, referring to Aoki.

"Nah! Fuck that bitch!"

"Because I can do better."

"You can," he replied dryly.

Tisa lowered her lips to the dick again and wrapped them around it. She slid her lips up and down his limp dick and cupped his balls, working desperately to awaken an erection. Still, it was to no avail.

She sighed with frustration and propped herself back upright on the couch. "You wanna fuck?" she asked him.

"I'm not in the mood to do anything right now, baby. Maybe tomorrow."

"Yeah, tomorrow," she said matter-of-factly.

AZ placed his member back into his boxers and stood up. He reached for his clothing and started to get dressed.

"Where you about to go?" she asked him.

"I gotta make a run."

"It's late."

"And? I gotta handle something," he barked.

Tisa knew not to get too much into his business, so she remained silent, but she wasn't happy about it.

AZ left the house and got into his car.

Tisa stared from the window. Her womanly instincts told her that he was up to no good and being sneaky about something.

AZ slowly steered his Benz into the parking lot of the Canarsie pier. It was a late night with a full moon, and the parking lot was light with cars. He parked at the end of the lot and killed the ignition. He then pulled out his cell phone and texted: I'M HERE.

Now all he had to do was wait. He smoked a cigarette while gazing at the ocean from his seat.

An hour later, Connor's car pulled right alongside AZ's.

Connor jumped out of his ride and pranced in AZ's direction. He slid into the passenger seat and slapped AZ across his face and frowned. "You know what you do to me! What the fuck I've been through! Now you wanna see me? What? To have sex?"

AZ knitted his brow and swiftly threw his hand around Connor's neck and started choking him. He growled, "First off, nigga, don't you ever touch me like that again! And, second, I had too much shit to take care of to come running after your bitch ass. You understand me?"

Connor barely nodded.

AZ released his hand from his neck and sat back in his seat.

"Well, I'm glad you're okay and alive. I love you, AZ, and I was so worried about you. You know you are my world, baby. Seeing you in that hospital, looking like that, it fucked me up."

AZ lit another cigarette. He sat in silence, pulling from the Newport and looking ahead.

"I don't know why I love you so much, after everything you done put me through, but I do. And you know that bitch Aoki and her friend had the audacity to put their hands on me. She had me banned from visiting you because she was scared of how it would look

AZ tilted in the direction of Connor all of a sudden and pressed his lips against his, and the two shared a passionate kiss in the front seat.

When they finally pulled their lips apart, Connor smiled. "Now that was nice," he said. "Is that your way of saying you missed me or to shut me up?"

"Both."

"You so stupid, AZ." Connor chuckled. "But you look good, baby."

"Things are changing, Connor."

"I hope not between us."

"I'm a different person."

"And what that got to do with our relationship?"

"I did things since I've been out the hospital. I—" AZ was ready to confess his sins to Connor, but he stopped.

"What is it, baby? What you need to tell me? I hope it ain't about that bitch you moved into your home. Why is she there?"

"Just for show."

"I can't wait for the day when you start showing me off, because you know I'm beautiful, nigga."

AZ ignored the comment. "I just need to relax," he said.

"Relax, huh. That bitch ain't been making you relax?"

"Nah. She can't do like you do, baby."

Connor smiled. "Of course, she can't, because you know I love you and want you more, AZ. When are you gonna come out of the closet?"

AZ cut his eyes at Connor and barked, "And commit suicide, nigga? You know the world I live in. Who I'm around and do business with are majority homophobic. If they ever find out about you and me, then we're both dead!"

"So we can run away together. Leave New York, go somewhere different, where our lifestyle is acceptable, Atlanta or Seattle. That's far way."

"New York is my home, Connor, and I aint' goin' anywhere. Don't you fuckin' forget that."

"You ain't gotta curse at me."

"I just need you to understand. It's a dangerous world I live in, and the Long Island suburbs you come from ain't gonna protect us from shit! If my peoples or my enemies ever found out about me, yeah, you gonna miss me fo' real."

Connor remained silent momentarily. AZ's words hit him deep. He would do anything to help or protect his lover, though AZ had never made him a priority in his life. But he understood that he had his reasons. It was just upsetting that they couldn't run off and get married, though New York was all about gay pride, gay rights, and advocacy for the gay community.

"Let me make you relax and think about me then, so when I'm gone, you won't forget how special I treat you," Connor said, smiling at his boo. He positioned himself in the front seat and unzipped AZ's jeans.

Unlike with Tisa, AZ was rock-hard, his dick upright like a missile ready to take off.

The minute Connor covered the hard dick with his lips, AZ titled his head back and moaned like he'd never moaned before.

Connor bobbed his head up and down in the front seat, deep-throating every inch, and making sure AZ get the pleasure he deserved.

CHAPTER 35

Tisa walked into her Pink Houses apartment looking fabulous in her tight jeans, cashmere top, and red bottoms. Penny, Stephanie, Lady, and Kim were right behind her. Tisa was looking like a million bucks with AZ's money, and she was running her mouth all around town about how AZ was taking care of her and would do anything for her because he loved her so much. She was just putting on a show for the projects, because deep down, she knew that all wasn't what it seemed with her man.

"So what you sayin'? Y'all ain't fuck yet?" Penny asked.

"We mess around. I be tryin' to suck his dick, but nah, we didn't."

"Yo, that's crazy," Kim chimed.

"A fine nigga like AZ? Shit, I would be havin' this nigga eat my pussy," Lady said. "He do that?"

"Nope!"

Kim laughed. "Damn! So you all sexually frustrated right now."

"I know I'm a bad bitch, and I be tryin' to please my man," Tisa said.

"You sure he ain't gay?" Penny asked.

"My nigga ain't gay!" Tisa said quickly.

"Shit. You never know. The way these niggas be on the down-low out here. You gotta watch ya back wit' these niggas, lookin' like 50 Cent but actin' like Nicki Minaj," Penny joked.

The girls laughed.

Tisa felt it was something else with AZ.

The girls were in the kitchen looking for something to eat. Since Gena's death, everyone was left to fend for themselves in the kitchen.

As Penny and Kim removed what was left to eat from the fridge, Tisa was leaned against the countertop. She sipped a bottle of water. "I think it's Aoki!"

"Aoki? Why's that bitch on your mind?" Stephanie asked.

"I think he still loves her."

"What? Why are you even worried about that bird bitch?"

"I'm not worried."

"You a hundred times better than that bitch," Lady said.

"And you got the upper hand. You got AZ doin' right by you, buying you nice shit, and he got you stayin' at his crib." Penny added. "Even though he ain't givin' you any dick."

The girls laughed.

Kim suggested, "Maybe he likes that freaky shit—what is it?—*S* and *M*?"

"Yo, that's white people shit," Lady said.

"That's that crazy shit!" Stephanie said.

Penny said, "Nah, he don't look like the type of nigga to be in some shit like that."

"Girl, you ain't gotta worry about AZ," Kim told Tisa. "That bitch Aoki, she old news, yesterday's trash. That bitch is lucky we ain't beat her down at the hospital or the funeral. I'm so tired of her and Ri-Ri."

"And you know what?" Penny said. "If that bitch even steps incorrectly, we gonna fuck that bitch up. You wit' us now, Tisa. Fuck them other bitches!"

As they lingered in the kitchen, talking shit about Aoki and Ri-Ri, the bedroom door opened up and Ri-Ri came out.

The girls were shocked that she had been in the apartment the entire time. All eyes were on her, but they weren't worried about her.

Word around town was that Ri-Ri was dead broke. After Gena's death, her life did a 180, and she'd been either staying in the apartment or at some nigga's place. Ri-Ri was still saddened by her mother's death and hadn't been hanging around Aoki lately.

Ri-Ri walked by the girls uncaringly.

Tisa glowered at her sister's presence. Usually, Tisa would gloat about the clothes, the money, and her relationship with AZ, mostly to make Ri-Ri jealous, but today, she didn't. She and Penny's crew just watched her leave the apartment.

"Damn! That bitch look bad," Lady said.

Tisa said, "Fuck that bitch!"

The girls shrugged her off and went back to their girl talk.

CHAPTER 36

Aoki was bored. She missed the action on the streets. She was an adrenaline junkie, and action made her pussy throb. As expected, AZ cut her off completely—no work, no pay. Tisa now had his undivided attention, although he liked men. Like Aoki once was, Tisa was nothing but a front to maintain his reputation around the way. If you're always with a bitch, then no one has a reason to question your sexuality.

Though Aoki still felt threatened by Oscar, a lot of time had passed, and so far she felt safe. She didn't think Oscar would retaliate against her. It was paranoid thinking. Her gut told her that she would've been dead already if he wanted to seek revenge.

Aoki finally allowed B Scientific to spend the night in her home. When he walked inside, he was impressed by the décor, the artwork, the large flat-screen, and latest amenities. She had style. The place looked a whole lot better inside than the outside. It was fully remodeled and decked out.

Aoki inviting B Scientific to spend the night was purely calculated. She needed work, to seek employment in his organization. Whether it be running drugs for him or murder for hire, it didn't matter. She needed that excitement back.

The two got comfortable in the living room. B Scientific popped open a Corona and was ready for round two with her, but she wanted to talk business to him first.

"So what you wanted to talk about?" he asked.

Before Aoki could open her mouth to speak, there was a sudden commotion outside the house. Blaring police lights caught their attention, and the harsh announcement of "NYPD! Open the door!"

There wasn't a knock, but there were two loud bangs as the front door came flying off the hinges and several officers came charging into the home.

B Scientific was slow to react, but Aoki took off running toward the kitchen to arm herself with a large knife.

Several cops rained down on them like lightning and hail, with their weapons pointed at them and shouting, "Don't move! Don't you fuckin' move!"

Every area of her home was swarming with cops, and they had a warrant to search the place.

B Scientific scowled and threw his hands up in the air, easily surrendering, and Aoki was growling in her Jamaican accent at the police. Quickly, they both were thrown to the floor and handcuffed.

An officer put his knee in B Scientific's back as he was restraining him, causing B Scientific to grimace in pain.

"Fuck dat warrant!" Aoki shouted.

One of the cops started reading the Miranda rights to them. "You have the right to remain silent. Anything you say can and will be used against you in a court of law. You have the right to an attorney . . ."

Aoki was being detained in the kitchen, while B Scientific was being detained in the living room. Aoki watched the cops tear through her backyard searching for two dead bodies in barrels. They'd received the tip from an informant.

For an hour, they ransacked her home but came up empty.

"We found nothing, sir," an officer said to his sergeant.

The sergeant frowned. "Nothing?"

"No bodies, no indication of any crime here."

Aoki smirked.

"We still have the gun." He turned and glared at Aoki. "I'm gonna wipe that fuckin' smirk off your face. Take her to the car. It's not over yet."

Two officers escorted Aoki to a marked squad car, and then they placed B Scientific in a different car. His handcuffs were purposely made tight to cut into his wrists and make for a painful trip to the local precinct.

B Scientific shouted, "Y'all muthafuckas ain't got shit on me! Fuck y'all!" He stared at Aoki in the backseat of the squad car and shouted her way, "Whatever it is, it ain't gonna stick, Aoki! I'm gonna get my lawyers on it, and we'll be out in a couple of hours!"

At the precinct, they both were placed in separate windowless interrogation rooms, furnished with a table and three very uncomfortable chairs. The room Aoki sat in had a large mirror on one side, facing her. It was undoubtedly a two-way mirror. The lighting was harsh fluorescents, and the room was cold, as if the air conditioning was purposely turned on high.

Aoki sat handcuffed to the table, keeping cool. Thirty minutes went by. Why was she there? What were they charging her with? Her intuition had paid off. She was relieved the bodies were gone, but she wasn't out of the fire yet.

She heard the muffled sounds of people talking outside the door. Definitely cops. The door opened, and two suit-and-tie detectives, both clean-shaven, middle-aged white men, entered the room. She had never seen them before. Their suits looked a little ruffled from a long day.

They took a seat across from Aoki at the metal table.

"I'm Detective Pine, and this is my partner, Detective Meaner."

Aoki sat stone-faced.

They wondered why on earth anyone would say she killed her parents and had them hidden in the backyard for years. Though the accusation seemed far-fetched, their investigation led them to believe it was quite a coincidence that both parents had disappeared at the same time, and interviews with the neighbors made them speculate foul play. Aoki was too old to be placed in Child Services but not too young to face a lengthy prison sentence.

Her beauty intrigued the detectives. She had an innocent-looking face, but her eyes weren't so childlike, but icy and unsettling.

Before the men could continue with their interrogation, she asked for Sergeant Snashall. "Me want to talk to him," she said.

Detective Pine said. "Well, you're out of luck, young lady. He's not in the building, and besides, he heard about your arrest and decided to leave early. Seems like he didn't want anything to do with you."

Sergeant Snashall had promised that he'd given Aoki her last break. He didn't want anything else to do with her. She'd chosen her path, and there were consequences with those choices.

"Fuck it! Me have nothin' else to say. Me want a lawyer."

Frustrated, both men stood up, with Detective Meaner exclaiming, "Fine. Have fun in Central Booking!"

In the other interrogation room, B Scientific was hard-core. Two different detectives sat across from him, grilling him with question after question, but he refused to answer any of them.

"You take ownership over the gun, and we'll let your girlfriend go free," the detective said.

"I don't know what the fuck you talkin' about. What fuckin' gun?" B Scientific replied.

"Fine! Have fun in the pokey, asshole! Because they sure gonna have fun with you."

"You think I'm gonna have a problem in jail with my reputation, then you're fuckin' stupider than you look, nigga!" B Scientific replied.

The cop wanted to leap across the table and beat the shit out of him, but he held his composure and removed himself from the room.

Both Aoki and B Scientific were processed at the local precinct and then transported to Central Booking downtown. For transport, B Scientific was hooked up to a chain gang with seven other guys, and Aoki went in separate transportation with the ladies.

Aoki arrived at Central Booking and was thrown into a 12 x 15 cell with various groups of women. There was a metal toilet in the back corner that had a four-foot wall around it. The cell was also bright and cold. It was early morning, and the sun hadn't risen yet.

Around six a.m., a woman came to question Aoki. She asked her basic questions like her age, where did she work, and about her parents. Aoki was stubborn and hated the white bitch standing on the other side of the cell. She cursed at the woman, being difficult, and sent the woman scurrying away.

Aoki was allowed one phone call, but she didn't know who to call. B Scientific was locked up with her, and friends were no longer friends. She couldn't trust anyone. Her three best friends and the man she loved were the only ones who knew about her parents. One of them had snitched! She thought long and hard, and the most likely culprit was Tisa. She had motive.

She refused to call anyone, but her instincts told her that whoever came to bail her out was most likely the person who'd ratted her out.

CHAPTER 37

B Scientific was called from the small cell and led to a holding area behind the courtroom to meet with his lawyer. Still dressed in his street clothing, he sat on the small stool and looked at his attorney seated across from him. David Sparrow was the best that money could buy—the Johnnie Cochran of his day. B Scientific was smart enough to have him on retainer. Sparrow was known for his courtroom skills and his connections. He was a pit bull in the courts, snarling and barking at prosecutors and witnesses against his clients, and would go down fighting for his clients.

"I need to get out of here," B Scientific said.

Sparrow grimaced. "A gun charge! Are you stupid?"

"There's more to it. That gun, when it's taken to ballistics, will come back with a body on it," he confessed.

"Are you out of your mind, Bryant? How foolish! Why didn't you get rid of a dirty gun?"

"It was a mistake. I fucked up!"

"Yes, you did! But I don't need to know any more."

"Can you get me out?"

"It's a challenge, but it's possible. It can take a few days for ballistics to return, so right now, let's work on your arraignment. Fortunately for you, the gun was found in the house and not on you personally, and the house was clean. More good news—it wasn't your home; you were just a guest there. The gun is the only obstacle for now."

"Okay."

Sparrow locked eyes with B Scientific and asked him the inevitable question. "So, how close are you to this Aoki?"

"I need to bail her out."

"She can hurt you."

"Why?"

"So far, the police files have no one taking possession of this gun, and now that you tell me it might be connected to a crime scene, this one will come back and bite you in the ass and leave a serious gash."

B Scientific sighed. "She can't go to jail."

"And can you?"

He rubbed his chin. It was something he did when he had to make a dreadful choice. At first, he pretended to be totally against what his lawyer was saying, but deep in his mind he knew he couldn't do twenty-five years to life. B felt he was in his prime.

"Listen. At your arraignment, you will plead not guilty."

"Of course," he said. It was a no-brainer.

"This Aoki, she has a better probability of beating this gun charge than you do. No jury would think that she's the real owner of the gun and a murderer. She looks totally innocent like a doll. But you, you have priors, Bryant. Think over your options, and in the meantime, it wouldn't be wise to post her bail. That action alone could link you, and the DA could try the cases together."

B Scientific slouched and sighed heavily. He knew what needed to be done.

❦

Aoki was brought before the judge in the courtroom just before noon—and just before lunch. She was alone. She couldn't afford a lawyer, so she was court-appointed one, a young white boy in a bad suit with cheap shoes and fuzzy hair. He looked more like a surfer in a suit than a litigator.

On one side of the courtroom was a table where the powers that be gathered. On the other side was a table where the defense lawyers gathered. Aoki was led toward the bench, where she stood in silence.

Her defense lawyer shuffled some paperwork, and the white elderly the judge read a gun charge against her and asked her how old she was.

Aoki gave her age.

The judge's eyes lingered on her.

Her lawyer did his best, and Aoki was assigned $5,000 bail. He looked at Aoki like he had cured cancer. She didn't even have five *hundred* dollars to her name. She was broke. The judge might as well have remanded her without bail.

Aoki was escorted back into lockup. It was a small accomplishment nevertheless.

She was antsy until her bail was paid. *B Scientific kept his word to get me out,* she thought. She was processed out immediately. When she walked out of Central Booking, there he was with open arms, smiling widely and so happy to see her—Emilio.

How did he know about her arrest so soon? She didn't make any phone calls.

"Baby, oh my god, are you okay? I'm glad you're out. I missed you," he said.

Her eyes burned into him and he didn't know why. "How ya know suh fast?" she asked him.

"What?"

"'Bout me arrest. Me called no one."

"I came by the house to check up on you when your phone kept going to voice mail. A neighbor told me what happened. You know I worry about you, Aoki."

Maybe you worry about me too much, she thought.

"I made some phone calls immediately and reached out to a bondsman. I only paid ten percent of five thousand, so it was just five hundred dollars. It was nothing to get you out. You won't skip out on me, right?"

Aoki wasn't in the mood to joke. "Thank ya," she said.

"It was no problem. I know you would have done the same thing for me."

They climbed into his small car and drove off. Emilio continued running his mouth. Something about him was off—something that rubbed Aoki the wrong way.

"So who's this Bryant, and why was he in your house?" he asked.

"Him just a friend."

"A friend, huh?"

"Yes."

"You fuckin' him?"

Aoki cut her eyes at him. "Emilio, now not de time. Me had a long day."

"You know I love you so much. I just want it to be us."

"Emilio, me tired and just need some rest."

"You can come back to my dorm. It's quiet, everybody's on break, and it's out the way. Your place is just too risky."

Aoki pretended to be grateful, but in the back of her mind, Emilio was jealous and was emotional. As far as she knew, it was he was the one who called the cops on her. He did know about the bodies in her backyard and became emotional about it that day, leaving her. He'd threatened her, but then suddenly, there he was, coming back into her life the day AZ was there to kill her.

She took a warm bath with him.

He ordered Chinese food, and they ate and talked.

Aoki did everything to read him, and to her his words and his body language were off. He was hiding something, or not telling the whole story.

"I'm glad they didn't find those bodies in your yard."

She'd moved them, but told no one. How did he know what the warrant was for? He seemed too concerned about it. "Someone snitched," she said.

"But you're here, with me, and I'm gonna always have your back, baby."

Her heart was shattering into pieces, and she was aching greatly. She loved him, but he had to go. She had to kill him. He knew too much, and she didn't trust him suddenly. AZ was right—he had probably come to her home to kill her.

Now, it was her turn to react.

CHAPTER 38

Aoki's life was becoming unhinged. AZ was against her; B Scientific, God knew what he was up to; and the police were so far up her ass, she could taste the shoe polish. She knew it was time to clean house before her rivals got the jump on her. It was time to bring the Killer Dolls back into action. The first on her list was Emilio.

Aoki and Ri-Ri were dressed in colorful wigs and clothing to fit into the NYU student scene, dark shades covering their eyes. They were seated in a stolen car, nothing traceable to them. It was dark and late evening in Lower Manhattan, and traffic around Washington Square Park was thick.

It was the right moment.

They observed Emilio walking to his dorm. He had a backpack on and moved unhurriedly toward the building. He was with a pale white, pretty, young woman; she looked like a student. They were laughing and talking while walking.

Aoki frowned. *Is he fuckin' that bitch too?*

She and Ri-Ri got out of the car and followed him slyly. They walked briskly in his direction, their heads down, fitting perfectly into the area with other students. The last thing they wanted was to stand out.

Aoki removed the knife she carried. It was sharp and long enough to pierce into flesh and create severe damage. She gripped it tightly, while frowning.

Emilio, too busy with Snow White, was unaware of the danger lurking. His eyes were on her, and he was too close to her for Aoki's comfort. They reached the dorm, and he was a gentleman to the white bitch, holding the door open for her to enter.

Aoki's anger grew and grew. She wanted to make him feel agonizing death. As he was about to walk into the dorm lobby behind his white, cheery friend, she acted quickly and repeatedly plunged the knife into the side of Emilio's neck. He didn't even see them coming.

He jolted from the force of the unexpected strike. He clutched his neck, and blood squirted out like a fountain. His eyes opened wide, and he spun around to face a disguised Aoki. There was no mistaking it. It was definitely her behind the colorful wig and dark shades. As he clutched his neck, stumbling to stay standing and feeling himself growing weak, his eyes searched for some meaning to the attack on him. His knees buckled.

A sharp scream came from the snow bunny he was with.

Aoki gave him no reason. She glanced at him with coldness.

He couldn't see her eyes. He dropped to his knees and collapsed right there in front of her, choking on his own blood.

Aoki and Ri-Ri hurried away, and a crowd started to run to Emilio to assist him. There were more screams and confusion ensuing.

The girls made their escape.

Aoki never told Ri-Ri why she wanted Emilio dead, but Ri-Ri knew it had to be hard on her. She'd loved him once. Whatever he had done, Ri-Ri figured he must have done something to hurt her friend. She didn't ask any questions. She simply went along with the program.

The next day, the murder made the newspapers with the headline, NYU student stabbed to death, suggesting the Killer Dolls had struck again.

B Scientific was out on bail, but he wasn't out of the fire yet with a pending gun charge and possible murder case against him. He and Aoki both were caught up in a bad situation. Someone had to cop to the gun and explain the body on it once ballistics came back.

Though shit was bad, he couldn't stop thinking about Aoki. It bothered him that he didn't pay her bail, but someone else had, and that troubled him. Was it another nigga?

While he was being chauffeured through Brooklyn in his Escalade, he called Aoki. He wanted to make things right, to pick up where they'd left off.

Of course, it went against Marcus' advice. Marcus had warned him to leave her alone. But like always, B Scientific couldn't. It was like she had cast a spell on him.

Hearing her phone ring, he was anticipating an answer. She did.

"Hey, beautiful," he said.

"Hey," she answered dryly. "What ya need, B Scientific?"

"I need you, baby. I just wanted to talk to you and let you know that I got your back with this case. I hired a powerhouse lawyer for you, so you ain't gotta worry. I was gonna bail you out, but someone beat me to it. Who was it?"

Aoki rolled her eyes at the subtle bullshit he was throwing at her. "De only ting dat matter is dat I'm home."

"Yeah, you right. But I do wanna see you."

"Ya do?"

"Baby, you know I miss you so much. You're my fuckin' heart, Aoki."

She pretended to believe his game, told him what he wanted to hear, but in truth, her heart was cold again.

Three men claimed to love her, and none gave a fuck about her. Her once best friend, AZ, was now like a stranger. Why was it so hard to find true love and loyalty? There wasn't a thing as true love in her reality, just fraudulence and users. The answer was, it didn't exist. Her parents were together forever, and it didn't stop her father from killing his wife.

"You know I wanna see you so bad. Let me take care of you," he said.

"Where? At ya apartment?"

"Why not?"

"Me not gon' lay in de same bed wit' ya as ya ex-girlfriend did. Me don't even get down like dat."

"A'ight, I'll get a hotel room. That's better for you?"

"It is."

"I'll pick you up. What time?"

"Me meet ya."

"You sure?"

"Yes."

B Scientific promised to call her back with the time and the location. He was excited; Aoki wasn't. She had already made up her mind.

CHAPTER 39

Aoki pulled down the visor to check her makeup in the mirror. She looked flawless in a pink wig and cherry red lipstick. She wore a pink minidress and long satin gloves under a trench coat. Her legs appeared to stretch endlessly in a pair of stilettos, and she smelled like flowers and honey.

She was parked outside the Marriott in New Jersey. It was a breezy night with a half moon shining above. She lingered on her image in the sun visor and put on her shades. It was time to play.

She grabbed her small bag of naughty treats from the passenger seat and climbed out of the truck. She walked into the hotel lobby with her head lowered, her huge shades covering her eyes, her stilettos click-clacking against the marble floor. She walked toward the elevators with conceit.

She stepped into the elevator with two older men and pushed for eleven, and they pushed for twelve. Aoki could feel the men eyeballing her from head to toe, hypnotized by her beauty. They were either in town for the convention, or going back to their rooms to be with their wives. Either way, they were in awe, and she was making their night just being in their presence.

"You're beautiful, miss," one said.

She managed to smile.

The elevator stopped, and she stepped off, but before the door closed, she turned around and blew them a kiss. It was her way of having a little fun.

She continued toward the room. She found the room door, but before she knocked, she took a deep breath and checked her clothing again. She knocked, and B Scientific opened the door immediately, like he was waiting right by the door for her. He was clad in one of the hotel's white terrycloth robes and naked underneath.

B smiled widely, excited to see her. It was amazing how she had him sprung and strung. He was a powerful man, but still, when he was around her, he was like a horny virgin, desperate for his first time.

"Damn! You're gorgeous. I knew you wouldn't let me down." He opened her trench coat to take a peek at the goodies underneath.

She smiled, and they hugged and kissed right there in the doorway, and then she walked into the hotel suite.

He wanted to have a long, romantic night with her. The expensive suite had all of the latest amenities. He went all out for her, from the scented candles burning to the rose petals scattered across the bed.

Aoki pulled out handcuffs and blindfolds.

He thought they were gonna have kinky sex. "Something new?" he inquired.

She nodded.

They kissed passionately again. He ran his hands across her body. He squeezed her ass. She made his dick so hard that it felt like a small statue underneath the robe.

She fondled him warmly, her fist sliding back and forth against him. Moaning, he couldn't wait to get started. He peeled away her coat and removed the long satin gloves. He pulled up her dress to see that she had on no panties.

"You always know how to turn me the fuck on."

"Lay down. Let's have some fun," she said.

He didn't argue. The man was like a dog ready for his Scooby Snacks, his mouth like a dog's tongue lapping for some action.

Aoki pushed him against the bed and straddled him. She pulled out the handcuffs.

B Scientific was reluctant at first, but the right touch and the right kiss in the right places made him change his mind.

But he refused to be blindfolded. He needed to see what was going on.

With his hands cuffed to the bed, Aoki continued to toy with him, gyrating her hips into him, feeling his erection poke against her pussy.

"Me gon' do things to ya dat gon' make ya scream out," she said.

B Scientific liked the sound of that.

Aoki wanted to do one more thing to him, gag him.

Reluctantly, B Scientific agreed. This kinky shit was new, but somewhat fun to try out for him.

She placed the cloth into his mouth and suddenly, B Scientific found himself restrained fully. He couldn't move or speak, all for love and pussy.

Once he was secured, Aoki got off the bed.

B looked at her strangely. He wanted her badly and was tired of waiting around. He tugged at his handcuffs. He couldn't speak because of the gag. He followed her every move with his eyes.

While he watched, she turned up the television to a loud volume. Her actions were alarming, but he wasn't too worried. The bitch was a freak.

She walked toward the bed and straddled him again. She removed the gag from his mouth.

He said, "Aoki, what the fuck you doin'?"

"It's comin'. Be patient."

She reached into her small bag again, fumbling around for something inside, while at the same time B Scientific had his eyes on her, his fists tightened inside the cuffs.

"What you got next for me?"

She simply smiled, awkwardly though. From the look in her eyes, he knew something wasn't right. Maybe it was a mistake letting her restrain him to the bed. His trust for what she was doing was starting to thin out.

"You know what, Aoki? Just uncuff me. I ain't liking this shit right now."

"Ya mine now. What's wrong? Don't ya trust me?"

"Just get me the fuck out of these cuffs!"

She gagged him again. Whatever he had to say was muffled and incoherent.

B Scientific's eyes widened with fear when Aoki pulled out a large, sharp knife. He desperately tried to break free from his restraints, but to no avail. He couldn't even shout out.

"Good bye!"

Aoki didn't hesitate to plunge the knife deep into his throat several times, causing him to thrash around violently. His blood was thick, and everywhere, coating the bed sheets in crimson. And he bled out quickly.

Aoki lingered on top of the body and exhaled. She gazed into his dead eyes, and honestly, she felt nothing. He was nothing but a job, a contract she'd placed and implemented herself. Not too long ago he would have done the same thing to her.

Two down, one to go.

She stood up and looked at the body. *Good riddance*, she thought. Killing him was the simple part. Not getting caught was the difficult part. But the more she killed, the better she was at it.

Aoki meticulously cleaned up any evidence and collected her things and his things, robbing B Scientific of his jewelry and five thousand in cash. She left the suite quietly, acting like nothing had happened.

CHAPTER 40

The newspaper covered the story of the Killers Dolls terrorizing the streets of New York yet again. This time a drug kingpin was found murdered in a New Jersey hotel.

B Scientific's crew was furious and wanted revenge, and they had the Killer Dolls on their radar. Marcus was beside himself. His friend was dead, and he was ready to burn down the city to find his killer.

The cops were doing a thorough investigation, and the only thing they had to go on was the hotel footage of a slim woman wearing a pink wig, dark shades, and a long trench coat. It was the same modus operandi. She left behind no evidence. The city had put out an alert on her and a reward of two thousand dollars for any information.

Aoki was no fool. She knew it was time to leave town, but there were other affairs she had to deal with. When the time was right, she'd be gone.

Tisa walked into her mother's apartment and found Ri-Ri in the bedroom smoking a joint, listening to the radio.

She tossed the paper at Ri-Ri. "So this is what y'all been doin', huh? Y'all killed B Scientific! What the fuck!"

Ri-Ri was caught off guard by her sister's accusation. The headline on the *Daily News* was about B Scientific's murder in New Jersey. She wasn't there when it went down, but she was sure that Aoki had implemented the murder.

"Emilio too! So who's next? AZ? Looks like anything connected to Aoki is dying out there!" Tisa shouted. "So who the fuck is payin' y'all? Huh?"

"Tisa, you need to shut the fuck up and mind your business!"

"Fuck that! Y'all fuckin' wrong, and I'm not gonna stand around and have Aoki kill off these people and come for my man."

"You need to stay in your lane, you little bitch!"

"No, because y'all got my nigga worried!"

Ri-Ri shouted, "She's not comin' after AZ. You don't need to worry!"

"How you know that? What the fuck y'all got planned? Am I next?"

"No!"

"How you know Aoki won't come after me? Huh, Ri-Ri? Do you still trust her?"

"She's our friend."

"Our friend? She ain't been *my* friend in months. Did you even know about B Scientific and Emilio?"

Ri-Ri was there for Emilio, but B Scientific was the bewildering murder. She wasn't so sure about Aoki anymore. She was becoming a lone wolf, acting out on her own and didn't enlist her to the B Scientific hit. They did everything together. Or used to.

When the murders hit the papers, AZ became super paranoid, thinking he was next on Aoki's list. Tisa was by his side and noticed his apprehension. She wanted to know why he was so paranoid over Aoki.

AZ knew that Aoki was a ruthless killer. B Scientific, Polo, and more, her list was extensive. She was dangerous, and she needed to be put down somehow. He was thinking he should kill her before she killed him. He wanted Tisa to get back into Aoki and Ri-Ri's good graces and infiltrate them. He needed to know everything about Aoki.

Word around town was, she had gone underground. The hood was hot, and people were paranoid. There was a war ensuing on the streets, and folks didn't want to get caught in the crossfire.

AZ felt he had some housecleaning to do on his own. Things were changing, and with B Scientific dead, he knew now was his chance to step up and fill that void. It was his time, and nothing was going to stop him.

AZ also felt that the people in his life were becoming more of a risk to him than a service. His only true friend was Heavy Pop, but even their friendship was becoming a bit strained. He was doing one thing, and Heavy Pop doing another.

AZ had Connor to please him, but he started to feel threatened by him too.

Connor had always said that he understood where AZ was coming from, but then he was continuously pressuring

AZ to come out of the closet. He'd been begging AZ to leave the game alone, telling him he could take care of him until he found a legit job, maybe a career elsewhere, until he was able to get back on his feet. Connor had even gone as far as to threaten to expose him.

"It's for your own good, AZ. You can't keep hiding from yourself. If you love me, then you would do this."

AZ didn't like the way Connor was talking. There had been a lot of pillow talk between them, so Connor knew a lot of his darkest secrets. It bothered him.

AZ was on the rise in the streets, but he had deep, twisted issues within himself. He felt betrayed by so many, and he wanted to become someone new.

With B Scientific gone, AZ was ready to become the boss of bosses in the city. Aoki was the biggest threat to him. He needed to take care of her before she took care of him, and he needed Tisa's help in finding the killer bitch.

Tisa was desperate to see Aoki. She wanted to talk to her. She convinced Ri-Ri that she wanted reconciliation between them. She used their mother's passing as an excuse, and a way for the sisters to reunite.

"I don't wanna fight wit' you anymore, Ri-Ri," Tisa said from the bottom of her heart. "Mama's gone, and I can't lose you too."

The sisters hugged and made peace. Now all that was missing was Aoki.

Tisa started to come around Ri-Ri more, and she was always asking a lot of questions, mostly about Aoki.

Then again, Ri-Ri needed her family around her. She was alone and losing her mind. Some nights she would lock herself in the bedroom, smoke weed, and cry. She had done unspeakable things, and in a way, they were starting to eat away at her like a virus, attacking her from the inside out.

Tisa coming around to make peace felt like a blessing to Ri-Ri. Though Ri-Ri and Tisa were cool again, Aoki was a different story. She was cold and elusive.

Aoki completely abandoned her home and found shelter at a motel in Long Island. It was cheap and far away from Brooklyn, but not far away from her troubles. She stayed there with her small arsenal, preparing herself for anything. The last time she was at her Brooklyn home, someone had left a black rose on the front steps. She didn't know what it represented, or who left it, but she took it as a threat.

The rose was just the beginning. The men in black continued to spook her, and she was determined to kill them if she saw them again. She wasn't about to take any chances with her life.

Emilio and B Scientific were gone, and the only two people close to her that she felt posed a threat were AZ and Tisa. They knew everything.

When Ri-Ri called to tell her that Tisa had started coming around and the two of them had made peace and reconciled, Aoki saw this as opportunity for herself. She just couldn't be sure about Tisa anymore. All the threats she'd made about snitching to the police made Aoki wonder if she was the one who'd snitched to the police about her parents.

Tisa was a liability, and she had to go. The only thing was, she couldn't die at the hands of the Killer Dolls. Ri-Ri wouldn't stand for it. Though Tisa had been a bitch and Aoki couldn't trust her, Ri-Ri wasn't going to tolerate having her only sister murdered, especially after losing her mother.

Aoki decided to carry out Tisa's death on her own. It couldn't wait. The time was now.

Knowing that Tisa had become a drug mule for AZ, Aoki followed her around the city. She was adept with surveillance. Tisa traveled from borough to borough, moving drugs via train, just as the three of them had done in the past.

Aoki followed Tisa for days, waiting for the right moment to strike. Her murder had to look accidental. She didn't want Ri-Ri to suspect any foul play. Though they weren't around each other as much, Ri-Ri was still a friend and was still useful to Aoki, so Aoki couldn't afford to make an enemy out of her. Not yet, anyway.

Funny thing was, the past few days, Aoki had been getting calls from Connor, but she refused to answer. She had no time for his drama. She figured he was only calling her to beef about AZ, but he was beefing with the wrong bitch. Tisa was the new bitch in AZ's life.

It was a half hour before midnight on a weekend when Aoki followed Tisa into a Bronx subway station on Jerome Avenue. Seeing that it was late and the weekend, the train station platform was almost empty, except for a few stragglers here and there waiting for the next 4 train to Manhattan.

Tisa was on the platform walking with her backpack and a pistol and razor for protection.

Aoki followed her, dressed like a woman down and out on her luck in baggy, old clothing, tattered coat, a scarf, and glasses. No one paid Aoki any attention.

Tisa stood near one pillar, looking down at the screen of her smartphone, and not paying attention to her surroundings.

Aoki stood by the other pillar on the platform. She'd always warned Tisa that when you're a drug mule, you had to be on-guard twenty-four/seven, especially carrying weight or cash. Danger could come at you from anywhere at any time.

In total, there were six people waiting for the 4 train on the long platform, including Aoki and Tisa, and each person was in their own world, one reading a book, one listening to music, the other staring off into space, and a man reading a newspaper. Aoki planned on moving before they could figure out what went down. She would be long gone.

Aoki didn't have long to wait. She knew the train would be pulling into the station soon. She removed a syringe from her pocket. It was filled with a liquid called M99, also known as torphine. She slowly made her way toward Tisa, the bitch still on her smartphone.

Aoki readied the syringe and walked closer. When she was right next to Tisa, she bumped into her, and plunged the syringe into Tisa's neck. It was a quick pinch. Aoki apologized with her head lowered, looking submissive, and hurried away.

It took several minutes before the drug started to take effect. Tisa started to feel disoriented and queasy. Something wasn't right. Her vision became blurry. She started to hyperventilate. Her body felt like it was coming apart.

The 4 train started to approach the station, its lights becoming brighter and brighter. The sound of the train coming sent Tisa into frenzy, and before she knew it, she collapsed, plummeting forward just enough to be struck by the moving train.

The blow was intense, sending her body flying like a rag doll. Her remains became contorted beneath metal and steel. She had been crushed.

As the screaming and chaos ensued, Aoki walked out of the train station and jumped into a cab.

CHAPTER 41

Ri-Ri was floored when she heard the news about Tisa's death. She burst into tears and nearly collapsed. She was told it was an accident. Witnesses were saying that her sister had collapsed suddenly and fell forward toward the tracks, where the train crushed her Tisa's body.

Ri-Ri was inconsolable. They had only just recently reconciled and now this. To have her mother and sister die in one year was just too much.

Friends came by the apartment to give their condolences and support.

Aoki came by the apartment with flowers and counterfeit tears, telling Ri-Ri how sorry she was to hear about Tisa. "Whateva went down between us, she was still a friend," she said to Ri-Ri.

The autopsy results on the body were weeks away. The body had been so badly mangled, it was hard for Ri-Ri to identify her. The drugs and cash found in Tisa's backpack—several grams of cocaine, a pound of weed, and five thousand dollars—had police wondering who she was working for and if it really was an accident.

While Aoki was with Ri-Ri, her phone rang again. She decided to answer the call. It was Connor, exclaiming through the phone, "Aoki, please, don't hang up on me. This is important!"

Aoki didn't want to speak to him. She didn't care about him or AZ anymore. She didn't care if he outed AZ. She hung up on him, not giving him the chance to speak. Fuck AZ! Fuck Connor!

She continued to ignore his phone calls. Right now, she was consoling a friend, but there wasn't much consoling she could do.

Gena's death then Tisa's death and Ri-Ri's guilt pushed her to have a mental breakdown, and she had to be admitted to the psych ward on 72-hour hold.

Muthafuckas from the Pink Houses were falling out like flies.

CHAPTER 42

With Ri-Ri out of commission in the psych ward, Aoki felt it was her responsibility to give Tisa a proper burial. Knowing she couldn't go to AZ for financial assistance, she had to sell the jewelry she'd stolen from B Scientific to pay for it. Though it didn't cost a lot, it was a nice send-off. She was buried in the same cemetery as Gena.

It seemed like all of the Pink Houses had come out to her funeral. People cried, feeling a sense of hopelessness, that there were too many deaths in the community, and though the cops were saying Tisa's death was an accident, the people in the community felt like they were cursed. With a drug war raging between B Scientific's crew, now run by Marcus, and AZ's people, the streets were being painted red with blood as the gangs fought over turf

From afar Aoki stoically watched the gravediggers lower Tisa's casket. She had nothing to say and didn't care to give a eulogy. Tisa's death was both personal and business.

Now that Tisa was gone, it was time for Aoki to focus her attention on AZ, who had insulated himself from the streets and the danger, by making himself less visible. AZ's power and influence had increased since B Scientific's murder, and he had become a killer himself, but he still had killers on standby, his influence spreading on the streets. Aoki felt like she'd created a monster.

Leaving the funeral, Aoki walked toward her truck parked on the street. It was a chilly afternoon with dark clouds above, looking like it was going to rain soon. She moved carefully and stayed alert. She had her blade on her, and in her vehicle a loaded Glock 19 and a sawed-off shotgun. She noticed law enforcement close by. They were definitely monitoring the funeral *and* her. Aoki kept cool. As she exited the cemetery, two detectives from Homicide approached her.

They called out her name and wanted to have a talk with her, and they weren't aggressive nor disrespectful.

"Ah what ya want?" she asked, sick and tired of running into cops.

"Do you know of a *Connor*?" one of the detectives asked.

"Who?" Aoki pretended to be stupid. "Vaguely. Why?"

"He was murdered the other night, and yours was the last number he called," the second detective said.

"What!" Aoki was shocked to hear about his demise.

"He was gunned down in his car."

They produced pictures for her to see. Connor was hooked in the front seat of his car and lifeless, his blood pooling everywhere. He was shot three times in the head on a Brooklyn street.

The pictures they showed her transfixed Aoki. It was gruesome, but in her heart, she'd done worse. But it was still a shock to her that Connor was dead.

"Him call, but we didn't speak," she told the detectives.

"Is there a reason why he was calling your cell phone so many times?"

"Him was gay! But me don't have no reason. Him was strange too."

"Strange how?"

"Look, him was no friend of mines. We had our differences and me stayed away," she said, already feeling like she'd said too much.

Aoki knew the culprit was AZ. She figured Connor was a liability to AZ's livelihood and life because he knew too much, so AZ had him executed.

The detectives asked Aoki a few more questions, and then they left. Connor's murder left a cold chill up and down Aoki's spine. AZ was on a different level—one that she wasn't expecting from him. He had transformed into a devious, sadistic demon that she would have to face sooner or later. AZ wasn't her friend anymore. He had become a cold-blooded killer just like her.

After the funeral, Aoki decided to chance it and stop by her old house to collect a few personal items she'd left behind. It was night, and the block was quiet. She parked a block away and crept to her house. On the front porch was a FedEx parcel addressed to her. After assuring everything was clear, she grabbed the envelope and walked inside a dark house with a pistol in her hand.

Aoki walked into her bathroom, closed the door, and clicked on the light. She didn't want anyone passing by to see any lights on that would indicate she was home. She tore it open with unsteady, shaky hands and saw that it was from Connor. She was taken aback. She sat down on the toilet and started to read his words.

Bitch, this is Connor! Your shady ass ain't picking up your phone and I can't leave all this in a thirty-second voice mail. I'm reaching out to you because despite our differences, you always been real with me, Aoki, and I know you and AZ been friends for a long time. I don't care anymore that you fucked him. But AZ has lost his damn mind. He's not who you nor I thought he was. Even though he has hurt me time and time again, I still allowed him in my heart, and in my bed when he wanted some dick. I can't help it, because I'm in love with him.

Well, during our many nights together, fucking and making love however he wanted it, and having numerous pillow talks, he would always confide in me. He told me a fuckin' mouthful, and his confessions left me in awe! He admitted to me that he hired you and your female goons to murder his rivals. I can't fuckin' remember their names, but I'm sure you do, Aoki. He even told me that you and your hood rats are The Killer Dolls.

I guess you're asking why I am telling you shit you already know, right? Well, I got more news for you. Now don't get mad and want to kill me, if I'm not already dead, but the night Emilio shot AZ, AZ was actually going to your house to murder you. I know this for a fact! He has become a killer! He is dangerous (eyes rolling). He swore that's what he planned on doing. Only, Emilio got the drop on him.

Each day from his hospital bed he plotted to make you unknowingly murder the man you loved. That was his ultimate revenge.

I, honestly, never thought you would do it. Never, ever, ever. How could a person murder the person they loved? And now, I understand how easy it truly is, but I'll get to that point in a moment.

He also tipped off the police to those bodies in your backyard. I couldn't believe what he was telling me … bodies in the backyard. He said that you had murdered your parents years ago and kept them around like a souvenir. I'm like, What kind of horror show y'all people from Brooklyn are putting on?

Anyway, I begged AZ to knock all this revenge shit off, but he refused to listen to me. He said you broke his heart by rejecting him and he was going to make you pay. He claimed that you were the only person that was ever there for him, (forgetting about me, smdh) and that you treated him like he wasn't worth your love. He said when you looked at him, you saw a gay man, not a man, and it made him furious. He always had "closet issues."

Now, let me get to the real reason why I'm writing you this letter. I'm reaching out. I feel that we're both in danger. He's after me, and I know that he is now able to kill people. He confessed that he had murdered one of his drug clients who owed him money, and some crackhead. I swallowed hard when he told me this.

After you killed B Scientific, he said you was tying up loose ends and that he was going to do the same. I made a joke to him and said that I'm lucky I'm not a loose end, and the look he gave me could have turned my hair white from fear.

I know this sounds like speculation and innuendo, but I found a list in his handwriting with five names, and three have been already crossed off. The names on the list were B Scientific, Emilio,

```
Mack Ten, Connor, and yours, Aoki.
I'm terrified, Aoki. How can I go
to the cops with this? I have no
proof but just a handwritten list
with some names crossed off.

    Please believe me when I say
that we both are in danger. AZ
is now officially a mad man. I'm
coming to you for help, girl. I'm
so scared and I'm trying to reach
out any way I can. I want to live.
Call me back when you get this
letter. I've been avoiding him for
days. You should too.

    Connor
```

Aoki couldn't believe what she'd read. She was so shocked and heartbroken. *It was him the entire time, with his bitch ass!* She'd killed Emilio, believing she couldn't trust him. The only man she loved and who loved her was now dead because of AZ. Four of those names had been crossed off that list, and she refused to be the fifth. AZ needed to die!

She tried to stand up from the toilet, but her knees buckled and she fell back down and began sobbing. Visions of Emilio came gushing back and it was too overwhelming. She'd truly loved that man, and yet she'd plunged a knife into his neck and allowed the life to drain out from him. He was going to make something out of himself, and she snatched all that away.

A deep sadness swept through her. If there was one thing she knew, it was that she would never forgive herself for what she did to him. He was so good, and loyal, and she honestly didn't deserve his love. His *true* love. She seriously thought about ending her own life, but not before making the man responsible for making her take away her beloved pay for his actions. A life for a life. She was more determined than ever to hunt down AZ and destroy him. She gathered everything she needed; she wasn't coming back to the house. Gripped with vengeance, she stepped outside in the dark that night with a scowl that probably could scare away the devil himself. She planned on seeking him out and killing him slowly and painfully. Watch the man she once called a friend bleed out slowly and die like a rat.

Aoki descended the stairs and marched toward her car, but she hadn't taken three steps before a dark, shadowy figure emerged from behind her. Before she could react, she was tasered from behind, knocked in the head, subdued, and thrown into the trunk of a vehicle. She had fucked up. AZ had gotten to her first. Aoki spent less than an hour in the trunk, feeling the turns and when the car braked for a red light or stop sign. She had no idea where she was being taken, but she was sure her fate was sealed. She also didn't know how many of them there were, and she had nothing to protect herself with.

She was driven to the marsh area in Cross Bay, a known

body-drop for the mob back in the eighties. The car came to a complete stop, and the engine cut off. The trunk finally opened, and Aoki tried to fight them off, but there were three of them. She was roughly dragged out of the trunk, kicking and screaming, cursing out AZ. But she soon realized that the people that grabbed her weren't black.

She was thrown to the ground, and one of the men pulled out a gun and aimed it at her. "Oscar says fuck you," he said, and then he fired a round, shooting her in her chest.

The pain was unbearable. Aoki laid still, her eyes closed.

From the backseat of the vehicle, Oscar, smoking his cigar, observed Aoki's murder. He said no words. He watched his men pick up her body and toss it into the water, where the undercurrent was strong.

EPILOGUE

Aoki woke up in great pain, with no recollection of where she was or what had happened to her. She didn't know the date, nor how much time had passed. She was disoriented. All she saw was a white room and a few doctors standing around her, checking her vitals. They looked at her more like she was a subject clad in a simple white hospital gown than a patient, their eyes distant. Did they save her life? What were they doing to her? She had so many questions swimming in her head, and no one was saying anything to her.

Once her eyes were fully opened, one of the doctors turned swiftly and marched out of the room. It appeared that he was eager to reach someone.

Moments later, a distinguished-looking man in a dark suit walked into the room. He had a mysterious air about him. He was dark, and had a thick goatee and titan shoulders. He was one of the men that had been following her around town. At first she'd assumed they were feds, or mobsters, but it was obvious he was more than that.

They locked eyes.

"You will survive; the bullet just missed your heart. You're a lucky woman, Aoki. We've been watching you and your work for some time now," he said.

Aoki had no idea what he was talking about. She remained silent. Who was he? She didn't trust him at all.

"The Killer Dolls. I'm not impressed, but you do show potential," he said.

Potential for what?

He continued telling her everything he knew about her. He read the police report about what had allegedly happened to her parents and told her his organization had found the bodies in the storage unit she'd rented out under an alias.

"They have been properly disposed of," he told her.

Aoki felt she was fucked. *If this man isn't law enforcement, then who is he?*

"And your gun charge, well, that's been taken care of too," he said.

Aoki was still a bit groggy, but she was listening to him intently.

"I know you're wondering who I am. I know so much about you, but you don't have a clue why I'm here. Well, I'm part of an agency. We're connected and powerful. If you join our agency, then you will be taken care of, and we will take care of your problems with the cartel that wanted you dead, meaning, you can have your revenge on Oscar."

Aoki was definitely listening. Of course, she wanted Oscar dead. AZ too. But they didn't mention his name.

The mystery man continued talking. "If you choose to go back to your former life, then you can go back to

Brooklyn and live your life as you've been living it. You do not owe us anything so far. The surgery . . . consider it pro bono."

"Are you police?" she asked.

The man chuckled. "Absolutely not. But we do restore order."

"Who are you then?"

"The Commission."

Don't Let the Dollface Fool You

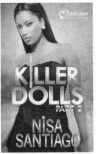
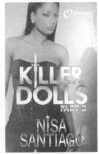

DON'T MISS THE NEXT EPISODE

MAFIO$O

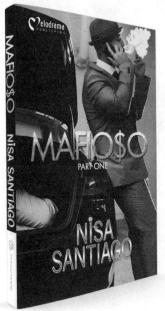

Ambitions as a Mobster

Scott West and his wife Layla have an infatuation with the Mafioso way of life. Armed with what they've learned, they assemble their own family based on the careers of the most successful mobsters and are now in charge of a powerful crime family. Their six children—Meyer, Bugsy, Lucky, Bonnie, Clyde, and Gotti—are all being groomed to manage the family business.

Al Capone's legacy taught Scott to run his drug empire upon fear, helping him prosper as a daunting opponent. When challenged by Deuce, the daring Baltimore crime boss, Scott has to play the game for real as they clash in a mob-style power struggle. When the smoke clears, only one will have a seat at the head of the table.

The enthralling new series by Nisa Santiago

MAFIO$O

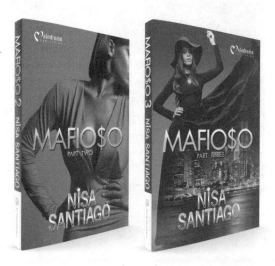

The enthralling new
series by Nisa Santiago

FOLLOW
NISA SANTIAGO

FACEBOOK.COM/NISASANTIAGO

INSTAGRAM.COM/NISA_SANTIAGO

TWITTER.COM/NISA_SANTIAGO